Praise for The Bluestocking's Secret Obsession:

"Captivating and well written, including delightful characters. I enjoyed the romance and its lovely happy ending. I recommend reading!" ★★★★★ Amazon review

"Another super well written story by this author… Could go on about how fabulous this book is but it is a MUST read. Curl up and enjoy." ★★★★★ Amazon review

"I loved this book. I do enjoy this author's writing. Friends to Lovers is one of my favorites, and a good pen-pal romance is hard to come by." ★★★★★ Amazon review

"I absolutely loved this story and could not put it down. I definitely want Benjamin to be my pen pal!!" ★★★★★ Amazon review

"Captivating… emotionally gripping, with its 'friends to lovers' theme, sensuality and suspense… I especially enjoyed the honest, heartwarming and sensual correspondence between the two throughout the book." ★★★★★ Goodreads review

"I couldn't sleep because I couldn't put it down… MM Wakeford writes an intoxicating tale of falling in love." ★★★★★ Goodreads review

"I have never read a novel which uses letters to tell such a passionate tale. This story is very well written, and I couldn't stop reading because I had to know what would happen next." ★★★★★ Goodreads review

"Very original story. Loved it." ★★★★★ Chirp review

THE STANTON LEGACY

Interconnected steamy historical romances set in England and America from the 1830s to the 1860s following two generations of the powerful and wealthy Stanton family.

Book 1: The Viscount's Scandalous Affair
An illicit affair set in late regency London between two unlikely lovers whose emotional and bumpy journey into love ends in a happily ever after.

Book 2: The Vixen's Unlikely Marriage
A steamy romance set in Victorian England featuring a marriage of convenience between two unlikely characters, a beautiful vixen and a virtuous clergyman, who nevertheless find themselves falling in love.

Book 3: The Bluestocking's Secret Obsession
A slow-burn but steamy friends-to-lovers romance set in Victorian England and America in the Civil War.

Book 4: The Viscount's Forbidden Love
An MM romance set in Victorian England with plenty of heart, angst and steam—and it does have a happy ending.

Spin-off novellas:

Mr Templeton Finds Himself a Wife
A steamy romance featuring two jilted lovers who find a second chance at love.

Miss Stanton Meets Her Match
A steamy age-gap, enemies-to-lovers romance.

THE BLUESTOCKING'S SECRET OBSESSION

A HISTORICAL FRIENDS-TO-LOVERS ROMANCE

THE STANTON LEGACY
– BOOK 3 –

M.M. Wakeford

First edition.
978-1-7395071-3-8

Cover designed by Sweet 'N Spicy Designs

www.mw-author.com

STANTON FAMILY TREE

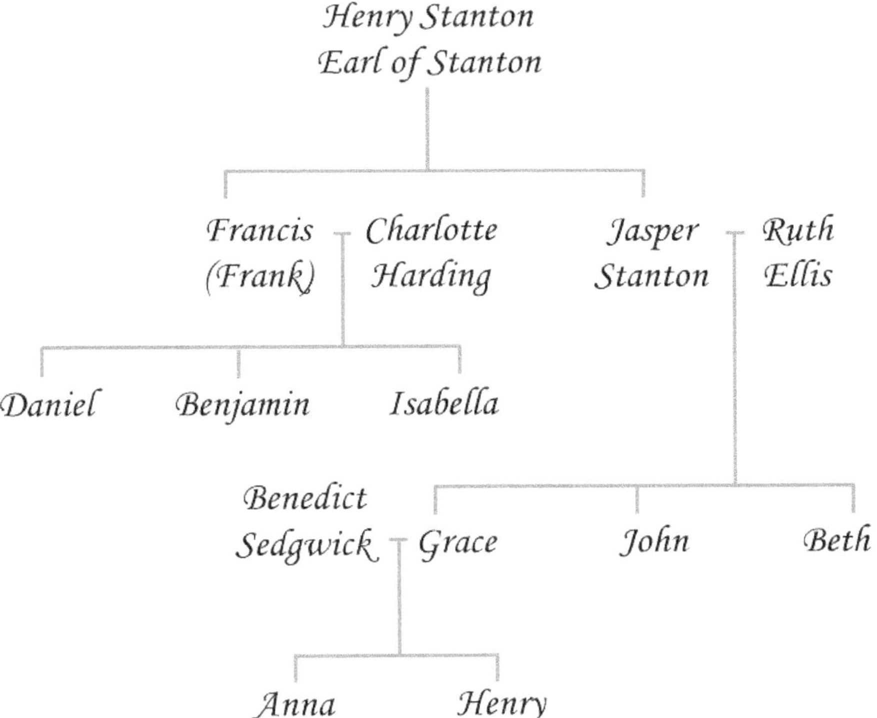

PREFACE

This is a historical novel written for a mature audience. There are sexual scenes that make this story unsuitable for anyone under the age of 18. Although it is part of a series, it can be read as a standalone, though for maximum enjoyment, I would recommend reading the books in sequential order.

PROLOGUE

BENJAMIN

"If any man cannot feel the power of God when he looks upon the stars, then I doubt whether he is capable of any feeling at all."
— *Horace*

December 1860, Oxfordshire, England
EVERYONE WAS GATHERED outside to witness the magnificent fireworks being put on display at the Stanton Hall Christmas ball. Everyone, that is, except for himself. Only a minute ago, Benjamin Stanton had sneaked back into the great house that belonged to his grandfather, the Earl of Stanton.

Now, he flew up the servants' staircase, not wanting to call attention to his movements, and made his way rapidly down the long corridor which led to the library. He had plans for tonight. While everyone was distracted by the lavish entertainment outside, he was to have an assignation with Daphne Phipps. He had met her on his arrival in England two weeks ago. She had sat to his right at church, and they had exchanged discreet glances throughout the service.

He had subsequently made it his business to find out who she was and to pursue her acquaintance. Great had been his delight to discover that Daphne, daughter of the village draper, was far from being an angel. A pretty little thing with a pert nose and comely curves, she had welcomed his advances with sly smiles and coy flutters of her eyelashes. In the ensuing weeks, Benjamin had made several visits to the draper's under false pretexts and flirted with Daphne, culminating in a quick fumble with her behind a wooden screen one day when they found themselves alone in the shop. It was then that he had proposed she meet him in the library on the night of the Stanton ball, when everyone else would be engaged in watching the fireworks outside.

He slowed his footsteps as he approached the library door. Very quietly, he pushed it open. It was dim inside, the only light coming from a small oil lamp on a side table. He looked around for Daphne and smiled as he spied a figure seated in the far corner by the window. He shut the door behind him and without a sound, tiptoed into the room. The closer he got to the seated figure, however, the more obvious it became that this was not Daphne. This person was tall, perhaps a foot taller than the draper's daughter, and her hair was dark, arranged in an artful bun on her head, not in blonde ringlets. He saw that she had her face in her hands and that her shoulders heaved.

What could be the matter? And who was this mysterious lady? He cleared his throat, not knowing what to say. At the sound, she froze then dropped her hands to her lap, revealing a tear-stained face and luminous grey eyes. All at once, he recognised her. It was Miss Cranshaw. He had met her once when she had accompanied her brother, the Earl of Stanton's land manager, on a visit to Stanton Hall.

"Are you quite alright?" he asked, then rebuked himself for the stupidity of that question. Of course she was not alright.

"I–I shall be," she stammered, dabbing at her eyes.

"Here, take this," he said, handing her his handkerchief.

She took it and wiped her tears. "Thank you," she murmured.

She made as if to return it to him, but he demurred. "No, no, do keep it," he said. He went to sit on the chair facing her, leaning forwards on his elbows. "Will you tell me what is troubling you?" he asked gently.

She used the handkerchief once more to wipe at her eyes then put it down in her lap with a self-derisive huff. "Mere foolishness on my part, I'm afraid."

He waited for her to continue. When she did not speak, he enquired with stubborn persistence: "What sort of foolishness?"

She sighed and looked away. It did not look like she would answer him, so he was surprised when she said: "The foolishness of hankering for someone who does not merit or return such sentiments."

"Ah. I begin to see." He eyed her with sympathy. "I have not myself ever been in love, but I am sure it must be painful to have unrequited feelings for another." At the tender age of twenty-two, Benjamin had not yet met any female that set his heart aflutter and whom he could imagine falling in love with in the way that his father and mother loved each other. He supposed, if ever he took the time to wonder about such things, that someday he would meet this person. There was plenty of time still for that, and he was in no hurry.

His was a carefree and happy existence, having grown up on the prosperous farming estate in Ohio that his father and uncle had built with their own hands after leaving England to seek their fortunes in America. They had done so to break free from the authoritarian Earl of Stanton, their father, who had used the enormous wealth at his disposal to exert control over his sons. Naturally, this exodus had caused a rift with the earl, which took many years to mend. Now, however, they were all back in England to attend to his grandfather, who was gravely ill. Notwithstanding his illness, the earl had decided to hold a sumptuous Christmas ball, keen to celebrate the return of his family, temporary though it might be.

Benjamin was brought back to the matter at hand by Miss Cranshaw's voice, which wobbled ever so slightly. "Then you should consider yourself fortunate not to have lost your heart to another, for I cannot recommend it."

"Was there something in particular that occurred tonight to upset you so?" He was curious to know what could have sent the outwardly sensible Miss Cranshaw to hide in the library and cry.

She toyed with the handkerchief in her hands as she spoke: "I went out earlier for a walk in the gardens accompanied by Mr Sedgwick, who as well as being the curate of this parish is a childhood friend of mine. We were there to observe the sky in the hope of seeing a meteor shower—astronomy is a particular pursuit of mine, you see. Instead, we came upon the person who holds my affections in a passionate embrace with a lady. You will pardon me if I do not name the individuals. I promised Mr Sedgwick that I would not spread any gossip."

"No, of course. Quite right." Benjamin nodded in understanding, though his curiosity had been aroused. "I suppose this encounter tonight has dashed any hopes you may have had with regards to this person you hold dear."

"Oh, I have long known it to be hopeless," she smiled sadly. "And yet it makes no difference. I continue to yearn for him."

Benjamin could not imagine how one could persevere in harbouring a passion for someone in the face of evidence that it was hopeless. In his experience, if a girl showed no interest in his flirting, it was best to move on to greener pastures. After all, there was no shortage of pretty girls in the universe. What was the point in wasting one's time and effort on someone who did not deserve such attention?

There again, he had never been in love. Perhaps, it was different when the heart was engaged. He tried to think of something useful to say, searching through his mind for a pertinent proverb. His mother often quoted maxims from her beloved classical philosophers, and they had become as familiar to him as they were to her. In the end, he settled on reciting this from Seneca the Younger: "True happiness is to enjoy the present without anxious dependence on the future."

At Miss Cranshaw's blank look, he elaborated. "You say you yearn for him. Perhaps you dream of a rosy future in the loving embrace of this person who has captured your heart. You may imagine yourself carrying his name and bearing his children, if only he could have a change of heart and truly see you. In all truth, nobody can say what will come to pass. It could be that this person is destined for you, and it could be that he is not. None of it matters though, because you do not live in the future, but in the here and now." He laughed a little self-consciously, all too aware that he was beginning to sound like a bore. "What I am trying most inelegantly to say is that happiness does not come from dwelling in the past or the future, but in enjoying the present moment."

"I suppose so," said Miss Cranshaw looking doubtful.

"Take me, for example. I will have you know, Miss Cranshaw, that I came up to the library for an assignation with a young lady who shall remain nameless. Instead of encountering that lady and enjoying a glorious embrace with her, I came across your good self. I could be forgiven for feeling some disappointment that my plans have gone awry, but there is no joy in dwelling resentfully on what could have been. So next, I ask myself, what would make me happy at this present moment? And the answer is simple. It would bring me joy to wipe that sad expression from your face and make you smile."

At this, she huffed and pressed her lips together, though he detected the glimmer of a smile. "What is it with all these secret assignations?" she grumbled. "I am tempted to believe that everyone but me is engaging in illicit activities when no one is looking."

"Maybe not everyone, but I would not be surprised if there are a good many people doing things in private that would be very much frowned upon in public. It is the way of the world."

She studied him. "Mr Stanton, you are a cynic."

He laughed. "Call me Benjamin, or Ben. No, I do not think I am a cynic, merely a realist." He stood and held out his hands to her. She took them and allowed him to help her to her feet. He looked down at her with a smile. "So now, we come to you, Miss Cranshaw—"

"Sarah," she interjected. "If I am to call you by your given name, then you must do the same with me."

He inclined his head. "Very well. So now, we come to you, Sarah. Put aside your woes about the past or the future and bring your attention to what would bring you joy this very minute." He held up a hand. "And before you say it, something other than having a certain man fall to his knees before you avowing his undying love."

Sarah's face took on a faraway expression. He presumed she was imagining that very thing happening. In an instant, it was gone. She took a steadying breath, murmuring, "Here and now, what would make me happy?" She was quiet, thinking about it.

Benjamin observed her as she furrowed a brow, contemplating the matter. She was tall and angular with smooth, pale skin, not the buxom shape he usually favoured. His gaze fell momentarily to her cleavage, covered in the pale blue silk of her gown. He discerned the slight outline of her breasts and pictured them in his mind—small nubs that would easily fit inside his hands. He felt himself grow hard at the thought. *Damnation! What was the matter with him?*

With an effort, he dispelled these unruly thoughts just as she looked back up at him and said, "I believe, right this minute, seeing a meteor shower would bring me joy. I was so sure my calculations were right and that there would be one tonight."

"Well, I cannot promise you a meteor shower, Sarah, but the next best thing. I hear no expense has been spared for tonight's fireworks display which is about to begin. How about we go out and watch?"

She touched a finger to her still-puffy eyes. "I am not sure I am in a fit state yet to be seen," she prevaricated.

"That is not a problem," he said swiftly. "Come with me." He held out his arm, and reluctantly, she placed a hand on it.

He led her out of the library and walked her to the end of the corridor. There, he proceeded to pull open the large sash window, glancing back at her with a grin. "Do you trust me to keep you safe, Sarah?"

"No," she responded reflexively.

He gave her a reproachful look, but continued undeterred, "Outside this window is a wide ledge that leads to a flat part of the roof. There is, I have discovered, a spot where the curvature of the slate tiles is such as to form a bench of sorts. I have been out there a time or two and enjoyed a marvellous vista of the grounds below. From there, we will have an uninterrupted and private view of the fireworks. Do come."

Without waiting for her reply, he swung one leg over the window sill and stepped out onto the ledge. He turned to face her, holding out his hand and speaking reassuringly, "The ledge is wide enough to stand on comfortably, and I shall keep hold of you at all times. Do not be afraid."

She shook her head. "This is madness."

"Don't think, just do," smiled Benjamin, citing another of his mother's philosophers.

"And now you are quoting Horace at me," replied Sarah. "Next, you shall be telling me to seize the day and put the least possible trust in tomorrow."

Benjamin's grin grew wider. "Seize the day, Sarah."

"Oh, very well," she huffed. Carefully, she pulled up the skirt of her dress and lifted a slim, stocking-clad leg over the window sill. With his assistance, she came to stand on the ledge. It was indeed quite wide, though she appeared to avoid looking below to see how far she might fall were she to lose her balance.

"It is but two steps to the right," said Benjamin. "Keep hold of my hand." Slowly, he guided her off the ledge to the flat part of the roof, then walked her carefully to the spot he had described. It was indeed shaped in such a way as to provide an unorthodox seat. Cautiously, she lowered herself down to it, shivering slightly at the cold feel of the tiles beneath her.

Benjamin settled himself at her side and noticed the shiver. "I am sorry," he murmured. "I should have thought to bring a blanket. Are you so very cold?"

She shivered again but replied, "No, I will be fine for a short while."

"You are a very poor liar, Sarah," mused Benjamin. He unbuttoned his top coat and draped it around her shoulders just as a loud bang was heard, followed by a flash of bright colours. Together, they watched the fireworks light up the dark winter sky. A minute into this, something extraordinary happened. Above them, a dot of bright light zoomed across the sky. Then it happened again and again.

"What was that?" asked Benjamin.

"A meteor shower." Sarah's voice exuded awed satisfaction at having her wish granted. For several minutes, they were silent, observing the show nature put on for them, nearly forgetting the man-made entertainments that were occurring concurrently.

"Incredible," murmured Benjamin.

"People call them shooting stars, but that is not really what they are. They are meteoroids or rocks in space falling towards Earth and burning up as they hurtle through the sky."

Benjamin turned his gaze towards her. "You seem peculiarly well informed," he remarked.

"Did I not tell you that astronomy is a particular pursuit of mine? I have what some would call an unladylike interest in science and engineering. On various occasions, I have been called an eccentric, 'an odd one' or a bluestocking by the good people of Stanton Harcourt."

He continued to observe her curiously. "Well, you are a little odd, but in a good way. It reminds me of Mama, who is herself considered something of a bluestocking. She likes nothing better than to bury herself in a book and quote classical philosophers at us whenever the situation demands it."

"Aha! That explains why you've been spouting Seneca and Horace at me this evening," exclaimed Sarah.

"Yes, it does rather. And though I am not quite as wont to do so as Mama, I do think that these philosophers have a thing or two to teach us. Aren't you glad now that you seized the day and came out onto the rooftop with me?"

She smiled. "Yes, I am, improper though it may have been."

"And I would hazard a guess that you forgot about the man that broke your heart for a least a few minutes."

A shutter came down over her expression. "I suppose I did."

"Stupid me! Now I have reminded you of your heartbreak when I was striving for the opposite."

She rested a hand on his arm. "You did help to distract me from my woes, and for that, I thank you."

"I am glad. Now, I can see you are still shivering, so I think it best we head back inside." He stood and held his hand out to her. She took it and got to her feet, handing him back his topcoat, which he quickly shrugged back on. Together, they stepped carefully back towards the window and climbed inside the house. Once they were in, Benjamin brought the window sash down again and turned to her. "Are you ready now to rejoin the ball?" he asked.

She nodded. "Yes, I am sure my brother, Ambrose, is wondering where I am."

"I shall let you go down first, lest our presence together occasions any gossip. Before you go though, I want to thank you for keeping me company this evening."

She could not help but laugh. "Surely it is I who should be thanking you? You have been excellent company, Benjamin, and a true friend."

"Good. I like the idea of us being friends. I do not think I have had any other female friends since growing into manhood, apart from my cousins. Will you allow me to call on you, as a friend, in the days to come?"

She bit her bottom lip in concentration. He noticed it was fuller than the top. "I would not like to call undue attention to myself," she said finally.

"You live in the cottage that lies at the edge of this estate, do you not?"

"Yes, Ivy Cottage."

"Well, if I should walk from the main house to you, I am hardly likely to encounter any gossips from the village. The grounds of Stanton Hall are extensive, so we should be able to take long and private walks together. That is, if you do not mind more of my company? You would be doing me a great favour, Sarah, for life here is rather dull, what with Grandpa being ill."

"Will you not be needed to attend to the earl?"

He shrugged. "Only some of the time. It is mainly Papa and Uncle Jasper who spend their days with Grandpa, and he tires easily, so there is not much for me to do. Will you take pity on me?"

Her lips quirked into a faint smile. "Very well. Goodnight, Benjamin."

"Goodnight, Sarah."

He watched her go, a strange feeling of elation blossoming in his chest. True, he had not had the pleasure of an illicit romp with Daphne Phipps tonight. But he had made a new friend, and was that not better than the fleeting pleasure of a carnal encounter?

PART I

PRELUDE TO WAR

CHAPTER 1

SARAH

"Love will enter cloaked in friendship's name."
— Ovid

AT FIRST, SARAH did not hear the knock at the door, so absorbed was she in reading a most interesting pamphlet by a French chemist named Louis Pasteur, describing a novel theory about microbes causing the decay of organic matter. According to Pasteur, it was tiny organisms in the air, invisible to the eye, that were responsible for spoiling beverages such as beer, wine and milk. He advocated the heating of such liquids to a temperature above 60 °C to kill these microbes and prevent putrefaction. How interesting! She determined at the soonest opportunity to conduct an experiment on this and test the veracity of Pasteur's claims.

There was a second knock and this time, Sarah heard Elsie open the door followed by the sound of a male voice. This was curious. Who could it be? Soon, Elsie was peeping her head timidly around Sarah's private parlour door. "There is a visitor for you, miss," she said. "A Mr Benjamin Stanton. I have showed him to the main parlour."

"Thank you, Elsie," Sarah told her maid. She stood, smoothing the folds of her dress, excitement shooting through her veins. She had not had occasion to speak privately again with Benjamin since their encounter at the Christmas ball. The following day, the Earl of Stanton had taken to his bed and breathed his last breath shortly thereafter. Sarah had attended the funeral two days ago and paid her respects to the grieving Stanton family, but had exchanged little more than a few words with Benjamin.

She hurried to the main parlour where Benjamin stood, hat in hand. "Mr Stanton," she said, walking towards him.

He gave her a reproving look. "I thought we had agreed to dispense with such formality," he told her. "Hello, Sarah, how do you do?"

"I am well, thank you, Benjamin," she breathed, her cheeks a little pink. "Do please take a seat. May I offer you some tea?"

He shook his head as he sat himself down on the nearest chair. "No need, thank you. I have come, Sarah, to invite you out for a walk in the park. The weather is dry and not too chilly today. How about it?"

"Do you mean right now?"

"Of course I mean right now," he laughed. "That is, unless you have something better to do."

Louis Pasteur's germ theory could wait. A walk with her newfound friend was more important at this moment in time. "Let me fetch my coat and bonnet," she said, rising to her feet. A minute later, she was back and ready to go.

With a warm smile, Benjamin escorted her out the front door and gave her his arm. She slipped her hand through it and followed his lead as he headed in the direction of the small lake on the southern part of the estate. They took a pebbled path that cut through grass and woodland, and once they had walked a short distance along it, Sarah spoke: "I am so sorry for your loss, Benjamin. Tell me, how is your family bearing up?"

His expression became serious. "Papa and Uncle Jasper are keeping busy with estate matters, especially now that Grandpa's will has been read. I believe it helps to distract them from their grief. We are being stoic, but of course, our loss is still fresh in all our minds."

"And you, Benjamin? How is it with you?"

He glanced at her in surprise but did not slow his stride. "It is a sad time, of course," he said. "However, I was never very close to Grandpa, not in the same way as Daniel or my cousin, Grace. I liked the old goat well enough, but he never spoke much to me." He gave a short laugh. "I suppose that might explain the terms of the will."

"I heard of it," murmured Sarah. Her brother, Ambrose, had been present at the reading of the will yesterday and had told her all about it when he came home. He had explained how the late earl's substantial fortune was to be split between four of his grandchildren. Daniel, the eldest and now the new Viscount Stanton, had inherited Stanton Hall as well as the London townhouse. Isabella, Grace and Beth Stanton had been granted sizeable estates, but Benjamin and John, the remaining two of the earl's grandchildren, had merely received £2,000 each. It was not a sum to sneer at, to be sure, but it paled in comparison with the wealth the others had received. The late earl's reasoning for this, apparently, was that both Benjamin and John would become heirs to the estate their fathers had built in America.

"So, you will have heard that my brother, Daniel, is now an extremely wealthy man, with a great estate to go with his new title," said Benjamin in an even tone.

Sarah examined his profile searchingly, taking in the pleasing symmetry of his nose and the firm line of his jaw. She was not usually very good at reading people, yet she sensed his perturbation. "Yes, I have heard," she said quietly.

"I am happy for him, of course," continued Benjamin. "When you think about it, Stanton Hall could not have been granted to anybody else, apart from Papa."

"Yes," agreed Sarah, "I can see that." She paused then went on, "I can also see that it has created a disparity between yourself and your siblings. They are now wealthy in their own right while you are still dependent on your father for your income. Is that not so?"

He shot her a startled look. "How well you understand," he marvelled. Letting out a deep breath, he added, "It is not that I envy Daniel or Bella, or at least not much, but as you so rightly say, there is now a disparity in our stations which I fear will create an invisible barrier between us. Daniel is now a man of stature, a viscount with a great estate who can do with his life as he pleases, whereas I must still do my father's bidding. I am not yet my own man."

"If you could do as you pleased," probed Sarah gently, "then what is it that you would do?"

He looked out to the distance as he said, "Before coming to England, I had recently completed a Bachelor of Science from the University of Pennsylvania. There was not enough time to decide on a course of action with regards to my future, though I had thoughts of finding myself a position as a railroad engineer or something of that ilk."

"A worthy career, with many good prospects I would think," remarked Sarah.

"Well, but that is all over for me, as I shall have to take my place at Papa's side now that I am to be his heir instead of Daniel." Although Benjamin spoke calmly, there was an undertone of bitterness to his words. "I shall have to set my sights on becoming a gentleman farmer just like Papa." He flashed a quick smile. "I will not complain, for I have gone from a landless second son to being the heir to a large estate. Some would say I am extremely fortunate."

"And so you are," reasoned Sarah. "My brother may work for his entire life, but on the wages of an estate manager would never make the kind of wealth which you will be acquiring in due course. That should put your good fortune in better perspective."

He laughed. "By Jove, Sarah, it is good to talk to you. I am certainly put in my place. The world we live in is not a very fair one, is it?"

"No indeed, but we must make the best of what we are given. That is what my brother always says."

He sobered instantly. "Your brother is right, and so I shall make the best of things. Now, enough talk about me. Let us talk about you."

"There is very little to talk about," said Sarah modestly. "I live a quiet life in a small village and am well on my way to becoming a spinster maid. There is not much of interest to discuss that concerns me."

"I disagree!" cried Benjamin. "For one, your interest in scientific pursuits promises that you will have something of note to say on such matters. For another, there is the story behind this attachment you have formed for this unnamed person, which I should like to hear about. When and how did this attachment begin?"

They had by now reached the lake, and Benjamin guided Sarah towards a wooden bench positioned to take advantage of the view. He gallantly swept it with his handkerchief before inviting her to sit. This she did while thinking of an appropriate response to his question. Strangely, she felt an urge to be forthright in her answer, even though her friendship with Benjamin was still so very new. "It happened three years ago, not long after we came to live here, Ambrose and I," she said finally. "I made the acquaintance of the gentleman in question at a reception hosted by the late earl. He was so handsome, so witty and charming. It was all I could do not to stare. I had never in all my years come across a gentleman such as he."

"So, you were bedazzled by his good looks and charm."

"Yes, I suppose so," replied Sarah. "And then, each time I subsequently met him, which was not often as we do not mix in quite the same circles, he had the identical effect on me. It is like coming across a rare breed of a rose amongst a sea of ordinary dandelions."

"And in that time, have you also come to know his character?" asked Benjamin. "It would not do to form a long-lasting attachment based solely on someone's looks and charming manners." He disguised the rebuke with a grin. "Now I am all for good looks and charm. Many have been the females that have hooked me with a coquettish bat of their eyes, but none of that interest lasted very long. For an attachment to endure over the years, I would think more would be needed, a meeting of like minds perhaps."

"I have had the opportunity to study his character over the years," replied Sarah, a little uncertainly. "While he is something of a flirt with the ladies, I have also come to know that he is generous and kind. Also, Ambrose tells me the gentleman has always been fair and honest whenever he has had business dealings with him."

Benjamin studied her curiously. "And in all that time, this gentleman has never shown any sign that he reciprocates your interest in him?"

"I am not sure. He has charming words to say, but he is that way with other ladies too, so I do not know that it means anything."

Benjamin stared at her, his brown eyes glinting with an unknown emotion—was it amusement, or something else? "Sarah," he said in an almost gruff voice. "If a man is interested in a lady, then it is usually evident in his marked attentions or warm looks. I had thought that females have an intuition about this sort of thing."

Sarah looked down at her lap. "I am sure most do, but that is the one area where I am lacking. No doubt it is to do with the life I lead and my own unusual disposition, that I find it hard to deduce what others might be thinking."

She glanced up and caught what she thought was a sympathetic gaze. She decided it was time to change the subject matter. "Let us talk instead about scientific things," she said quickly. "I have been wondering. Do you have any experience of working with steam engines, given what you said earlier about wanting a career as a railway engineer?"

"Yes," he said agreeably, ready to change the subject too. "It was during my time at the University of Pennsylvania. One of my fellow students there had an uncle who owned an engineering works that manufactured steam-powered locomotives, and in my spare time, I would go there, observing all with great curiosity." He smiled beguilingly. "It was not long before I managed to wheedle my way towards being allowed to assist one of the engineers in his work."

"How lucky you are!" blurted Sarah, then felt herself blush. "What I meant to say," she continued in a more measured tone, "is that you were most fortunate to gain such an apprenticeship if you mean to work in this field."

He regarded her steadily. "Yes, I have been fortunate. Is this something that interests you too, Sarah?"

She looked away, her face still pink. "It is not the kind of work considered appropriate for females," she mumbled. "Had I been born a man though, I would have liked nothing more than to do the same as you."

He stood then and held out his arm to Sarah, indicating they should start walking again. She rose to her feet and slipped her hand through his arm as they began their slow journey back towards Ivy Cottage. After a while, he mused, "No, the world we live in is not a fair one." He thought some more. "There is something of a similar nature that you could do though."

"What is that?" wondered Sarah, intrigued.

"Have you ever thought of building yourself your own small railway at home?"

"I have heard of such novelties for children, but I am not sure how I would go about it—and in any case, I would be much more interested in creating the real thing in miniature than a mere toy," replied Sarah, her interest aroused despite herself.

"I agree! I could work on it with you. First, do you have a room at home that you could use for such a venture?"

Sarah did not need to think about it. "I have my own private parlour at the back of the house. It is where I read and conduct my experiments."

"Perfect," beamed Benjamin. "Now, onto other matters. Broad or the standardised gauge?"

After a moment's consideration, she replied, "I rather like that at Oxford, they have both gauges. If I were to follow suit with a mixed gauge for my project, then I would be less restricted in what I choose to represent."

Benjamin nodded pensively. "That makes sense. Next, we shall need to think about the track design of your miniature railway and what scene you might want to depict."

"How about the approach to Hanborough station?"

"Good thinking," said Benjamin approvingly. The rest of their walk was devoted to discussing this proposed miniature railway. By the time they arrived at Ivy Cottage, Sarah was in the grip of a strange new set of emotions. There was, of course, excitement about this project she was about to embark on with Benjamin and also joy at the discovery of a like-minded friend, but above all that was a sinking feeling of sorrow that this wonderful new friend would soon be leaving for America, likely never to return.

CHAPTER 2

SARAH

"Every heart sings a song, incomplete, until another heart whispers back."
— Plato

Two months later

THEY ARRIVED AT church a trifle late, just moments before the service was about to begin. Ambrose guided her quickly to their pew seats. No sooner had they settled themselves down than Sarah Cranshaw glanced through the crowd, looking for one person.

At first, she did not see him. *Damnation!* Why did they have to get here so late? Church service was the one time in the week when Sarah was afforded a long and unimpeded view of Philip Templeton. She shifted in her seat, craning her neck sideways. There he was! She let out a quiet sigh. Her gaze settled on his handsome profile and on the broadness of his shoulders in the immaculately tailored coat he wore. Could there be a more perfect looking man? Not in her estimation.

She had fallen under his spell from the moment she had first met him three years ago, although she had tried many a time to cure herself of this affliction, especially after coming upon him in an embrace with Grace Stanton at the Christmas ball—now Grace Sedgwick of course, since her marriage to Benedict. Sarah still could not fathom why her old friend had married that flighty girl with questionable morals, but she kept her doubts to herself. To all appearances at least, the marriage seemed to be a happy one. Nevertheless, seeing Mr Templeton passionately kissing Grace should have put a stop to Sarah's infatuation once and for all. It had not. Every time Mr Templeton's fine form graced her sight, Sarah's heart still beat a little faster, and her eyes glazed momentarily in admiration of him.

It seemed ridiculous that she, a sensible and intelligent being, should form an attachment based primarily on someone's looks. Surely she should be looking beyond mere appearances and into Mr Templeton's character before forming a deep attachment to him. This was what Benjamin Stanton had implied on that first of several walks they took together before he had left for America. Though he did not know the identity of the man she had confessed to admiring, he had questioned her about this attachment and voiced his doubts as to whether it was based on a true knowledge of character rather than on surface appearances.

To this, Sarah had had little to say except that she knew Mr Templeton to be generous and kind. And so here she was, at the ripe old age of twenty-five, still unmarried, hoping against hope that one day, some eligible gentleman might come to see her worth.

It was not as if she had rejected a whole host of other suitors in favour of waiting for Mr Templeton. She lived comfortably at Ivy Cottage with her brother, but she had no money of her own. At most, Ambrose would be able to settle £50 on her, should she ever marry. Even worse for her marriage prospects, she was considered eccentric—the bluestocking of the parish— and she had no great looks to recommend her. Tall and thin, her figure did not conform to the standards of beauty of the day. Her facial features were regular enough but unremarkable. All in all, it did not make for high prospects of marriage. The only other gentleman who had ever shown an interest in her—and for whom she had felt an attraction—was Benjamin Stanton. But

Benjamin had viewed her merely as a friend who shared his passion for railways and besides, he was long gone now.

Throughout the service, Sarah lent half an ear to the sermon preached by her childhood friend, Benedict Sedgwick, while at the same time keeping her attention on Mr Templeton. The hand that brushed his hair back from his noble forehead, the uncrossing of the legs stretched out before him, the scratching of something on his cheek, the stifled yawn—all these gestures were noted and catalogued by the ever attentive Sarah. He looked a trifle weary today, she thought. Had he slept well? Perhaps he was ailing. That dreaded influenza had been taking its toll on many of the good folk in Stanton Harcourt. Her brother had himself only just recovered from its ill effects this past week. She most sincerely hoped that this was not the case with regards to Mr Templeton.

In her worry, she forgot discretion and stared across at him, a crease in her brow. If that was indeed the case, she would make sure to speak to Mrs Turner, his housekeeper, when that lady came to the village on her errands, and to advise her on the simple but effective broth she had prepared as remedy for her brother when he had been sick.

A hand coming to rest firmly upon hers brought these wayward thoughts to an abrupt halt. It was Ambrose. She darted her gaze to his, and he gave her a look that was clear in its meaning. She should not be staring so at Mr Templeton. Chastened, she brought her gaze back to Benedict standing at the pulpit and tried to pay attention to his sermon.

She and Ambrose had never spoken of it except in the vaguest of terms, but she knew that he was aware of her infatuation with Mr Templeton. He would never presume to tell her what she should do, although she suspected that privately, he did not think her attachment to Mr Templeton wise or desirable. But that was neither here nor there. She loved her brother dearly, and he was the only family she had left following the passing of their mother and father, both within a year of each other. However, Ambrose was so steeped in his bachelor ways that she did not think he had much of an understanding of romantic love, so she would not be taking advice from him on the matter, even were he to volunteer such advice.

The service came to an end, and they all rose to their feet. With the deftness of long practice, Sarah manoeuvred herself to be within Mr Templeton's path as he made his way out of the church. On seeing her, he smiled amiably. "Miss Cranshaw, how do you do?"

"Thank you, I am well," she answered calmly, her tone belying the thoughts that had been passing through her mind not a few moments ago. To the world, she presented such a sensible and well put together front that it would be hard for anyone to imagine that beneath it all, she suffered from a great obsession for the man standing before her.

He looked over her shoulder and greeted her brother. "Cranshaw. You seem well recovered from your previous indisposition."

"Indeed I am," responded Ambrose jovially. "Nothing can keep me down for too long."

They moved along with the throng until they found themselves outside the church. Mr Templeton bowed politely in their direction before heading away. And that was the sum of the weekly interactions with her beloved, unless there was a particular social occasion, a dance or a dinner party, at which they were both guests. Great may have been Sarah's devotion to Mr Templeton, but it was a passion conducted from afar. She stifled a sigh, knowing it would probably be another week before she had a chance to see him again.

There were times when she wondered how it was that such a passion as she had for Mr Templeton could be sustained from so little personal contact with him. A heretical voice in her head would point out, most inconveniently, that perhaps she worshipped an illusion, a figment of her imagination. Through the week, she would daydream of his masculine beauty and charming manners. On seeing him in the flesh, reality never quite matched her imaginings, but still her pulse raced with excitement, and her desire for him felt very real. So embarrassingly real in fact, that she often returned home with an uncomfortable dampness in her drawers.

That Sarah yearned for Mr Templeton and felt intense desire for him did not mean that she lived an unhappy life. She was much too practical and had far too many interesting scientific pursuits to sink into a sentimental decline. She had also taken to heart the words spoken to her by Benjamin, two months ago in the library of Stanton Hall, to enjoy the present and not pay too much heed to the past or the future. So, when she saw Mr Templeton, she found joy in her proximity to him, and when she was away from him, she tried her best to find pleasure in other aspects of her life.

Now, standing with her brother outside the church building, she did not let herself feel bereft or miserable. She took a deep breath in, willing the pounding in her heart to subside—though the damp drawers she could do nothing about. In accordance with the scientific bent of her mind, she had researched this strange occurrence and learned that this dampness was produced by females when physically aroused in order to provide lubrication for the act of sexual intercourse. It seemed that in the presence of a virile man such as Mr Templeton, her body was fooled into thinking she was about to engage in that sexual act. Sometimes, the dampness was also accompanied by a throbbing feeling down below, as it did now. Not for the first time, she wondered what it would be like to have conjugal relations with a man and to fulfil the physical need elicited by this throbbing. Would God ever grace her with that knowledge?

It was best not to dwell too long on the thought. *"Live in the present,"* she reminded herself. For now, she had a luncheon at Stanton Hall to look forward to. Most Sundays, except when they joined Benedict and Grace Sedgwick at their home in

Mulverley Grange, Ambrose and Sarah were invited to break bread with Daniel, the new Viscount Stanton, at his magnificent stately home. Since the late earl's passing, Ambrose had spent considerable time working with the new viscount on estate matters, as a result of which they had formed a close friendship. Now, every Sunday, Daniel expected them to join him and the rest of his family for luncheon. This was always a delight for Sarah, firstly because the Stantons had a marvellous cook—that game pie served last week had been divine—and secondly because it meant she could spend time in the vast library and borrow a book or two to read.

Ambrose turned to his sister with an affectionate smile. "Well, that is that. Let us be quick and make our way to Stanton Hall. I do believe it might begin to rain soon, and I would much rather not get wet if I can help it."

Sarah was in full agreement with this. She did not wish her brother to catch a chill when he had only just recovered from the influenza. "Yes, if we walk briskly, I am sure we can avoid the coming downpour," she said looking towards the grey skies on the horizon ahead.

They began their journey arm in arm. It would take them to the edge of the village and along a tree-lined avenue that went past their cottage, leading on to the main house. At a brisk pace, they would reach their destination within fifteen to twenty minutes.

They had only been walking for a short while when a clatter of hooves made them both glance towards the road. A smart-looking carriage flew past them then halted a few yards ahead. Its door opened and out jumped Daniel, Viscount Stanton. In quick strides, he reached where they stood, an angry frown marring his handsome face.

"What do you mean by this, Ambrose?" he demanded.

"If you could elucidate what 'this' is alluding to, my lord, I would be happy to explain myself," responded Ambrose mildly.

"Do not 'my lord' me, and you know perfectly well what this is about," thundered the viscount.

"Perhaps you mean me to explain why my sister and I are walking towards Stanton Hall. I believe it is because you have invited us to dine there," said Ambrose smoothly.

The viscount narrowed his eyes. "What I wish you to explain, Ambrose, is why you are traipsing around in what is soon to be a rain storm, when there is a perfectly good carriage to take us all to Stanton Hall."

As Ambrose went to answer him, the viscount held up a hand. "Later, Ambrose. Let us not tarry in the middle of the road." He bowed to Sarah. "Miss Cranshaw, good day. Forgive my poor manners. Would you do me the honour of letting me escort you to the carriage?"

Sarah gave a quick curtsy. "Thank you, my lord." In truth, she was relieved that the viscount had caught up with them, for the cold air had precipitated in her brother a worrying new bout of coughing. She placed her hand on the viscount's proffered arm and let him help her into the carriage. A moment later, both men joined her and soon they were on their way again.

In the carriage sat Isabella Stanton, the viscount's younger sister, who greeted the newcomers with a polite inclination of her head. "Mr Cranshaw, Miss Cranshaw, good day," she said, adding, "We looked for you outside the church, but you had already gone. You must know that it makes no sense for you to walk when we are all going the same way and can share the carriage."

"That is very kind of you, Miss Stanton. However, we did not wish to presume," spoke Ambrose. His words were followed by an extended fit of coughing. Sarah stroked his back soothingly as he held a handkerchief to his mouth. When at last it was over, he murmured, "Pardon me."

The viscount's lips pressed into a tight line. "Ambrose," he gritted. "I have told you many times how much I abhor standing on ceremony. For the avoidance of doubt, you are to presume that we expect you and your sister to ride with us in the carriage whenever we go to church." He paused and scowled. "In any case, should you have ventured out today? It seems to me you are not yet over your sickness. I will not thank you for spreading the infection to me or to my servants."

Ambrose looked contrite. "I am sorry, my lord. You are quite right and perhaps it would be best if you were to excuse us from joining you for luncheon today. We are nearly at Ivy Cottage. Please do let us out here."

The viscount made a noise somewhere between a huff and a growl but did not deign respond to this, and the carriage continued on its way to Stanton Hall. Isabella smiled kindly at Ambrose. "I will let cook prepare a hot infusion of ginger and honey for you as soon as we arrive. It will help soothe your tickly throat."

"Thank you, Miss Stanton," replied Ambrose, a little pink with embarrassment at the fuss being made over him. "That is very kind, but I assure you there is no need to go to the trouble."

The viscount huffed again but did not speak. The rest of the passengers continued the short journey in silence. At last, the carriage stopped in the grand driveway of Stanton Hall and all four persons inside descended from the vehicle. With quick bounds up the front steps, the viscount hurried into the house ahead of them. Sarah saw him summon Siddons, the butler, and confer with him quickly. A moment later, he was back, escorting the ladies inside.

"We will go to the main parlour," he said. "It is less draughty than the drawing room." They made their way there, finding a servant adding kindling to the warm fire burning in the hearth. They settled themselves down, the viscount indicating that Ambrose should sit on the armchair closest to the fireplace. Shortly thereafter, another servant walked in bearing a tray with tea and that promised ginger infusion for Ambrose. Her brother took it gratefully, casting a quick smile at the viscount.

Sarah too glanced approvingly at her host. When the late earl had taken sick, both she and her brother had wondered with some trepidation about their future on the estate. Would the earl's heir keep Ambrose on as estate manager? What manner of landlord would he turn out to be? In the weeks that followed the earl's death, their questions had been answered and their fears allayed. Daniel made it clear that Ambrose would continue in his position as estate manager. In addition, he displayed a commendable interest in the running of the estate, spending hour after hour in Ambrose's company, trying to learn as much as he could about the land and properties he had inherited.

What neither Sarah nor Ambrose had expected was that they would be drawn into the social circle of the viscount and included as guests whenever he hosted lunch or dinner parties. Having grown up in America where his family's titles meant very little, and having spent his childhood outdoors, pitching in to work on the land his father had claimed, Daniel had no time for social snobbery. He determined very quickly that Ambrose Cranshaw was a man he liked and respected, and he therefore thought it fit to include Ambrose and his sister as equals in his social circle.

Sarah's musing were interrupted by the arrival of Benedict Sedgwick with his wife, Grace, followed by a surprise guest— Walter Sedgwick, Benedict's father. Sarah rose to her feet in delight at seeing Walter again. Their closest neighbour when growing up, Walter was like family to her. She embraced him warmly, exclaiming, "Uncle Walter, this is a lovely surprise!"

"Sarah, my dear," replied the elderly gentleman. "It is good to see you."

The next few hours flew by as the happy group ate, joked and reminisced. The Stanton cook once again surpassed herself, this time with an extremely flavoursome and tender haunch of lamb. Afterwards, they all reconvened back in the parlour for some brandy, before the Sedgwicks took their leave. Sarah sat back in her chair feeling relaxed and replete. It had been a very enjoyable afternoon. She supposed she and Ambrose ought to be making their way back home too. She glanced across at her brother only to find his eyes shut, his deep breathing signalling that he had fallen asleep in his armchair.

Daniel followed her gaze and said softly, "Let him be for now. There is no rush for you to get back, surely."

"Well, if we are to walk back, then we should be going before it begins to get dark."

"You will be taking the carriage," said Daniel in a voice that brooked no disagreement.

"In that case," murmured Sarah, "we can stay a short time longer. Perhaps I can peruse the books in the library while Ambrose rests."

"Of course, and Miss Cranshaw, I hope you know that you are welcome to borrow a book from here any time you wish."

"Thank you, my lord, that is very kind."

Daniel sighed in exasperation. "Oh do please stop with the 'my lord'. Can we not be easy in each other's company? I do hate all this ceremony."

Isabella chimed in, "Oh yes, please let us be at our ease. I feel like we are almost family already. When we are alone, away from the rest of society, let us go by our given names."

"I would be happy to," smiled Sarah.

"Then Sarah, off you go find yourself a book. We will remain here with Ambrose until he wakes."

Sarah stood, and with a quick nod in their direction, made her way out of the parlour. In the library, she walked along the shelves, inspecting the extensive collection of books which had been lovingly curated by the previous earl. She soon found a book of odes and verses by Horace, which she pulled down from the shelf, remembering how Benjamin Stanton had quoted them to her only a few months ago. Taking it over to a chair by the window, she sat and began to read.

In another twenty minutes or so, a soft knock on the door heralded Daniel's entrance in the library. "Ambrose is awake and insists on returning home at the soonest opportunity," he said. "I volunteered to come fetch you."

"Thank you." Sarah stood quickly, picking up the book she had been reading and another one she had chosen.

Daniel's eyes fell on them. "Good. I am glad you have books to take with you, for I meant what I said earlier. You require no invitation to come here at any time and help yourself to whatever book you wish."

"I am very grateful, my lor—Daniel," she said, correcting herself.

"Before we go down, Sarah, I have something for you." He fished a letter out of his pocket. "It is from Benjamin. I would recognise his scrawl anywhere." He handed it to her, saying, "He mentioned before he left that he planned to correspond with you from America, and that for the sake of discretion, he would address his letters care of me at Stanton Hall."

Sarah took the letter, feeling a strange burst of pleasure. On saying goodbye to Benjamin all of two months ago, he had suggested they start a correspondence with each other, but she had not truly believed that he would follow through with this suggestion. "Oh, how thoughtful of him," she now said. "Not that there is any need to hide this from Ambrose. He does not interfere with such matters as with whom I might be corresponding."

"In that case, next time a letter arrives, I will give it straight to him to pass on to you. Just so you know, Isabella and I will be sending return missives to Ohio in another day or two. If you wish, I could include a letter from you along with ours."

"That would be wonderful, thank you. I will make sure to write my letter and bring it over tomorrow."

"Good." He studied her a moment more. "Perhaps it is not my place to ask, Sarah, but I cannot help my curiosity. Just what is the nature of your relationship with my brother?"

"We are friends. That is all. Is that so very unusual?" Sarah raised a brow in response. Seeing as she had been friends—and only friends—with Benedict all her life, she did not think there was anything untoward in her new friendship with Benjamin. She ignored the inconvenient recollection of instances when she had felt an attraction to him. They were friends, nothing more. Nonetheless, she knew society frowned upon such things and impugned the possibility that men and women could have purely platonic relationships.

"It is unusual for Benjamin," replied Daniel. "I have not ever seen him befriend a lady just for the sake of being friends. Come to think of it, I myself have never done so either. It is not very common to see in our society."

"Well," retorted Sarah, "I do think that is a shame, for there is no earthly reason why men and women cannot be friends."

Was she protesting too much? It seemed not, for Daniel smiled and responded, "I quite agree. Now, let me return you to your brother before he sends out a search party."

The two of them returned to the parlour and soon thereafter, Sarah and Ambrose took their leave, returning to Ivy Cottage in the Stanton carriage, at Daniel's insistence. Benjamin's letter to Sarah lay tucked into the pocket of her coat, waiting to be read. She was intensely curious about its contents, for despite what she might have said earlier in the library, she was not much used to receiving mail from gentlemen. But it was more than that, she knew. In the short time of their acquaintance, Benjamin had made an unforgettable impression on Sarah. She had thought of him often in the last two months, each time with a deep sadness that their budding friendship had been cut short so soon. She was eager now to learn his news and feel, if only for a brief moment, a reconnection with him.

First, though, she made sure that her brother was settled comfortably in his room and brought him some hot broth to drink before bed. Then she went to her own room, added some kindling to the fire burning in the hearth and lit her bedside candle. Once that was done, she undressed and washed, put on a sensible nightgown and got into bed. Now, finally, she could read at leisure the letter that had arrived for her. As she carefully unsealed the envelope and took out the two thick sheets it contained, it occurred to her in passing that she had not had one single thought of Mr Templeton since leaving church earlier that day. She would remedy this omission very soon and resurrect sweet memories of her brief encounter with him. But first, she had a letter to read.

CHAPTER 3

LETTERS EXCHANGED BETWEEN BENJAMIN AND SARAH, FEBRUARY 1861

February 1ˢᵗ, 1861

Dear Sarah,

Very little happened on the journey back home, and I applaud myself for not falling down dead from seasickness as I did on the boat to England. Papa was relieved to find the farm in good order, having been under the management of his foreman, a capable man named Tom Shaw, and the whole operation overseen by our neighbour, Robert Ellis, who is also brother to my uncle Jasper's wife. So you see, Papa needn't have worried quite so much.

However, worry he does, especially with recent developments in the southern states of America. You may know perhaps that the election of President Abraham Lincoln in November of last year has precipitated the secession from the Union of several states in the south, the latest one being Louisiana. This is all to do with Lincoln's opposition to the spread of slavery into the new territories. It seems the protection of that dreadful practice of enslaving other human beings is the reason why several states in the south have decided to secede.

What this will mean for us, I hardly know, but rumours are rife that a war between the Union and the seceded states is brewing. Despite these rumours, everything here is calm and peaceful—the most pressing matters on people's minds are how long this current frost will last and what it will mean for our crops.

One thing that is different since our return is that now Daniel is no longer here, Papa has required me to learn more about the business side of things. I have been like his shadow, following him about as he meets with bankers, investors and grain merchants on his trips to town. It is a strange turn of events. As the second son, I never expected to acquire such responsibilities. Daniel was always the one at Papa's side, the heir to all this magnificence. And now, as we discussed, all this has changed.

I am not sure what to think of this change in my fortunes, though I will heed your advice and try to make the best of what I have been given. I do not want to disappoint Papa, who has built this estate from the ground up and wants to pass it on to his progeny, but neither do I know if I am truly cut out to be a gentleman farmer. I have found the business negotiations tedious, even though I see how important they are to our prosperity. Perhaps in time, I will become more accustomed to my new position.

I have thought much of you, Sarah, and wondered how you are. Have there been any further developments with regards to Mr T? Forgive me, but I have discovered the identity of the man for whom you have romantic feelings. You see, on New Year's Eve, we played a game of questions and commands, and I had the bright idea of commanding everyone to tell who they had kissed in their life so far. It was then that Grace confessed she had kissed Mr T at the Christmas ball, and I soon put it all together, guessing that it was the two of them you caught in an illicit embrace. I did not wish to mention it to you during our last walk, for fear of causing embarrassment, but now with the distance of an ocean between us, I wanted you to know that I know. I hope that you will be able to be candid with me in your correspondence. I do like the idea of our friendship knowing no bounds. Tell me whatever it is you are doing or thinking, with no fear of judgement. In return, I will regale you with unvarnished tales of my adventures. How about that?

So, in the spirit of frankness, let me tell you that since my return, I have embarked on a dalliance with a young lady named Chastity Hewitt. She is the youngest of three sisters whose family runs the general store in the village nearby and quite the minx—the antithesis of her name. Let me hasten by saying that this is no love affair, for neither of us have our hearts engaged in the matter. It is simply a little piece of harmless fun between the two of us. She came by the other day with a delivery of sugar and smoked fish, and I cleverly managed to spirit her to an empty barn to have my wicked way. How is that for forthrightness? I hope you are not shocked. No, I do not think you can be, for I feel that under your bluestocking exterior, you have an understanding of what draws men and women to each other.

And on that note, I will end this first letter. Write to me soon, for I am keen to know your news.

Your good friend,

Benjamin Stanton

28th February, 1861

Dear Benjamin,

I was so glad to receive your letter and to hear of your safe return home. You guessed right. It is indeed Mr Templeton for whom I hold a candle, hopeless though it might be. Do not worry though. I am not much dismayed that you have learned my secret, for now I have someone with whom I can talk with complete candour about it. It is a relief to be able to speak freely on this matter, for even though my brother and Benedict may have an inkling of my feelings for Mr Templeton, they will not ever speak of it unless I instigate the conversation. You are also right to say that the physical distance between us makes it easier to be frank, for I am not sure I would be quite this forthright with you in person! So please do keep writing and regaling me with all your unvarnished thoughts and adventures — I will endeavour to do the same.

I am not much shocked to hear of your dalliance with this Chastity Hewitt — it is the kind of thing many young men take the opportunity to do with women of loose morals — though that is not to say that I approve of such lewd behaviour. I hope you have a care as to what may be the consequences should this wretched girl ever become with child after you have had your wicked way with her. Now I will stop with the hectoring, for you are free to do as you please, and it is not my place to chastise you. Do not, I beg, refrain from being frank with me for fear that I may judge or prose to you about what you should be doing.

As for my news, there is little to report. I have not had the good fortune to be in Mr Templeton's company except on Sundays at church. I sit at my usual pew seat from which I can have a clear view of his handsome profile. To my shame, I spend the church service with my mind filled with thoughts of him rather than on the excellent sermon that Benedict is no doubt preaching. As soon as the service is over, I make sure to be in Mr Templeton's path as he negotiates his way out. Thus he has no choice but to acknowledge me—which he always does with a most pleasing manner. I must tell you, Benjamin, that the moment when he approaches me is wonderfully exciting, sending my pulse racing and my heart pounding. Then it is all over, and I must wait another week until I see him again.

Writing this, I am struck by how piteous I sound, grasping at what little crumbs are thrown my way. It is not an enviable state of affairs. Often after my encounters with Mr Templeton, I wonder what it would be like to be held in the embrace of a loving husband and to feel his lips on mine. How would it feel to join my body with a man who loves me and to fulfil our conjugal passion? Dear friend, you will not, I hope, mind my sharing with you the unvarnished, sad truth of my imaginings. Perhaps with your dalliances, you have had experience of what it is I am yearning for. But I think not. It is quite one thing to embrace someone you love and another to embrace one you are simply dallying with.

There, now you know the truth of it all between me and Mr Templeton. However, I do not want you to think I spend my days pining for what is not to be. In fact, you will be glad to know that I have remembered those words of Seneca you recited to me the night of the ball. I endeavour to live in the present and not have a care as to what the future may bring. While I may at times yearn for more, I am not unhappy. I have beyond what is adequate for my needs and live comfortably, which is more than can be said for many people in this world.

I must tell you also, while I remember, that your older brother has been everything that is kind and generous to Ambrose and me. Every Sunday, he invites us to partake of lunch with him, and he has given me free use of the vast library of Stanton Hall. He has also been so very considerate of Ambrose, who has been laid low with the influenza but is now thankfully recovered. The young ladies of Stanton Harcourt are all vying for his attention. I have not, however, noticed him show partiality for anyone.

Do correct me if I am wrong, but I believe it must have been a trial for you to grow up in the shadow of an elder brother so assured and gifted as he, and moreover one who would one day inherit not just a title but a vast patrimony. Ambrose tells me, in the most admiring of tones, that Daniel is a brilliant linguist, having mastery of Latin, French and German, and that he excelled in his studies at Yale. Dear Benjamin, such a paragon of a brother must be hard to live up to! I should know, for I have experienced this very thing myself with Ambrose, whose achievements I could never match.

And now you are being asked to step into his shoes. I sense your reservations about the new role you have been given. In your mind, you had set your sights on a different future than the one now being laid before you. To this, dear friend, I counsel patience. I do understand your desire to work in the field of engineering, for I too share this interest. I can think of nothing better than working as a railway engineer (or railroad, as you call it in America). Imagine designing new locomotives or overseeing the construction of suspension bridges, or even engineering new railway lines on difficult terrain and helping to bring remote areas of the country within easy reach. How admirable!

All this and more could still be ahead of you, though perhaps not immediately. You are still very young. I say this as one who is three years your senior—if you do not mind me bringing up the difference in our ages. In time, you may find a capable person to manage your lands for you, much as Ambrose manages the

Stanton lands, and to turn your attention towards these other pursuits. Patience, my friend. Write to me soon.

Your friend,

Sarah Cranshaw

P.S. The situation you describe regarding the secession of the southern states is concerning. I do hope a war can be averted, though I do not think that the evil of slavery can be allowed to spread. My thoughts and prayers are with you.

CHAPTER 4

LETTERS EXCHANGED BETWEEN BENJAMIN AND SARAH, MARCH TO MAY 1861

March 22nd, 1861

Dear Sarah,

It was wonderfully good to receive your letter, though the reading of it left me with mixed feelings. Much as you claim not to want to chastise, I felt, from the distance of an ocean and a continent, your disapprobation over my dalliance with Chastity. Perhaps I should not have been so forthright in writing of it to you, but then without frankness on my part, you would not have been able to reciprocate with your own unvarnished truth— which I so want to hear. I do not think I have been privy to such honest exchanges with anyone else in a long time. Daniel used to confide in me when we were younger, but this changed as we grew to adulthood and went to different colleges. I like the way you listen to my thoughts and seem to truly understand me in a way that no one else in my family seems to do.

But back to my affair with Chastity. Firstly, I think it will be short-lived, and worry not, I am being careful to ensure there is no junior Stanton produced as a result of it. I will spare you the details, but suffice it to say that it was that paragon you speak of, none other than my brother Daniel, who instructed me on the ways to go about having dalliances with damsels, for he is the master of such things, or so he tells me.

Dear friend, for that is what you are, I do believe that the true basis of friendship is the acceptance of each other with all our faults, and the ability to be honest about how we feel. I have never made any claims to saintliness. I stand before you a flawed human being with faults aplenty, one of which is my weakness for comely maidens. I will have you know by way of explanation (or mitigation), that to sink into the softness of a woman is one of the greatest pleasures known to man. It is a pleasure I am unable to resist, though I do believe there will come a day when my soul and body will belong to one woman only. I am certain you are right in saying there is night and day between the embrace of two people in love and the embrace of people merely dallying. I have not experienced the former, and perhaps when I finally do, it will feel so right as to make it impossible for me to ever kiss anyone else again but the one I love.

The other reason for my mixed feelings on reading your letter was your painfully accurate estimate of my relationship with Daniel. How was it you knew? It is true that it has been hard to grow up in his shadow, for he is so handsome and accomplished, and more so than this, enormously kind. I, on the other hand, am not quite so handsome and certainly not as accomplished, and arguably not as kind. But though it has been hard to live up to all his perfection, I try not to give in to that perfidious emotion known as envy. It is not always easy. I love him dearly, but can't help resenting him sometimes, which I know I ought not to do.

On to other matters. I am trying to heed your counsel on staying patient. Every day, I am learning more about the management of our estate and doing my best not to disappoint Papa. It is a struggle though, I will admit. I would much rather be draughting the design of that locomotive we spoke of before I left, or tinkering with the mechanics of a traction engine.

And now we come to the important matter of your feelings for Mr Templeton. I was very interested to read your description of what happens to you when you are near him. Have you ever considered, dear friend, that what you feel is lust rather than love? I do not wish to diminish your feelings in any way, but in reading your description, I recalled a young lady I once knew by the name of Clarissa. I felt no love for her but a goodly amount of lust. I do recall how it felt to be up close and breathe in her delightful scent, to get a glimpse of the curves in her decolletage and to have my heart pound in my chest with need of her. It was like my body was on fire, causing a certain male part of my anatomy to thicken and throb in reaction—do pardon my frankness but strangely, I rather like talking to you of such things.

I wonder if something similar is occurring with you when you are in proximity of Mr T. I can see that he is a very attractive and virile looking man who no doubt appeals to your natural womanly urges. Now when it came to Clarissa, I was able to slake those urges and realise that lust was all that this was, not love. You cannot do the same with Mr T, but if you were to do so, I am sure you would come to discover as I did that what you are feeling is lust, and then perhaps you could open yourself to the possibility of love with someone else. Think on it.

Your friend,

Benjamin Stanton

P.S. The situation over here seems to be worsening. The states that have seceded from the Union have come together and called themselves the Confederate States of America. There are also rumours that more states are likely to secede and join them. Much sabre rattling is going on between the two sides, but as yet no open confrontation. We await to see how this situation will develop, but both Papa and Mama are extremely concerned about where all this is heading.

20th April, 1861

Dear Benjamin,

Once again it was a thrill to receive and read your letter. How glad I am that we embarked on this uncommon friendship of ours, one as you say that knows no bounds. I have never before engaged in such frank correspondence, and it is marvellously liberating.

Now where am I to start? Perhaps with an apology. I am sorry that you felt a note of rebuke in my previous letter. It was wrong of me to judge. Perhaps it was occasioned partly by that perfidious emotion, envy, for the freedom you have to indulge in dalliances without fear of judgement. The world we live in has different standards of morality for women than for men. What would be considered the natural "sowing of wild oats" in a man would be painted in a much different light for a woman. I have never dared contemplate letting a man have his wicked way with me. It would be unthinkable! And yet I feel those bodily urges much as you do. There have been times, in my most private imaginings, when I have wondered how it would be to be whisked away to a deserted barn, like Chastity, and to be thoroughly seduced. How deliciously wicked that would be!

Dear friend, I have thought much about your situation. I understand how maddening it must be to not pursue the path you wish in life. Again, I counsel patience. However, I do wonder if there would be some benefit to you in speaking more openly with your father or even your mother about your ambitions. They must, of course, be aware of your scientific inclinations, but perhaps they do not realise fully the depth of your desire to be an engineer. Do not let your fear of causing disappointment make you hide something so fundamental to your happiness from them. Speak openly and express both your respect and love for them together with an exposition of what you would in actual fact like to do. I believe your parents are reasonable persons and that they desire the happiness of their children.

Now I come to your evaluation of my feelings for Mr Templeton. Here I will admit something to you that I have not told anyone else. Something happens to my body in addition to the pounding of my heart when he approaches me. It is strikingly similar to what you described as feeling for Clarissa — that throbbing of a male part of your anatomy. Only in my case, it is the throbbing of a female part of my anatomy, accompanied by a strange wetness in my undergarments. I blush as I write this and think perhaps I should rip this sheet and start this letter again. But I will not. I feel with you such a freedom to express myself in a way I cannot do with anyone else, not even Ambrose or Benedict. I do so cherish this openness between us.

Being of a scientific disposition, I have of course investigated the possible reasons for these physical symptoms I have just described, and learned that these are nature's way of preparing a woman's body for the act of sexual congress. So, it seems my reaction to an attractive man's presence is entirely lustful. From this, it would be sensible to surmise that indeed as you say, what I feel for Mr T is simply lust rather than love. And yet... surely if it were only lust, even someone as stubborn as me would not have sustained these feelings for so long? And also, I care about his wellbeing and fret over him. I tell myself these must be signs of the heart being engaged.

Now I have some fresh news to share in regards to Mr Templeton. Two nights ago, I attended the Easter dance in Whitney. It is quite a big event which is held there every year. What a crush of people it was—over a hundred by my count. Ambrose and I travelled there together with your brother and sister in their carriage. The first thing Isabella and I did on arrival was to get our dance cards from the master of ceremonies. She, of course, was much sought after for dances, but I did not do too badly either. And now for my big news.

I was standing in a circle with Isabella, Ambrose and Daniel when lo and behold, Mr Templeton joined us. He made his bows and looked first to Isabella then to me, begging each of us for a dance. So it was that sometime later in the evening, I stood for the polka with Mr Templeton, my first ever dance with him. And Benjamin, it was wonderful. Even now, two days later, my heart beats faster just remembering it. As he held me close and whirled me round the room, I felt I was flying through the air. So you see, my friend, how difficult it is to dismiss the feelings I have for Mr T as simply lust.

Even were it true, it is not as if there is any rival presenting himself for my affections. One of the joys of living in a small village such as ours is that one gets to know the society there intimately, but the drawback is that the range of one's acquaintances is limited. I know only a handful of single gentlemen, and none excite in me any particular interest or desire. Perhaps if I were in America, like you, I would meet more eligible men, or if I were one of those young ladies able to go to London for the season. Then perhaps, there would be opportunity for the heart to fix itself on someone else—though I am not sure that a city gent would suit me either. As that is not within my purview, then I must content myself with what I have here in Stanton Harcourt and enjoy each delightful encounter with Mr T, short as it may be, before I die an old maid. You will not begrudge me that, I hope!

On a last note, I am reading the newspaper reports about the situation in America, and it does not sound to me as if the differences between the Union and the Confederacy can be resolved amicably. I dread the thought of war and bloodshed, especially now that I have people I care greatly about in America — that means you and your family, in case my meaning was not plain enough. I have come to treasure this friendship of ours. You do not know how eagerly I wait for your missives. Keep writing, and keep safe.

Yours in true friendship,

Sarah

May 15ᵗʰ, 1861

My dear Sarah,

I too treasure this unusual friendship of ours and look forward eagerly to receiving news from you. And what news it was! I am glad you wrote and posted it, although you may have regretted your candour the next day. Do please persist with this rare and wonderfully forthright correspondence between us. I promise to honour it with a reciprocal honesty from myself, never to judge and to always treat your divulgences with the discretion they deserve. Moreover, I must tell you that reading such things as you describe happening to your body has a powerful effect on me, causing a similar response in mine.

But first, let me discuss your revelation about what occurs to your person when you are close to an attractive gentleman. You are quite correct that your body without volition reacts to his nearness as if it were preparing for sexual congress. Now let me share something with you. Whenever I am in the process of such an intimate act, I first ensure that the lady in question is well lubricated with her natural juices — that wetness you describe — before penetrating her with my male organ, for otherwise it is painful to her and unpleasurable to me. (I hope by now that I no longer need to apologise to you for my frankness.)

If she has not yet reached such a state of lubrication, I help her do so by stroking a small protrusion at the juncture of her thighs. This protrusion has a scientific name — the clitoris — and it is so sensitive as to bring much delight to the lady when it is stimulated. I stroke her clitoris in quick strokes back and forth or in a circular motion with my thumb. Sometimes, I also dip my finger in and out of her cunt in anticipation of what my cock will soon do — that way I can also gauge her state of readiness for fucking by the degree of lubrication. Am I teaching you some shocking new words? I make no apologies for corrupting you on this front, my dear Sarah. A man's cock is a common name for his male sexual organ, and a woman's cunt is the name for the internal passage that leads to her womb. And fucking is the wonderfully coarse word used for describing the sexual act itself. I have my brother, that fount of knowledge about intimate relations with women, to thank for this information which has stood me well.

Now I have a question for you of a very personal nature. Do not feel obliged to respond, though I very much hope that you do. Have you ever stroked yourself with your fingers down below and touched your clitoris, even though you may not have known it by name? Such a touch would have sent excitement through your body, and brought you to a state of pleasurable completion known as an orgasm. It will have felt like involuntary convulsions at the core of your body, followed by a deep sense of contentment. An orgasm is unmistakable if you have experienced it. If you have not, then perhaps next time you are alone in your room at night, you may give it a try. And please do tell me all about it. I think we have come far enough in our frankness to each other to be able to share such things. If you do, I promise to tell you more about how I too pleasure myself alone at night!

In any case, I want you to know that the feelings in your body that you experience when you are in proximity of Mr T are entirely natural and no cause for shame. And by the same token, should you follow my advice and experience an orgasm through the touch of your fingers to your intimate regions, then that too is nothing shameful. That part of your body was God-created for sensual stimulation. Think of it as a gift from your maker.

Now on the subject of your feelings for Mr T, I still maintain that it is lust that you feel, for the simple reason that you have not given me any indication that you have gotten to know his character beyond what can be observed on the surface. Consider it another way. In all probability, you now know me far better than Mr T, even though we have known each other for far less time. It is the substance of the discourse between us that has allowed us to go quickly from mere acquaintances to good friends. Do you really know what manner of a man Mr T is? Glimpses of him at church, the occasional dinner party and one thrilling dance at a ball do not, in my view, suffice to develop deep and enduring love.

However, have it your way and call it what you wish. I will not argue the matter any further. It saddens me though, that you feel unable to love someone else because of a lack of opportunity. Cannot something be done about that? I do not mean a season in London, for I know that is not likely in your circumstances, but how about finding ways to enlarge your circle of acquaintances? I wish I could be there to introduce you to new friends. Perhaps Daniel could help, seeing as he is now lord of the manor and able to entertain lavishly. Should I write to him and suggest he hold a house party, inviting the illustrious people he has met in London? Say the word and I shall do so.

You offer sage advice with regards to my father. I should speak to him of my aspirations and I will, though I have not yet found the right moment to do so. In the meantime, I promise to be patient. There is so much on Papa's mind at this time. He still grieves for Grandpa, and he misses my brother and sister. Added to that, his concern grows ever deeper over the conflict between the Union and the Confederacy, and what it might mean for us. Just a few weeks ago, Fort Sumter in South Carolina came under fire from Confederate forces, and we now find ourselves in a state of war.

I tell myself the time is not right to rock the boat with selfish talk of my personal aspirations. President Lincoln has issued a call for volunteers to serve in the Union army. Soon, no doubt, cavalry regiments will be calling for volunteers too, and when that comes to pass, I shall feel duty bound to offer my services in the military effort in order to protect our lands and our values from the encroachment of the Confederate states. I can see no other choice but to play my part in the drama that shall soon unfold. My own petty concerns seem small when set in contrast with the troubles of the nation. I have not yet told Ma and Pa of my plans. No doubt, it will be a difficult conversation to have with them.

On this worrisome note, I come to the end of this missive. I hope all is well with you, dear friend, and wish you to know that our correspondence is the thing keeping my spirits up in these trying times. Keep writing for however long it is still possible to do so, for once I am a soldier in uniform, there is no knowing where I shall be or how I can be reached. I am uncertain even as to how long it will take for this letter to arrive in England, as shipping has been disrupted by the war. I will continue to write whenever I can and keep you apprised of my progress. Will you keep reading my letters, even if there is no hope of your response reaching me? It will be a one-sided correspondence, to be sure, but I would much rather keep the thread connecting us intact than break it altogether. You and your friendship have come to mean so much to me.

Your true friend,

Benjamin

P.S. You will be happy to learn that my affair with Chastity Hewitt has come to an end. It was only lust, after all. I told you, did I not, that it would be short-lived.

CHAPTER 5

SARAH

"Short is the joy that guilty pleasure brings."
— Euripides

June 1861

SARAH PUT THE letter down, a sinking feeling in her chest. It had taken nearly a month for Benjamin's missive to reach her in the quiet Oxfordshire village in which she lived. During that time of course, she had heard the news about a war breaking out in America, and she had fretted, the safety of her newfound friend and his family paramount in her thoughts. Not even a chance encounter with Mr Templeton in the village could lift that worry from her mind.

Ambrose too shared her fears, working as he did so closely with Daniel, who was filled with worry for his family. Only yesterday, Daniel had told Ambrose that he proposed to return to America. It had taken all of Ambrose and Benedict's powers of persuasion to convince him to stay. They reminded him that his father had entrusted Isabella to his care in England, and that his uncle Jasper had also tasked him with keeping a protective eye on Grace. He would be doing them both a disservice by leaving. In the end, it had been the packet of letters that arrived from America that had dissuaded him. His father, mother and brother all wrote to him, making their wishes clear. He should stay in England and abandon all thought of returning to his old home.

That same packet had contained Benjamin's letter to Sarah, which she had just finished reading. She was not much surprised to learn that Benjamin meant to enlist in the army. From what she knew of him, it was the sort of brave thing that he would do. Surprised or not, it still sent a pang of fear through her heart. This war could take from her the wonderful new friend she had only recently found. She sighed and picked the letter up again, reading it one more time. Then she placed it carefully in the box that contained Benjamin's other letters and readied herself for bed.

As she went to get under the covers, she paused. No, she was not quite ready yet for sleep. Slipping on her robe and taking her a candle with her, she opened her bedroom door and walked down the hall to Ambrose's room. On her knock, his voice came cheerfully through the door, "Enter!" She turned the knob and went in.

Ambrose sat in bed, his spectacles on the bridge of his nose as he read from the book that he held in his lap. On seeing his sister, he carefully marked the page and set the book aside. His understanding gaze settled on her face. "I thought you might come by," was all he said. He patted the space next to him in invitation.

Sarah set her candle on the table and came to sit beside him, letting her chin rest on his shoulder. "So, what has you unable to sleep?" he asked. "Is it today's letter from America?"

"Yes, it was from Benjamin Stanton."

He nodded. "I assumed so. What does he have to say that has you so uneasy?"

"He is going to enlist in the Union army, just as soon as the call comes for cavalry volunteers."

"Yes, I know." At her look of surprise, he explained, "Benjamin wrote of it to Daniel too, though he has not informed either of his parents yet of his decision."

"And Daniel told you?"

Ambrose kissed the top of her head before answering. "We had a long conversation about it today. Benjamin wrote that he planned to volunteer with a cavalry regiment and that Daniel was absolutely not to follow suit. He laid it on thick, writing that it was Daniel's duty to stay in England safe and sound so that at least one of their papa's sons would remain unharmed."

Sarah huffed in frustration, "I can well imagine how Daniel took that!"

"He was agitated, to put it mildly. But then in the next portion of the letter, Benjamin asked his brother to just this once let him have the glory. There is, it seems, some rivalry between the two."

"Yes," replied Sarah with a sigh. "Benjamin has lived in his brother's shadow all his life. You see how it is, don't you?"

"Having a handsome, brilliant older brother? I'm sure you must know how it is," replied Ambrose teasingly.

Sarah feigned ignorance. "I'm sure I cannot know what you mean." Then she returned to the matter at hand. "I do hope Daniel heeds your words. No good would come of him going to America."

"I hope so too," murmured Ambrose. He turned to face his sister. "So, you are worried about Benjamin."

She nodded mutely. He regarded her a moment more, then enquired gently, "And what is Benjamin to you now? I thought, perhaps, that your affections were engaged elsewhere."

Sarah felt her face flush. "They are. That has not changed. Benjamin is a very good friend. That is all."

"I see." He pondered this a few beats then gave a light laugh. "You were never one to take the conventional path, were you? When I come to think of it, this is nothing new for you. After all, you have been friends with Benedict all your life."

"I do not know why it is considered so strange that a woman should befriend a man. We are not different species of animal after all. What unites us in our humanity is far greater than the minor differences between male and female."

He shrugged. "You are right, I suppose, but I have never had occasion to befriend someone from the opposite sex."

"Perhaps you should think of doing so," said Sarah with passion in her voice, "for I assure you it is a most interesting thing to be able to speak freely with a person of the opposite sex."

"I do that already with you," Ambrose said, sounding amused.

"Mmm, not quite the same. There are things of which I cannot speak with you."

"But you can with Benjamin Stanton?" asked Ambrose, a touch perturbed.

"Yes, with him I can."

"Well then," replied Ambrose, "I am glad for you that you have him as a friend. Let us hope and pray he is unharmed in this war."

Sarah felt a tightness in her chest as she was reminded once more of why she had come to see her brother. With a slight quaver in her voice, she said, "I cannot contemplate the prospect of him being harmed without feeling great pain."

He squeezed her hand gently. "Then keep him in your prayers, my love. That is all that you can do."

"I know." Sarah shifted herself to the edge of the bed and stood. "I shall leave you in peace now. Goodnight."

"Goodnight."

Back in her room, Sarah discarded her robe and climbed into bed. Then, she blew out the candle and settled herself for sleep. Yet still sleep would not come. She thought of her friend, miles away in a land rife with discord and strife. Closing her eyes, she recalled how he had looked, sitting on a rooftop beside her as he marvelled at the wondrous sight of a meteor shower. She thought back to his letters and the privilege he had accorded her in corresponding with such honesty—writing of things no one else had spoken of to her before. *"Have you ever stroked yourself with your fingers down below and touched your clitoris?"*

he'd asked. *"If you have not, then perhaps next time you are alone in your room at night, you may give it a try."*

Slowly, a little astonished at her own brazenness, Sarah slipped a hand under the covers and pulled at the fabric of her night gown, raising it to a point above her hips. She felt the cool kiss of the sheet on the heated core of her body and shivered slightly at the contact. Next, she guided a trembling hand down to her mound, grazing the wiry tuft of hair that grew in this most intimate part of her body. Still lower she went, parting her legs to open herself up to the touch of her fingers. The flesh there was soft and moist, delicate as the petals of a flower. She had touched it before in passing while cleaning herself, but never in the purposeful way she was doing now.

She rested her hand over this soft flesh. The weight of it felt pleasant and warm, like a comforting blanket. Eyes closed, she paid attention to the sensation of her touch there. After a time, she felt a compulsion to move her hips gently, swaying them against the contact of her hand. Back and forth she began to move, rubbing herself against the fingers gathered on her moist core. It was a novel sensation. It felt... oddly good. Then, without her volition, she did another brazen thing. She imagined she was Chastity Hewitt in an empty barn with Benjamin, and that the hand rubbing over her slippery core was his, not hers. She heard his rough voice whisper words of praise and encouragement. She imagined him kissing a line up her neck to her mouth, then his firm lips finding hers and raining kiss after tumultuous kiss.

The motion of her hips became a little faster, a little more frantic, as she chased something unknown. She felt that familiar throb down below, but it was stronger now, more intense. The throbbing feeling was building up like the crescendo of an orchestral symphony, getting stronger and stronger. Then all of a sudden, she felt it. It was akin to the clang of the cymbals at the climax of a symphony, followed by reverberations that echoed through her body so violently she could not help the moan that escaped from her lips.

Her chest heaved with panting breaths as she experienced her first orgasm, for this surely was what she had just felt. It was unmistakable, as Benjamin had told her it would be. Slowly, her breathing steadied. She lay in her bed, glorying in a sense of wellbeing and satisfaction. A question teased the edges of her mind as it wandered, preparing to drift away into the land of slumber. Was it wrong to have imagined her friend in the throes of her passion? Should she have reached an orgasm to thoughts of him touching and kissing her? Perhaps this would have to be her guilty secret. But no. First thing tomorrow, she would write to Benjamin and tell him all about it. She would not throw a veil over this little episode as that would do a disservice to the extraordinary honesty that had built between them. She would tell him all. He would understand. He was her true friend, but of course she did not find him more attractive than Mr Templeton. Or did she?

CHAPTER 6

BENJAMIN

"He who postpones the hour of living rightly is like the
rustic who waits for the river to run out before he crosses."
— Horace

Late July, 1861
THE HEAT OF the afternoon sun beat down upon him as he stood in the harbour to oversee a consignment of wheat from the Stanton estate being loaded onto the lake steamer, which was headed north to Buffalo. It was tedious work, but his father had entrusted him to do it, now that he had proved himself capable of such responsibility.

Benjamin lifted his hat long enough to mop with a handkerchief the sweat gathered along the back of his neck. He dropped the hat back on his head, letting out a long breath. The job was nearly done, and then he could stop at the harbour tavern for a drink and a bite to eat before riding home. Not for the first time, he wondered where he would be a month from now. The mobilisation of the Union's military forces was proceeding apace, and soon, it would be his turn to go.

He had not spoken of his plans yet to his parents. This was something else he would have to do and soon. His thoughts were uneasy. He knew the conversation ahead was going to be a difficult one, and he felt a spurt of guilt knowing he would be disappointing and hurting the people he loved. Yet was he to stay behind while others risked life and limb for their country? He could not do that.

An hour later, he was galloping along the rutted road on his way home. His thoughts drifted to Sarah, as they often did when he was alone, wondering what she was doing. Would she be working on the miniature railway he had started for her? Or was she daydreaming of her latest brush with Mr Templeton at church? He snorted, mildly irritated. He found her continuing obsession with the man displeasing. It was not as if he wanted Sarah for himself. After all, there could be nothing but a long-distance friendship between himself and her. And anyway, she was not at all the kind of girl he was usually attracted to. Nonetheless, he could not help feeling that Mr Templeton was not good enough for her.

It had been over two months since he had last received word from her. He wondered what she would have to say in response to his last missive, in which he had imparted knowledge about the sensual workings of the female body and suggested that she try touching herself intimately at night. Had she done so? Would she tell him about it? He longed for her to tell him in great detail.

He reached the bend in the road that preceded the entrance to the large Stanton estate, riding up the dirt lane and through the gravelled path to the stable. With easy grace, he jumped down from his mount and led the horse inside to its stall. Jimmy, the stable boy, came to help, bringing straw and water over to the parched animal. "Hey Ben, how'd it go? It's spitting hot out there," he said with an easy smile.

"Hotter than hellfire," agreed Benjamin. They worked together amicably, rubbing the horse down and cleaning out its hooves.

"Soon as I'm done here," said Jimmy, "I'm headed down to the lake for a swim. Want to come?"

Benjamin needed no convincing. He was covered in sweat and grime, and a dip in the cooling water of the lake was just what he needed. "I'm coming," he affirmed. He gave his horse one last friendly pat and let himself out of the stable. In quick strides, he walked over to the large, white-trimmed house with a shingled roof and long, inviting porch. It had been built by his father and uncle from the trees they had cut down to claim this land. Not for the first time, he felt a sense of pride for what his father—a viscount from a rich, privileged family—had achieved. He had turned his back on it all to start afresh in the New World and be with the woman he loved. Speaking of that woman… there on the porch sat his mother, her face buried in a book, as was her wont. She had not heard his approach, so immersed was she in whatever it was she was reading.

On soft feet, Benjamin took the steps up to the porch and let out a low whistle. Charlotte Stanton looked up at once, her face transforming into a happy smile at seeing her son. "Benjamin, you're back," she murmured. "I've been waiting for you." She reached in front of her for an earthenware jug and poured some cold lemonade into a clean cup. "You'll be wanting this, I'm sure," she said, handing it to him.

Benjamin took it gratefully and gulped the liquid down in one go. She smiled, "More?"

"Please," he said, throwing himself down on the seat beside her. He took the refilled cup, drinking this one down a little more slowly before putting it down on the table. "Thank you, Ma, I needed that. It's hotter than Hades out there. I'm going to head out to the lake in just a minute and cool myself down. Clean myself too. I must stink."

His mother wrinkled her nose. "You do a little, but I am used to it. You go have your swim. Ruby has a towel and a change of clothes ready for you inside."

"Thank you," he said, getting to his feet. As he went to do so, he was stopped by his mother's next words.

"Letters came today from England. Yours are on the salver in the hallway."

A thrill rushed through him, but he hid it well, replying in a measured voice, "Oh good. What news from Daniel and Bella?"

"They are well. Worrying about us, though thankfully Daniel has given up on the idea of coming here."

"Hallelujah," Benjamin murmured dryly.

His mother laughed, with a hint of sadness. "Much as I would love to see them again, I think it best they stay out of this mess we are in right now. It is bad enough I have to worry about you," she said, looking pointedly at him. *Had she guessed his plans?*

"You don't need to worry, Ma." He pounded on his chest with the palm of his hand. "Hale and hearty. That's me."

"Just make sure you keep it that way," she said sharply. Then in a softer voice, she added, "There is a letter too from your lady friend."

Benjamin nodded but did not respond. His family had shown teasing curiosity at the regular stream of letters exchanged between himself and Sarah Cranshaw. It was not something that could remain hidden, though he refused to elucidate on the nature of his relationship with her. It was nobody's business but his own. He was not sure why, but he just knew that what he and Sarah shared was private, and not just because of the candour of their communication.

He went inside and picked up the letters—one from each of his siblings and one from Sarah. He weighed Sarah's letter in his hand, pleased at the thickness of it. He wanted nothing more than to rip it open and read it on the spot, but he would not. It was best to wait until he was alone in his room tonight. Setting the letters back down, he went quickly to fetch the packet of clothes and the towel that Ruby—their housekeeper who also happened to be Jimmy's mother—had set aside for him, then headed outside once again, walking purposefully towards the small lake at the edge of their estate.

Once there, he stripped off his clothes, collected the small bar of lavender soap Ruby had packed for him and waded into the cool embrace of the water. *Ah, that felt better.* He soaped his body and hair thoroughly, cleansing away the stink of the day, then threw the bar of soap over on to the clothes he had discarded. Closing his eyes, he plunged underwater, rinsing off the suds. It felt peaceful under there, the water enclosing him in a protective bubble, as if he were a babe back in the womb of his mother. Soon, he would be embarking on a dangerous new stage of his life, and part of him wished, just for this moment, to stay inside this safe haven.

The peace was shattered an instant later as someone dived into the lake, creating ripples all around him. He came up to the surface with a splutter, just as Jimmy emerged beside him, shaking the wet hair out of his face with a grin. "Jimmy!" Benjamin cried in annoyance. "Did you have to do that?"

"You were under there so long I was starting to worry," replied Jimmy unabashed. "What were you doing?"

"Nothing. Just contemplating."

Jimmy looked at him as if he had grown two heads. "Contemplating? I'm not sure I even know what that means."

"It means, idiot, that I was having a peaceful moment underwater until you came and ruined it."

"Accept my apologies then," replied Jimmy, looking anything but sorry. "You got soap?" he asked, changing the subject.

Benjamin nodded with his head towards the pile of clothing by the lake. "Over there."

Jimmy swam back to the water's edge and fetched the bar of soap, then came back in, rubbing it all over his sturdy, tanned body. Once he was done, he threw it back where he had found it and plunged underwater to rinse the soap away. He rose to the surface again, rubbing his eyes and brushing the wet hair off his forehead.

Benjamin observed him silently for a while before asking, "Are you going to enlist?" The question had been on his mind for some time though to Jimmy, it might have seemed to come out of the blue.

His friend squinted under the bright rays of the sun. "Your pa says I don't need to—that I'm too important to the war effort here, and he can get me an exemption."

"He's right, I suppose. We've got a whole army to feed."

Jimmy said nothing more for some time, lying on his back and floating in the still water of the lake. Eventually, he roused himself to answer the question. "I've thought about it plenty, and I've decided. First chance I get, I'm signing up."

"There's talk of a cavalry regiment being mustered up at Camp Chase, just outside Columbus," Benjamin remarked, almost conversationally.

At this, Jimmy came upright in the water and stared at his friend. "I was thinking more in terms of being a regular soldier in the infantry," he muttered.

"If I pay for your horse and whatever equipment you need, will you join the cavalry regiment with me?"

Jimmy did not answer at once, thinking it over. Then, a slow smile spread over his face. "Yeah, I can do that."

LATER THAT EVENING, sitting at the dinner table with his parents, Benjamin finally broached the subject that had been on his mind for weeks. It was during talk of the latest developments in the war that, sounding more calm than he felt, he threw in the following remark, "Jimmy and I have decided we're volunteering for the first Ohio cavalry regiment. We'll be going to Camp Chase early next month to enlist together."

All conversation ceased as Frank, Earl of Stanton, stared at his son in fury. "You will do no such thing," he gritted. "I forbid it."

Benjamin swallowed, his hands balled into fists at his sides. He tried again. "Pa, I am of age and my own man. You cannot forbid me to do it."

Frank thumped on the table with his hand. "Then think of your mother! Will you make her endure worry and heartache over you, all for a cause that is nothing to do with us? Madness!"

"I'm sorry, Mama," Benjamin said, glancing over at his mother. "I do not wish to cause you worry, but please understand, I cannot be the coward that stays behind while others fight on my behalf."

Charlotte Stanton reached across the table to place a reassuring hand on his arm. "I know," she said, her voice tight with emotion.

"Charlotte! Surely you do not support this preposterous idea!" spluttered Frank, scowling at his wife.

She rose from her seat and came to place her arms around him. "Darling, Benjamin's mind is already made up. There is nothing much we can do but accept his decision."

"We can speak to him and convince him to change his mind!" retorted Frank, leaning into his wife's embrace.

"I won't!" cried Benjamin. "And Pa, you are wrong about this cause being nothing to do with us. When you left England and claimed this land, this became your home. I was born here and I am an American, regardless of my English descent. Moreover, Pa, there is a moral imperative to this cause, and you know it. We must stop the Confederacy and the spread of their barbaric practice of slavery."

"All I know, son, is that I have already lost someone dear to me this year. I will not lose another." With that, Frank disentangled Charlotte's arms from around him and stood up. He turned and left the dining room without another word.

Charlotte watched him go, pain and worry etched on her face, then came over to her son. Putting a hand on his shoulder, she said, "I will speak with him. Give him a little time to come round. This is going to be hard on all of us, Benjamin."

He looked at his mother in misery. "I am sorry, Ma."

She shook her head. "It is not your fault. This situation is outside our control. But understand, Benjamin. Your papa loves you, and he is hurting."

He put his hand over hers and nodded. She dropped a kiss to the top of his head, then left to go find her husband. Benjamin remained seated alone at the dining table, all thought of food gone. Setting his napkin down, he stood. Right this moment, he needed comfort, and he knew what would provide it. With quick footsteps, he made his way up the stairs. In his room, he settled himself on an armchair by the open window, picked up Sarah's letter and slit it open, pulling out several sheets of paper. Then, he started to read.

CHAPTER 7

LETTERS WRITTEN BY BENJAMIN AND SARAH, JUNE TO JULY 1861

14th June, 1861

Dearest Benjamin,

If, as you say, you will shortly be enlisting for the war, then this may be the very last letter of mine that will reach you for a long time. As I write this, I feel the need to make this missive matter as much as possible. But how can I make it so? What can I say here that will sustain our friendship over the course of months or years or however long this conflict lasts between the Union and the Confederacy?

I could tell you that your letters are my most treasured possession. That I keep them in a box under my bed, and that I often take them out to re-read. I could tell you also that it is through you that I experience a world beyond the small village in which I live. It is you who tells me things nobody else would consider speaking to me about. Why, who else would have taught me those wicked words—clitoris, cunt, cock and fuck? Words that I am sure will now become part of my nightly imaginings. I could also tell you about what I did last night.

I received your letter yesterday, and as is my wont, I waited until I was alone in my room in the evening to read it at my leisure. And what a letter it was! There was so much for me to take in, chief of which was the knowledge that my dearest friend was soon to go to war. I had, of course, already learned from reading the papers that hostilities had broken out between the Union and the Confederacy, and I had half expected that you would feel duty bound to join the war effort, so your revelation did not come as a great surprise to me. However, the news still hit me hard. I could not sleep for worry, so I went to see Ambrose and had a talk with him about it. There was not much he could say, though, to allay my fears. Only that I should keep you in my prayers, which I will. Every morning and every night, and probably several times a day in between, you will be in my prayers. Promise me something, Benjamin. Promise me you will come back safe and sound from this war. Promise it even though it is not something within your gift to promise. And once you have made this promise, keep it within you as a good luck charm to ward off any evil.

I apologise, dear friend, if I am coming across as overwrought and emotional. I shall try to hold myself in hand for the remainder of this letter. Let me continue with my recount of what happened last night. I returned to my room, yet still could not get to sleep. The words of your letter kept going round and round in my mind, including your question: "Have you ever stroked yourself with your fingers down below?" The answer to that question was no, I had never thought to do so—until now.

Emboldened, I let my hand slide down slowly to the juncture of my legs. I tangled my fingers through the small tuft of hair that resides there and burrowed deeper until I reached the soft flesh below. There I rested my hand, my attention directed to the sensation of my touch. I do not know what instinct propelled me to do so, but I started to thrust my hip upwards into my hand. It was a pleasing sensation, and the more I did so, the more I felt that familiar throb of my core, only much stronger. And here, I confess I did another bold and shocking thing.

As I felt the friction of my hand to my core, I imagined it was your hand that was there touching me, and that I was Chastity, lying on a bed of straw in the barn. Your lips were on mine and you were whispering sweet words of praise to me. "That's my sweet girl," you said in a voice laced with passion. "Rub yourself against my hand. Get yourself wet and ready for me." And so I rubbed myself frantically against your hand, and oh my, how good it felt! I could feel how wet I had become for you and could sense your satisfaction. Soon, your cock would be inside my cunt, and you would lose yourself in the pleasure of sinking into the softness of my flesh.

The throbbing in my core by this time had become so intense. Each touch of your hand to me was sweet agony. I needed you so! "Take me," I whimpered. "Plunge yourself deep inside me and join your body to mine."

"Oh Chastity," was your ragged reply, though in my head, I think I heard you say my name. Then your cock was entering me and oh Benjamin, it was as if I felt it for real. A deep convulsion came over me and I shuddered in sweet ecstasy. I knew then what it was to experience an orgasm. It took some time for the shudders to stop and for my breath to return to an even rhythm. A wonderful feeling of contentment washed over me and I could feel myself sink into blessed slumber.

But before I did, I had one last thought. Was it right that I had imagined myself with my dear friend in such a wicked way? On the back of that thought came another. I would have to keep this a secret, for what I did was too shocking to reveal even to you. But then, I realised what a mistake that would be. What has marked our friendship is this searing honesty between us. I would be doing you, and our friendship, a disservice by withholding this knowledge. And so, even though it may paint me in an unfavourable light, I have written in detail of what occurred last night. I hope this will not make you throw up your hands and think, "Oh no, that wretched girl has crossed a line that should not be crossed."

Please write and tell me that I have not, in my wicked lewdness, destroyed the fabric of our friendship. And Benjamin, do keep writing, no matter what. I promise to read all your letters, even if I am unable to reply. Take care of yourself, dear friend, and do not forget that promise. I pray to God this war shall be short and that you will soon return victorious.

Your loving friend,

Sarah

July 28th, 1861

Dear Sarah,

Thank God your letter finally reached me. I had almost despaired of hearing from you before I leave for the war. It is decided. In a week or at most two, I shall leave for Camp Chase, a Union military training camp newly set up on the outskirts of Columbus. Jimmy, our stable boy whom I have known all my life, will accompany me. That way, I shall have someone from home on this new journey I am taking.

As you might expect, my family did not take this decision well. Papa was near hissing with fury, although as Ma explained, it was fear for me and pain that induced it. She says in time, he will come round. He was so mad with me tonight that he left the dinner table, his meal half eaten. I hope he does come round, for I would not wish to leave him on a cloud of anger.

I read and re-read your letter, not least because I know it will be the last one I receive from you in a very long time. And here I will confess: your letters are my most valued possession too. I keep them safe in a hidden compartment of my desk drawer, but I shall be taking this last missive of yours with me to war and keep it close at all times. Once you receive this, I shall be gone, either at training camp or elsewhere I know not. I was more grateful than you know that you wish me to continue to write to you even though you will be unable to respond. I cannot promise correspondence with any degree of regularity, but whenever it is possible to send you a missive, I will. Of course, I shall write to my family too, but yours will be the letter in which I speak the honest, unvarnished truth. With Pa, Ma and Bella, I shall be forced to write with cheer so as to allay their worries about me. With Daniel, I shall have to inflate my glorious achievements and present my war effort in the most positive light—for such is the burden of inferiority I carry when it comes to my brother. But with you, I will be truthful. Brace yourself, my friend, for the picture I will paint will not often be a pretty one. War is a nasty business, or so I hear.

I do not know how well I will take to military life. I will be exchanging one set of constraints for another, for I will need to take orders from my superiors, but I hope at least to be given some independence out in the field. I do believe joining the army is the right thing to do. Some part of me views the coming days with great hope and enthusiasm—it will be a break from the tedium of overseeing grain consignments, and I feel a sense of righteousness at fighting for a worthy cause. Another part of me views the future with dread. I have never before killed a fellow man. In the heat of battle, when I have to shoot my gun or wield my sabre, will I be able to do it or will I hesitate?

Enough of this sombre talk. I want to talk about you and the tantalising revelations you shared. Congratulations, by the by, on your first orgasm. The first of many, I hope. I cannot tell you how pleased and grateful I was that you were willing to share this most personal experience with me, writing it all with your usual candour. Dear Sarah, I am honoured. Doubly so as I was with you in your mind as you experienced this first bliss.

Do not feel ashamed or worried for our friendship that you imagined me with you as you touched yourself intimately. Your knowledge of such things came from me, for it was I that told you about seducing Chastity in an empty barn and how I stroke a lady's nether regions to get her wet and ready for me before the act of penetration. It was only natural therefore that you took that knowledge and used it in your imaginings to bring yourself to a pleasurable peak. Our friendship is of a special sort, one in which we are unsparingly honest about what we do and feel. The product of such searing honesty is intimacy—for now you and I know things about each other that nobody else in the world knows.

So, in this same spirit of intimacy, I will tell you something. As I read of your first orgasm, I became lustfully aroused. My male organ swelled, and I was obliged to put your letter down so as to undo the fastenings of my pants and release it from its confines. When I had it in my hand, I began to stroke myself, thinking of you in your bed, a hand on your mound, your hips thrusting up as you imagined yourself in the barn with me. The thought of you pleasuring yourself to thoughts of me was intoxicating. I could not help myself. I urgently needed to reach my own orgasm by stroking myself repeatedly with a hand wrapped tightly around my cock. To help with this, I took out from a drawer in my desk a bottle of castor oil and poured a few drops into my palm. I keep that bottle there for this very purpose.

With a lubricated hand, I can rub up and down my engorged shaft in a fast motion that brings me intense pleasure.

Before long, I reached my peak. Do you know, Sarah, what happens to a man when he reaches an orgasm? I will tell you. My cock swelled even more until it was red and stiff and angry-looking. And in that moment of intense bliss, a stream of pearly liquid shot forth from the tip. As you may have read about it, this is the fluid in which lies my seed, were I to impregnate a lady with a child.

When it was over, I closed my eyes and laid my head back, feeling immeasurably content. What a contrast to how I had felt only a half hour before, telling Papa of my decision and receiving his blazing anger in return. I had come up to my room despondent and weary. But reading your letter and its aftermath (one of the finest orgasms I have ever experienced) had me all mellow once more. You cannot know how much it fills my heart to think that I will be in your prayers night and day. Keep me safe through your prayers, Sarah, and in return, I will make that promise to you. I will come back safe and sound from this war. I shall wear this promise like an amulet around my neck.

Afterwards, I roused myself to clean the mess I had made and to read your letter once more—only to get aroused all over again and to stroke myself to orgasm a second time.

So you see, now we are even. You thought of me as you pleasured yourself, and I thought of you as I did the same. What wicked things we do in the privacy of our rooms at night! I hope you won't mind knowing that I will take your letter with me as a precious memento of home and will be sure to read it again whenever the need for comfort is upon me. Farewell, dear friend. You have my unequivocal permission to continue imagining me touching you whenever you touch yourself at night. In fact, it is my express wish that you do so. Keep pleasuring yourself, dear Sarah, for there is little enough joy to be had in life otherwise. And keep me in your thoughts.

Your true friend,

Benjamin Stanton

July 28th, 1861

Dear Daniel,

I spoke to Papa today, and as expected, he did not take news of my decision well. I hate to be the cause of his pain, but my mind is unchanged. I shall be leaving for Camp Chase early next month to volunteer for the first Ohio cavalry regiment. Jimmy goes with me too.

I think, were you here in my shoes, that you would do the same. That does not mean I want you to rush over here and volunteer alongside me. Please, please stay in England, for to have both his sons embroiled in this war may be too much for Papa to bear, or Mama.

I shall write whenever I can and keep you apprised of my progress, though I do not know how often that will be. I leave in positive spirits, and in the knowledge that I am giving my services to fight for a worthy cause.

Take care of yourself, dear brother, and of our sister. May I also, as a special favour, commend you to keep a watchful eye on my dear friend, Sarah Cranshaw. She has come to mean a great deal to me. Be there in my stead should she ever be in need of help in any way. Goodbye for now.

With love always from your brother,

Benjamin Stanton

PART II

WAR

CHAPTER 8

BENJAMIN

"Though things are bad now, they will not always be so."
— Horace

July 1863

BENJAMIN WATCHED WITH puffy eyes as the coffin was lowered into the ground. He had pulled strings and spent precious gold to ensure Jimmy received a proper burial in an established cemetery rather than an unmarked mass grave, as was the case for many of the fallen soldiers of Gettysburg. Above him the sky was cloudless and blue, a brilliant sun sparkling on the horizon. Before him, the chaplain intoned the familiar words of prayer for the soul of the departed. There were few people here to commemorate the passing of Jimmy — just himself and Sergeant Stevens from his regiment, along with a nurse from the field hospital who had cared for him.

Benjamin had woken this morning with a pounding in his head, the result of overindulgence in whiskey last night. He had doused himself in water, swallowed a bitter cup of coffee, then dressed in full regimental uniform to see off his friend. As Jimmy was lowered into his final resting place, Benjamin stared without really seeing, his mind at work remembering his friend. The boy with an easy smile who had loved horses all his life. The cheerful young man who had accompanied him to war and kept him sane these past two years. *"Farewell, Jimmy,"* he thought. *"I shall miss you."*

Few lingered when the service was over. Everyone had things to do, including him. As they walked away from the grave, Sergeant Stevens spoke, "I understand Private Reeves's father and mother are employed on your family's estate in Ohio, is that not so?"

"Yes," replied Benjamin.

The sergeant sighed. "I would have wanted to grant you leave to go home and convey the news to them in person, but we are short of men and cannot spare anyone. I will be writing an official letter of condolence to them today. Should you care to write a personal missive of your own, we can have it sent out in the same packet."

"I would," said Benjamin.

The sergeant, a man of few words, nodded. "Good."

They reached their horses, mounted them and rode back to camp. A short time later, Benjamin sat down to write.

July 8th, 1863

Dear Papa,

I hope both you and Mama are in good health and that all is well at home. News of our engagement with the Confederate army at Gettysburg may have already reached you by now, and that we were able to repulse the Confederate advance towards Washington. I am happy to report that I am unharmed and in sound health.

However, I do bear some sad news. Our dear friend Jimmy passed away yesterday from an infection caused by a gun wound to the shoulder. I was with him throughout his final hours on this earth and offered him whatever comfort I could. He was given a Christian burial this morning, his final resting place in hallowed ground, the grave marked for posterity. He served his country with dignity and honour, and his sacrifice shall not be forgotten. A letter from Sergeant Stevens, notifying Jimmy's parents of his passing, should be in the same packet in which you receive this missive. I would ask, Papa, that you be the one to break the news to them.

I leave with my regiment tomorrow, as we pursue Lee's retreating army in Virginia. I hope this will herald the beginning of the end to this protracted war. Give my love to Mama.

Your loving son,

Benjamin Stanton

Benjamin sealed the letter carefully, then pulled out some more sheets of paper. They would be on the move tomorrow, and today was perhaps the last opportunity for some time in which to correspond with the rest of his family. He would write letters to England. He knew that a large convoy of patients from the field hospital would be transferred to Baltimore tomorrow. He could give the letters to Nurse Walters, who had tended to Jimmy and attended his funeral, and trust that she would post them for him from Baltimore. He began with a letter to his brother. It was short, for he could think of nothing more to say but the basic facts.

Once he had sealed this letter and the one to Bella which was equally short, Benjamin began another, this time addressed to Sarah. He paused for a minute, re-arranging his thoughts. This letter would not be short. There was so much he had to say. It was odd really. He had not seen Sarah in years, and only met her a handful of times before being parted from her. Yet he felt closer to her than to anyone else in this world. He could tell her anything. To her, he could speak his truth. He picked up the pen again and began to write.

July 8ᵗʰ, 1863

Dear Sarah,

I've been wondering lately about the fate of the letters I send you. Do they overcome the numerous obstacles in their way—the raid of railcars they are transported on, the destruction of ships on which they sail, and all manner of other troubles—to reach you? And if they do not do so, then what is the point of my writing? Is it simply a way to purge my thoughts, a journal of sorts never to be seen by anyone but myself?

If that is the case, then perhaps I may put down on paper the unspeakable thoughts in my head. Sarah, dear invisible friend, I am sick of it all. I am sick of this war, sick of my fellow man, sick of myself. I have lost count now of the number of lives taken by my own hands—a half dozen? Or much more? It is a travesty in itself that I cannot account for each one of these departed souls. Yet still they come back in my dreams to haunt me.

I cannot recall anymore what all this misery was in aid of. Some noble cause perhaps? In battle I charge my horse and see men on the opposing side that look just like me—only the colour of their uniform is different. They speak the same language as me, worship the same God. They cry the same cry as they fall to their deaths, their blood spilling on the fields of battle to mingle with that of their enemy. These men have mothers and wives back home as we do, and who is to say which side mourns their loss the most? A just and noble cause indeed.

I went to see Jimmy yesterday. He took a bullet to the shoulder during the engagement at Gettysburg a few days ago. Since then, he has been at Camp Letterman, a field hospital on the outskirts of the town. He has been housed in a tent, along with a dozen other wounded men. Despite the best efforts of the valiant medics and nurses, the stench of putrefaction and death could not be hidden. It permeated all surfaces.

Poor Jimmy. We were hopeful at first that he would pull through, but a gangrenous infection set in and ravaged his body. Yesterday morning, I sat with him, listening to him speak in his delirium. Much of it did not make sense. I am not sure he was even aware of my presence until he clutched my arm and stared at me with burning eyes. "Grace," he said. I thought at first he meant it as a prayer, asking for God's grace. But then he repeated over and over, "My child, my girl. Anna. Grace called her Anna." Then he fixed me with his delirious stare and demanded, "You will tell her one day about her pa. Promise!"

Such was his agitation that I could not avoid but do so. After that, he went quiet, his mind seemingly at ease while I tried to make sense of this revelation. I could only suppose that Jimmy believes my cousin Grace's daughter is his own. I do not know the truth of the matter, though I have always wondered about Grace's hasty marriage to Benedict. Could it have been because she was carrying Jimmy's child?

Be that as it may, a promise is a promise. I suppose one day, I shall have to speak to Grace and let her know Jimmy's final wishes, for soon after this, he took his last breath and was gone, another casualty of this miserable war.

Last night, I drowned my sorrows in whiskey and a visit to the local whorehouse. You may think it strange that I chose this way of honouring Jimmy's passing. I cannot explain it myself; I felt a compulsion. There was no great pick of whores to choose from, but I did not care. A woman of indeterminate age and melancholic eyes took care of my needs.

In the room she led me to, which reeked of body odour and cheap perfume, I threw myself atop her on the bed and ripped away the bodice of her dress to reveal her bountiful breasts. Then, releasing my aching member from my pants, I drove myself inside her, and even in these insalubrious surroundings, I felt the ecstatic relief of sinking into soft female flesh. Over and over, I plunged my swollen shaft into her body, seized by a frenzied madness, remembering just in time to have enough gallantry to consider her pleasure, until finally we both achieved our release.

When it was over, I dropped my head to her breast, overcome with shivers, and shed hot tears. The kindly whore held me to her while I cried, repeating in soothing tones, "There, there, it's alright." May God have mercy on her, and on me. Eventually, I calmed enough to get back to my feet and adjust my clothes. In acknowledgement of her kindness and my bestiality, I emptied the remaining contents of my purse, though this did little to assuage my guilt.

This morning, Jimmy was buried in a cemetery on the edge of the town. I have written home to inform my family, and now I sit to write to you—or is it to myself? No matter. What is done is done. Tomorrow, my regiment leaves this town. Now that we have buried our dead and taken the injured to be cared for in hospitals, we will continue our campaign, heading south in pursuit of the retreating Confederate army.

If you get this letter, Sarah, then I ask you to please burn it after reading, and with it burn all memory of my shame. I hope all is well with you. Perhaps you have finally had your wish and married Mr Templeton, or some other worthy person. Are you heavy with your first child? In which case, you will not be wanting to be importuned by my words. Erase them then from your memory, and should more missives of mine come your way, feel free to throw them in the fire without first reading them. I have no right to burden you with my misery.

Ever your friend,
Benjamin Stanton

CHAPTER 9

SARAH

"One loyal friend is worth ten thousand relatives."
—*Euripides*

August 1863

SARAH ENTERED THE church on her brother's arm and ran her eye over the pews for a sighting of Mr Templeton. There he was, in his usual place on the aisle of the fifth row. She followed Ambrose to their own seats three rows behind Mr Templeton, to his left. From there was a good vantage point for her to watch him.

She settled herself down for her favourite pastime of the week—observing the handsome Mr Templeton. This was a fixed feature of her life from which she had not deviated in five years. Why should she? It was not as if Mr Templeton had any great competition in the narrow confines of Stanton Harcourt society. In the unchanging and dull village life she led—quite apart from her scientific pursuits at home, that is—he was often the only source of entertainment. Thus, she sat through the service, listening to Benedict's sermon while at the same time casting her eyes on Mr Templeton's fine form.

Sarah sometimes felt as if she were living two lives. In the privacy of her own room at night, she took out Benjamin's letters, re-reading them often and getting caught up in a whirlwind discovery of her own passionate self through the secrets they had shared. Then day came, and she turned back into the prim spinster that admired the handsome Mr Templeton from afar as she had always done. He remained in pride of place when it came to Sarah's affections, at least of all the men she knew in England.

Once the service was over, she rose to her feet and slowly made her way to the aisle, timing it perfectly so that she came upon Mr Templeton on his path out of church. He gave her a cordial smile. "Miss Cranshaw, a pleasure."

"Mr Templeton," she said smoothly, "how do you do? Are we to see you at the Stanton soirée next Thursday?" She knew full well the answer to this, as her friend, Isabella Stanton, had shared with her the guest list for the soirée she and Daniel were hosting at Stanton Hall. It was to be a dinner, followed by a piano and singing recital of a musical piece by the American composer Henry Clay Work called *Kingdom Coming*, which celebrated the liberation of slaves from their Confederate owners and the Confederacy's defeat in the civil war. It was wishful thinking, for the war still raged on, with no side claiming victory as yet. However, both Daniel and Isabella Stanton were keen to have this piece performed, their way perhaps of supporting the Union from afar.

"Of course," replied Mr Templeton. "I would not miss it. I take it, Miss Cranshaw, that you and Mr Cranshaw will be in attendance?"

"Yes, indeed we shall," she said, her heart beating fast at his nearness. "It promises to be an interesting musical piece. I am told the lyrics are written in the plantation creole dialect and tell the story of slaves emancipating themselves from their owners as the Union army marches in."

"Quite the dramatic piece! I look forward to it and to renewing my acquaintance with your delightful self," drawled Mr Templeton, his lips quirking into a knowing smile at seeing the flush rise to her cheeks. She should not read much into it, for he was always like this with the ladies. Though she did wonder if the look he had given her was an indication that he knew of her feelings for him.

She managed to respond, as calmly as it was possible, "As do I, Mr Templeton. Good day."

He bowed. "Good day, Miss Cranshaw, Mr Cranshaw." With a final smile, he continued on his way.

She felt Ambrose lace his arm through hers and guide her away from the church, towards the waiting carriage. He assisted her up into it, and a moment later, they were joined by Daniel and Isabella. Soon, they were on their way to Stanton Hall. Not long after, Sarah became aware of Daniel's stare from across the carriage. She raised a brow in query. "What is it, Daniel? Why do you stare at me so?" she asked, familiar enough now with his company to speak directly.

"I am wondering whether or not it is appropriate to enquire…" He did not complete the sentence.

"What did you wish to enquire about?"

He sighed. "I have eyes, Sarah. I received a one-page letter from my brother that contained very little information apart from the fact that he is alive and in good health. Whereas you received a thick packet that must have included at least three or four sheets." He looked away in pained frustration. "I do not mean to pry. Your correspondence with him is your business. Yet… I would wish to know more."

"You are quite right when you say that my correspondence with Benjamin is my business alone," she said gently.

He nodded vehemently. "I understand. Forgive me. I simply wanted to know how my brother truly is. He will not tell me."

She looked down at her clasped hands. The truth was, she had been struck by the bitter tone of Benjamin's last letter. He had sounded weary and disenchanted, understandably so after the events he had recounted. But she could not share any of this with Daniel, not without betraying Benjamin's confidence. Before she could speak, Ambrose interjected on her behalf, "Daniel, you are putting my sister in a difficult position, and you know it. You are making her pit her loyalty to your brother against her friendship with you. That is unfair."

"What is unfair is that my brother, my own flesh and blood, is shutting me out of his life!" flashed Daniel.

"Oh Daniel," commiserated Sarah. "He does not mean to do so, but like it or not, before going to enlist in this war, there were expectations put upon him."

"What on earth do you mean?" retorted Daniel sharply.

"Goodness me, I expressed that badly. Let us just say that Benjamin felt that he had to present a certain face to all of you, irrespective of what he truly felt. I hope it is not breaking too much of his confidence to tell you this. In his last letter to me before he left home, he wrote that henceforth, he would have to present a cheerful front to his family in his letters, to spare them from hurt and worry about him. And with regards to you, Daniel, there was the added wish not to show you any weakness on his part."

"And to you he can show his true self?" Daniel murmured, sounding crestfallen.

Sarah let her silence be her answer.

"Why?"

"We all know why!" Isabella now spoke, wiping a tear that had slipped from her eye. "Ever since I can remember, there has been a rivalry between the two of you."

"I never—" spluttered Daniel, but Sarah interrupted him.

"It was never anything you purposely did, Daniel, but for too long, your brother has lived in your shadow, your achievements and talents always seemingly greater than his. Is it surprising that now, at this most difficult time for him, he does not want to betray any weakness to you?"

Daniel rubbed his eyes and looked away, but not before Sarah saw the stricken expression on his countenance. Ambrose, who was on the seat beside him, put a hand to his shoulder. "Do not be too hard on yourself," he spoke gently.

"Perhaps once Benjamin is back from the war, you may clear the air with him."

Daniel nodded. In a voice thick with emotion, he stated, "I must take this to mean that all is not well with him."

"War is by necessity an ugly business," spoke Sarah, careful of her words. "You must know that the Union and Confederate armies engaged in a battle at Gettysburg last month, and that both sides suffered many fatalities—in the tens of thousands if the newspaper reports are to be believed. And also that your childhood friend, Jimmy, was one of the deceased."

"Yes, I know." Daniel's voice was a harsh whisper.

"Then you have your answer. That is all I will say on the matter."

The carriage stopped then and brought the conversation to a natural end. Ambrose leaned out of the window to open the door and jumped down, ready to assist the ladies out. As they made their way up the front steps of Stanton Hall, Daniel came to Sarah's side and said in a quiet, urgent voice, "Pardon me, Sarah. It was ill-mannered of me to ask. I am glad Benjamin has you as his friend."

"I am glad of his friendship too. And Daniel, please also know this. In his letters, it is clear how much Benjamin cares for you and all his family."

Daniel nodded, and then, the subject was closed.

CHAPTER 10

SARAH

"The greatest pleasure of life is love."
— Euripides

LATER THAT AFTERNOON, as Sarah walked back to Ivy Cottage with Ambrose, she had occasion to think on the day's events. These must have been on her brother's mind too, for no sooner had they put some distance between themselves and Stanton Hall than he spoke, saying, "Daniel did not mean to badger you about Benjamin today. It is just that he is desperate to know what is going on with him."

"I could see it."

"You were quite right to keep Benjamin's confidence," he went on. "And Daniel understood, although he is cut up about it." He threw her a questioning look. "How bad is it with Benjamin?"

She sighed. "It is bad. Do not mistake me. He is in sound health physically. But Benjamin's is a gentle soul, and there is no place for gentleness in war." On further reflection, she added, "I often wonder what would have been if by an accident of fate, we had been born in America. Remember how Father considered emigrating there for a while, but Mother was set against it?"

"Yes, I remember it well," he said thoughtfully. "It makes me wonder how I would have managed. I do not know if you would class me a gentle soul, but I am not sure how I would ever go about taking another person's life."

"What if I were in danger and our home about to be attacked?"

He smiled. "You have me there. I suppose then, I would kill to keep you safe."

"As would I," responded Sarah. "War makes us do things out of necessity that we would otherwise never consider doing."

They had by now reached the front gate that led to their cottage. Ambrose unlatched it and let his sister through. In ponderous silence, they walked up the path to the door, which Ambrose opened. Once inside, he turned to her. "It is several hours yet until dark. What are your plans for the rest of this day?"

"I thought perhaps to work on my railway."

He placed an affectionate arm around her shoulder and kissed the top of her head. "I thought as much. Then, will you excuse me while I go read in my study?"

"Of course. I will bring a tray there later in the evening, and we can have a light supper together."

He smiled in acquiescence and let her go. Sarah climbed the stairs to her room. First thing was to divest herself of her Sunday clothes and put on the brown cambric gown she usually wore when doing her train modelling work. Once that was done, she headed down the stairs again to the small parlour room at the back of the house that was for her exclusive use.

In one corner of the room, a large table was set up with the miniature railway project that Benjamin had started with her two years ago. It would take months or even years to complete, but Sarah was in no hurry. Most days, she spent a few hours here, adding new sleepers to the track she was building or working on a model of the Iron Duke, a favourite locomotive of hers.

The work was laborious and long, as Sarah had to fashion most of the parts herself. In this, she was using the skills of jewellers and clockmakers. The rails she had fashioned from brass rod and the sleepers were made from kindling wood, into which she had inserted pins. She then soldered the rails to the pins, carefully measuring to ensure that they were the right distance apart. The finished track, which ran from one end of the table to the other, was very nearly complete.

Far more of a challenge to build was the locomotive. Here, she had used the services of the clockmaker in Witney to help fashion the parts she required—wheels, valves, piston rods and so forth—based on the detailed drawings she had furnished him with. For the tender and the cab, she had procured thin sheets of brass from the ironmonger, which she cut, bent and soldered to the shape required.

It was a labour of love, and one of which she was proud. Strangely, it gave her a feeling of closeness to her friend who was mired in war on the other side of the world. Benjamin. As she sat at her modelling table and began to work, her reflections returned to him. Over the past two years, she had received nearly a dozen letters from him. The first few had been imbued with a youthful optimism, high spirits and a dash of salacious humour as he shared intimate details of his sexual conquests and wondered about her progress in pleasuring herself at night. As ever, his missives were distinguished by their searing honesty. She had longed to write back to him and give an account of her nightly adventures, but of course, she could not.

Over time however, she had noticed a subtle shift in the tone of his letters. As the novelty of being in uniform wore off, he began to hint at his fatigue with it all. One turning point, of course, had been his first kill. The face of the man whose life he took haunted him for weeks. It had been a young man, perhaps no more than twenty years old. They had come face to face in battle and both raised their guns. His had been fastest to discharge, hence why he and not the young Confederate soldier was alive to tell the tale. That first kill was soon followed by others, as is demanded by war. With each life snuffed, something too was extinguished in Benjamin, his natural optimism replaced by something darker—a bleak outlook of his fellow man.

Then came his last letter. It was written in the aftermath of the bloodiest battle in the war so far. Throughout it all, miraculously, he had remained unharmed. His friend, Jimmy, was not so fortunate, succumbing to a bullet wound some days later.

In the aftermath, Benjamin had taken himself to the nearest house of ill repute, desperate to seek comfort for his grief in the soft flesh of a woman. With unsparing detail, Benjamin told of how, drunk on whisky and rage, he had sunk himself repeatedly into this unknown woman, wanting desperately to achieve release. Afterwards, he had laid his head on her plump breast and cried. The whore, an older woman of a kindly disposition, had held him to her and soothed him. Sarah had read the letter and wept.

That night in bed, she had stripped naked and touched herself, all the while imagining she was that kindly whore and that Benjamin had come to use her. She'd pictured herself being taken roughly by him while she held him tight, whispering soothing words of love, feeling his heavy weight upon her and the whisky on his breath. With each furious thrust of his cock in her, she had held on even tighter, subsuming his anger and despair into her welcoming body. Her hand on her clitoris had stroked roughly, frantically, in an echo of Benjamin's brutal thrusts, and she had orgasmed so strongly it had left her breathless.

Afterwards, she had extinguished the light and slept, her dreams crowded with an amalgam of visions—a bloodied battlefield followed by smoky rooms filled with desperate soldiers and whores rutting together, then Benjamin crying on her naked breast. She had awoken in a sweat and with a pounding heart. Drawing a deep breath, she had got out of bed and washed away the evidence of her orgasm. She had dressed with care and headed for church with her brother. Then, seating herself on the eighth row, she had looked at Mr Templeton and allowed herself to drift into the easy familiarity of her infatuation with him, sealing away the pain, anguish and ecstasy of last night into a hidden compartment of her mind.

She sighed now, thinking about it. This was how it had been with her these past two years since Benjamin had first introduced her to the wicked art of pleasuring herself. At night, she escaped into delicious fantasies, playing herself into the role of whatever buxom widow or comely maid Benjamin described to her in his letters. She would touch herself, imagining it was his fingers on her, his cock inside her, and she would reach her orgasmic peak. She had tried once or twice to imagine herself with Mr Templeton, but that had not worked. It was Benjamin that owned her at night.

Thoughts of Benjamin when the evening came co-existed with tantalising thoughts of Mr Templeton during the day. It was as though she led two separate lives—one as an upright spinster who daydreamed of the handsome but unattainable gentleman she loved, and one as a voluptuous vixen who filled her mind with wicked thoughts of her friend while pleasuring herself at night. If ever she were to marry, she supposed then she would put a stop to this strange double life she was leading, but as that prospect seemed unlikely, she thought it fair to continue to indulge in her nightly secret obsession for a faraway friend—one she was unlikely ever to meet again.

CHAPTER 11

BENJAMIN

"Everything changes; everything flows.
What we were or are; tomorrow we will not be."
— Ovid

Two years later
CORPORAL BENJAMIN STANTON of Company C of the 1st
Ohio Cavalry Regiment manoeuvred his horse through a small
gap in the trees at the top of the hill. He lifted his field glasses
and examined the expanse of wooded fields ahead. From east
to west, he scoured for signs of movement. *Over there.* He
sharpened the focus of his lens and looked more closely. Yes,
there they were. He stayed where he was for some time,
studying the men in the distance with cool, dispassionate eyes.
When he had seen enough, he put away the glasses, turned his
horse and began the journey back towards his regiment.

Early on in his service, he had distinguished himself for his
skill in reconnaissance. His sharp eyes missed nothing. He
could identify the approach of enemy forces sometimes days
ahead of their reaching their destination. Weaving through
enemy territory, using the cover of trees to disguise his
movements, he became skilful at obtaining vital intelligence for
his commanding officers. He liked this aspect of his work. It felt
blessedly peaceful to be alone, away from everyone, just himself
and his horse, sleeping under the stars.

He did not trust himself around others anymore, ever since Gettysburg and its carnage, and the mad haze of rage that had driven him to a whorehouse to pound himself relentlessly into one of its whores, only to then cry like a babe on her breast. That day, gentle, considerate Benjamin of yore had been nowhere in sight. He barely recognised the man he used to be. Nowadays, he was quick to become enraged, especially when whisky was involved. Therefore it was best he stay well away from his fellow man.

Some hours later, he rode into camp and found Sergeant Stevens, conveying to him the intelligence he had gathered. He was checked by the sergeant as he was about to leave. "Corporal Stanton, a moment of your time."

"Yes, sir."

"Good news. I have received confirmation from Major Patten that 1st Ohio Cavalry Regiment is to be mustered out of service in the next few days. Consider today your last scouting mission and start packing your bag. You're going home, son."

Benjamin stood rooted to the spot. He had known, of course, that this day was coming, ever since General Lee's surrender last April. And yet the thought of going home after over four years of absence struck shock through him. This peripatetic military life had been all he had known for so long, that he was not sure how he would go about being in the civilian world again.

"You don't seem happy about it," remarked the sergeant.

Benjamin pasted on a smile. "I am sir, just taken aback for a moment."

The sergeant eyed him up and down. "You may wish to consider tidying up your appearance somewhat, Corporal, starting with a visit to the barber. You do not want to give your poor mama a scare when she sees you after all this time."

Benjamin put a hand to his beard, which was untrimmed and wild-looking. He had not been concerned with his appearance for a very long time. Perhaps the sergeant was right. "Understood, sir," he replied.

Sergeant Stevens nodded. "Dismissed."

Benjamin saluted and walked out of the sergeant's quarters, a requisitioned building on Mulberry Street. As he emerged into the bright sunlight, he blinked and shaded his eyes from the sun. For the last four months, his regiment had been on garrison duty here in Macon, Georgia. Not for much longer though. Soon, he would be going home.

Briskly, he set a pace heading down the street. There was a barber shop three blocks away. Best start the process of civilising himself now. A few minutes more and he was entering the premises, all conversation halting at the sight of a Union soldier in their midst, particularly such a fierce-looking man. The barber approached him hesitantly. "May I help you, sir?"

Benjamin stroked his beard. "I need a haircut and a trim to my beard," he said in a clipped voice.

"Of course, sir. Please take a seat." The barber led him to a chair that faced a large mirror. Benjamin sat and glanced at his reflection. He had not had occasion to look at himself in months. The face that looked back at him was that of a stranger. It was not only the dark unruly beard with threads of silver, nor the lank hair that fell to his shoulders. The eyes that looked at him were the eyes of a man decades older, lined from countless hours of squinting into the sun, the skin around them tanned to a mahogany brown. And then of course, there was the scar, a little memento from the Battle of Jonesborough last year. The bullet destined for him had missed his skull by mere inches but gouged a line across the top of his left cheek bone. He looked nothing like the twenty-three year-old man who had left home, bright-eyed and hopeful, all of four years ago. Would Mama even recognise him?

The barber soon got to work, trimming Benjamin's hair and clipping the beard to a much more acceptable length. The end result was not transformative, but at least he looked more respectable. He paid the barber and left, returning to his quarters to start preparing for his departure.

IT TOOK A week to complete the journey home, riding on trains and horse-driven wagons full of other delisted soldiers. He kept to himself, unable to join in with the boisterous laughter around him. He was glad, of course, that the war was over. He wanted to see his family again. Beyond that though, he could not contemplate what he was to do with himself in the days to come. Resume his old position of gentleman farmer as if nothing had happened in the intervening years? He recoiled at the idea.

In Ashtabula, he went to the port tavern, his old haunt, and ordered himself a beer along with something to eat. Curious glances were cast his way, but nobody recognised the Union soldier as the Benjamin Stanton of old. He enquired about renting a horse to ride the remaining distance to his home and paid what seemed an extortionate amount for the privilege. An hour later, he was away, riding along the familiar rutted road that cut through acres of wheat and corn fields. A small glimmer of joy seeped into the dark recesses of his mind as he saw familiar sights that told of home.

He rode into the gravelled entrance of Stanton House and stopped at the stable. A boy, no more than sixteen, came out, looking enquiringly at him. Benjamin dismounted and studied his face, trying to place him. Giving up on the effort, he grunted, "Who are you?"

The boy gave a contemptuous snort. "Never you mind. Lost your way, soldier?"

Benjamin's lips tightened into a grim line, but he declined to answer. Instead, he threw the reins at the boy and turned to walk towards the house.

"Hey! What do you think you're doing?" called the boy after him.

Benjamin ignored him and walked on, taking the steps up to the deserted porch two at a time. He was checked by the unmistakable cocking of a shotgun and a strident female voice calling, "Stop right there!"

He halted, arms up in the air in the universal sign of surrender.

"If you've come thinking you can steal from here while the men are away, think again," continued the voice. "You just turn around now and go back the way you came."

"Ma," he called out, his voice gritty from lack of use. "It's me."

There was a pause, then, "Benjamin?"

"Yes, Ma." The nuzzle of the gun was lowered and disappeared from the gap in the window. A moment later, the front door flew open, and his mother rushed to him.

"Benjamin!" Charlotte Stanton may have been short in stature, but she hurled herself at him with the force of a hurricane, clutching wildly at his jacket. His arms encircled her, and he held her tight as she wept with joy. "My boy! My boy is finally home!" she cried over and over.

The commotion had alerted others in the household and those next door in the house that belonged to Uncle Jasper. Soon, he was surrounded by a bevy of females exclaiming at his return and embracing him. He heard a voice, which he recognised as Auntie Ruth, call to the stable boy, "Go get the men, quick. Tell them Benjamin's home."

Eventually, he was ushered inside and made to sit, the women fussing over him, plying him with drinks and offers of cake, his mother exclaiming at how thin he had become. Questions came at him a mile a minute, until Auntie Ruth told everyone to stop pestering him. She shooed his cousin Beth away, who was twittering excitedly at his side. When the din had quietened down, he sat, hands trembling in his lap as his mother took an inventory of the changes that had occurred to him. She pointed to his cheek. "What happened?"

Ah. He'd forgotten how the scar must look to those around him. He rubbed the edges of it with his finger. "A stray bullet at Jonesborough. I suppose there won't be any more doubt now that Daniel is the handsomer of the two of us," he replied whimsically.

His mother scolded in annoyance, "As if that matters!" She placed her small hand to his ravaged cheek. "You will always be beautiful to me, my darling boy." Then, he was embracing her again, unable to stop the trembling in his body and the wetness of his eyes.

"I love you, Ma," he mumbled.

"And I love you, dear boy. Precious, precious boy."

A door slammed and there was the sound of brisk strides in the hallway. Benjamin pulled away from his mother and looked towards the parlour door. There, stood his father, staring at him with dark, burning eyes so like his own. He got to his feet. "Papa," he said, with a touch of uncertainty.

Frank, Earl of Stanton, approached his son with slow, deliberate steps, never taking his eyes off Benjamin. He came to a halt a mere breath from him, still staring. "Son," he finally ground out in a roughened voice. "Welcome home."

Then Frank Stanton took his beloved son into his arms and held him so tightly that he nearly squeezed the breath out of his chest. Both men stood in this tight embrace for a long time, neither wanting to let go. The moment was broken by the sound of Jasper's amused voice behind them. "That's all well and good Frank, but now may I have my turn to welcome Benjamin?"

With a gruff sound, Frank dropped his arms from around his son and stepped back, letting Jasper come forward and clasp his nephew warmly. "Welcome back, Benjamin. We have missed you," he said.

"And I you," responded Benjamin, before turning to greet his cousin John. He was overwhelmed, surrounded by such warmth and love after being deprived of affection for so long. It felt foreign. He wished he could be alone in the quiet of his room to re-order his frazzled emotions.

As if sensing this, his mother remarked, "You must be tired from your long journey, darling. Would you like to go rest for a while? I'll have some hot water sent up so you can wash."

He nodded gratefully and with an awkward smile, addressed everyone, "I will see you all later. We can talk more then." He stood and made his way to the door. There, he paused and turned, addressing his mother. "Is there any news from England? How are Daniel and Isabella—and the Cranshaws?"

She smiled, her eyes brimming with love. "They are all well and constantly ask about you. Your papa will be sending word to them today that you are home. I am sure they will want to visit here as soon as they can."

"It will be good to see them," he agreed and walked out of the room, a light sweat forming on his brow. Up the stairs he went, along the corridor, second door on the right. He opened it and went inside. His room was pristine, all his belongings in the same place he had left them four and a half years ago. He closed the door behind him and leaned against it, taking in deep gulps of air, anxiety engulfing him. God help him, what was he to do with himself now? All of a sudden, the future felt too overwhelming. Soon, his siblings would come, and they would see the change in him. No more was he the happy-go-lucky Benjamin of before. What he was now was… something else. And before long, his pa would expect him to resume the work he had done before on the estate. It was all just too much to think about.

He took another deep breath and recalled those words he had once said to Sarah: "True happiness is to enjoy the present without anxious dependence on the future." He should take things a day at a time and not worry about what would come next. It was easier said than done.

CHAPTER 12

SARAH

"Time gliding by without our knowledge cheats us, and nothing can be swifter than the years."
— Ovid

September 1865

SARAH EXAMINED HER reflection in the dressing table mirror. She was not in the habit of doing so, having long ago given up on any claims to vanity, but she was curious to see whether the face staring back at her looked like a confirmed old maid now she had reached the grand old age of thirty.

She saw large grey eyes and a clear complexion with no lines or wrinkles to show her advanced age. She smiled to herself. Perhaps there was still a residue of vanity in her after all. She finished brushing her light brown hair and with the efficiency of long practice, pinned it up in a neat bun. Satisfied, she rose to her feet and made her way down the stairs to have her breakfast.

The dining room table was laid out with fresh coffee, bread, butter and some slices of cold ham. There was no sign of Ambrose, who was in the habit of leaving for his work duties as estate manager in the early hours of the morning. Sarah was used to eating breakfast alone, except on Sundays, when her brother joined her. She ate quietly now, thinking of the day ahead.

In the mornings, on Tuesdays through to Fridays, she tutored Rosemary and Fanny Collins in French, Literature and Classics. They were the daughters of a retired naval commander, Colonel Collins, who had settled in the locality a few months ago, renting Gorston Manor, which had been vacant since its last tenant, old Mrs Nugent, had passed away last year. Shortly after their arrival, he had made enquiries about a suitable person to tutor Rosemary and Fanny, respectively seventeen and eighteen years old, and Daniel had suggested Sarah for the job. She was not in any need of additional funds, for Ambrose was well paid in his role as manager of the Stanton estate. However, Daniel had thought that Sarah would welcome the opportunity for useful employment, and in this, he was quite right.

Sarah embraced her new position with relish. Her two new charges were quiet, self-effacing girls who were keen to learn. The pay was generous, and the three hours a day she spent at Gorston Manor were not onerous, leaving her plenty of time still to indulge in her own pursuits.

Having finished her breakfast, she called Elsie, the housemaid, to clear the table and had a quick discussion with her about the day's duties. With this done, she slipped on her boots and coat, tied on her bonnet and headed out to Gorston Manor, which was an easy twenty-five minutes' walk from Ivy Cottage. The day was dry, with an occasional hint of sunshine breaking through the bank of clouds in the sky. She walked briskly, letting her mind wander.

She was stubborn in her habits, so of course, the first stop in her ruminations was her beloved Mr Templeton. She had observed him closely in church yesterday and concluded that he was aging well, like a fine wine. Perhaps it was because she had only recently turned thirty and was thus more preoccupied with the concept of aging than usual, that she had scrutinised his countenance looking for signs of his advancing age. He would be thirty-eight years old now, she knew, an age that to her once might have seemed approaching decrepitude. How silly! Thirty-eight was not so old at all, especially when it gave a gentleman a dashing thread of silver at his temples and in his whiskers.

In an instant, her thoughts skipped to Benjamin. She wondered if he too looked older now, after several years in the army. Logic dictated that he would, though she could not picture it. It had been nearly five years since she had last seen him. She could recall him clearly as he had been on that last day when he had come to say goodbye—smooth-shaven, showing off the fine cheekbones and firm jaw that all Stanton men seemed to have, the malleable mouth that curved into an engaging grin, and those dark brown eyes of his that shone with every emotion he felt. She knew that face well, for she thought of it every night.

It was odd that when it came to stimulating her senses at night, it was not Mr Templeton, but a man she had not seen in years, that dominated her thoughts. She stroked herself and reached her orgasms to dreams of Benjamin, imagining herself with him in bed, in a barn or in a deserted meadow doing all manner of wicked things. She read and re-read his letters often. They were infrequent, due to the war in America, but he still wrote whenever he could with raw honesty about himself.

There had been no repeat of the incident at Gettysburg with the kindly whore. Benjamin wrote that he knew well enough to avoid the whorehouses, where the women were often diseased and desperate—but more than that, he realised how desperate and vulnerable they were. It had been a sign of his own desperation that night that he had overcome his usual disgust of such places and gone there. More like an act of self-loathing, suspected Sarah, that he was still alive with blood on his hands when his friend had not been so fortunate.

His letters this past year had been imbued with a deep sense of melancholy and loneliness. She wished sometimes that she could reach out and hold him to her, whispering in his ear that he was not alone. He wrote to her, baring his soul, without receiving any word in return. He did not even know that she read his letters and treasured them. Her heart ached for her friend's pain.

On the move from place to place with his cavalry regiment, enduring difficult conditions and blood-soaked battles, there was rarely any time or opportunity for frolicking with women. He was mostly celibate, he wrote, obtaining sexual release through the stroke of his own hands. Then in his last letter, he had written of how he had met and had a lone assignation with a widow, a Mrs Davis, who lived not far from where he was quartered in Macon, a small town in Georgia. His regiment had been stationed there since April, giving him a touch more stability than before — though he was often absent for days on solo scouting missions.

Benjamin's letter had arrived just a few days ago, dated July 1865. Now, as Sarah walked to Gorston Manor, she recalled the one passage in the letter that she had read and re-read so many times that she almost had it memorised.

I arrived at Mrs Davis's house at the appointed time and rang the bell. I was shown in by her servant, who told me that the mistress awaited me in her bedchamber. "First door on the right," she said, pointing upwards. Without further ado, I strode up the stairs to said bedchamber, knocked briefly on the door, and entered.

Inside, I saw Mrs Davis laid out on the bed, naked as the day she was born, reclining on one elbow. She gave me a sultry smile and said, "Corporal Stanton, what took you so long? I have great need of you." So saying, she splayed open her legs, revealing to me the delightful folds of her cunt. I needed no second invitation. I pounced, laying my lips on those muskily scented folds. But Sarah, here's the thing. As I did so, I thought of you, or more accurately, I thought of how I would describe this all to you in my next letter. My poor girl, you have never experienced the delights of having a man worship your cunt with his lips, have you? Or perhaps, if you are married now, you have, but then you would not be reading this letter.

On the off chance that you are still unmarried, and that you are reading this, then let me describe it to you. The taste of a woman down there is unforgettable—or perhaps you have tasted yourself? Wicked girl! Do it, if you have not yet done so. Back to Mrs Davis. I put my mouth to her soft, fragrant cunt and I licked, lapped her up as if she were the most delectable morsel. With each lap of my tongue, she writhed in pleasure beneath me, secreting more of her delightful juices. Her clitoris was engorged, such was her state of arousal, and after a time, I surrounded the stiffened bud with my mouth and sucked. You should have heard her cries of pleasure. It was not long before she spent in my eager mouth.

A moment later, I had freed my swollen member from my pants and plunged into her steamy depths. And Sarah, as I did so, I imagined you in your bed, the lights out late at night, touching and tasting yourself to dreams of me licking your cunt, sucking your sweet little bud and then pounding you relentlessly with my hard cock the way I pounded Mrs Davis. It was the thought of you, dear invisible friend, that drove me to the peak, a climax so intense that I shook from it.

Dearest Sarah, it is the very strangest thing, but every time I am with a woman, you are there with me too in my mind as I imagine writing to you of it, as I envision you in your bed pleasuring yourself to thoughts of me. It is probably all an illusion in my mind. You are most likely in your staid marriage bed, all thoughts of me far from your mind, but a man can dream, can he not?

If he only knew how true his words were, thought Sarah as she turned off the main path to take a shortcut through the woodland that belonged to Mr Johnson, a local squire. She was trespassing, but it was only a short way until she emerged onto the lane that led to the entrance of Gorston Manor, and this route saved her at least ten minutes of walking. It was then that she heard the sound. A whimper. She stopped in her tracks and listened. There it was again. Was it an injured animal? No, the sound was distinctly human. With care, she stepped in the direction from whence it came.

As she rounded the side of a thick oak tree, she saw a boy, no more than ten years old, lying on the ground, his right foot caught in a man trap. It was one of the newer, humane traps, without teeth to cut into a person's flesh, designed to catch poachers in the act. The metal chain of the trap was firmly attached around the trunk of the nearest tree, preventing a poacher from escaping.

But this was no poacher. It was just a small boy in pain, by the sounds of his cries. She approached him carefully, looking down at her feet to ensure she did not step on any other trap. Really, it was too bad of Squire Johnson. Why anyone could have been caught in the trap, including herself, but this poor boy was the unlucky one. She was clearly not the only one to cut through the wood to save time on her journey. Feeling the beginnings of righteous anger in her chest, she knelt down by the boy. "Now, now," she said, "do stop crying and tell me your name."

The boy hiccupped and spoke in a tearful voice, "Mattie. My name's Mattie."

"Well, Mattie, let me take a look at your leg." With a gentle hand, she palpated his leg and immediately saw the problem. When the trap had caught his foot, the boy must have stumbled and fallen at an awkward angle, causing a fracture. Already, the flesh around his ankle was badly swollen. She examined the metal trap around his foot and saw that the only way to release it was to unlock it with a key, most likely in the possession of Mr Johnson's gamekeeper. What was she to do? She thought quickly.

"Mattie," she said softly. "I am going to go find someone to help release you from this trap. In the meantime, I want you to lie as still as you can. Try not to move your leg. Can you do that?"

He sniffed. "Yes."

"Very well." She stood. "I will be back as soon as I can." Carefully, she walked towards the lane, looking down at her feet the whole time, fearful of setting off another trap. A few minutes later, she emerged onto the rutted track of the lane and began to walk rapidly in the direction of Gorston Manor. She had not gone far before she heard the sound of a horse's hooves. Before long, a rider appeared in the distance. She waved at him to stop, and it was only then that she saw the rider was Mr Templeton.

He brought his mare to a stop before her and doffed his hat. "Miss Cranshaw. Are you in any trouble?" he enquired.

She spoke quickly. "Not myself, no, but there is a little boy beyond in the woods that needs our help. His foot has got caught in one of Squire Johnson's traps, and he must have fractured it as he fell. I need help to release him from that trap and get him to a physician as soon as possible."

By now, Mr Templeton had dismounted his horse and was passing the reins around the thick branch of a tree. Once it was secured, he went to one of the saddle bags and removed from it a pistol that was securely wedged inside one of the pockets. He loaded the weapon as she looked on, explaining as he did so, "A shot from this should sever the chain holding him trapped."

"What a good idea," she said approvingly, then frowned. "Only it will alert the gamekeeper, who will come to investigate. I do not want the poor boy to be found and charged with a crime."

"It is a risk we shall have to take. The gamekeeper is usually filling his belly at the village inn around this time, so we should be fine. In any case, I will carry him straight to my horse and we can be away soon after. Now, which way do we go?"

Impressed at his decisiveness, she led him back the way she had come, saying over her shoulder, "I did not see any other traps on my way out, but do be very careful where you step."

"I will."

Stepping cautiously, they made their way back to where Mattie lay, his tearful eyes wide with surprise. "His name is Mattie," said Sarah, touching the boy's head gently.

Mr Templeton smiled and crouched down at eye level with the child. "Mattie, my name is Mr Templeton, and I am here to help you. I want you to stay very still as I fire my pistol to break the chain and release you. It is very important you do not move though, are we clear?"

"Yes, sir," mumbled the boy.

"Good."

Mr Templeton then stood and pointed his pistol at the middle link of the chain. He grinned at Sarah. "You may wish to cover your ears," he said as warning. She did as he instructed, as did Mattie. "Ready? One, two, three." The pistol went off with a bang and a small cloud of smoke. Mr Templeton looked down at the chain. "I think that did the trick," he said. Placing the pistol on the ground, he pulled at the rings of the chain, and with a small clang, they came apart. "There we go, all done," he said in satisfaction. "Now let us get out of here." He disarmed the chamber of the pistol and handed it to her. "Miss Cranshaw, please hold this while I carry Mattie back to my horse. Do not be afraid. It is quite safe."

She snorted and took it from him. "I am well versed in the workings of a pistol, Mr Templeton."

He smiled admiringly. "You really are quite an intrepid female, Miss Cranshaw."

She flushed in pleasure at the praise, but Mr Templeton was already turned away, bending down to lift the small boy into his arms. "Careful now, this may hurt a little," he said in a surprisingly gentle voice. The boy went to him trustingly, putting small arms around his neck. Mr Templeton straightened to his full height and began to walk towards the edge of the wood, all the while keeping his eyes tracked to the ground. In a minute or two, they reached the lane and the waiting horse. With strong arms, Mr Templeton lifted the boy into the saddle, then nimbly mounted behind him. He looked down at Sarah. "I will take him now to Dr Benson. Will you be alright on your own?"

"Of course," she replied calmly. "I was on my way to Gorston Manor, which is but a few minutes' walk from here."

Mr Templeton nodded. "Very well, I shall leave you to walk there. I would suggest, Miss Cranshaw, that you avoid this perilous shortcut in future and take the long way around. I should hate for this to happen to you."

"On this, I am in full agreement." She hesitated. "Mr Templeton, you will let me know how he gets on?"

"Of course. I shall ride over to Ivy Cottage later today once I know the boy is in safe hands and give you a full report. Now, we better make haste. Good day, Miss Cranshaw."

"Good day," she murmured.

With a light tap of his shoes to the flank of his horse, he was off. Sarah watched him go, then remembered that the gamekeeper, alerted by the sound of the pistol, could be on his way. She set off hurriedly in the direction of Gorston Manor. She arrived there only a few minutes later than normal, and only slightly dishevelled, not occasioning any comment from her young charges. Her mind half on the events that had occurred that morning, she managed to get through the lessons of the day. Just before midday, she bid the Collinses goodbye and walked back home, electing sensibly to take the longer route.

It was not much later that there came a knock on the door and Elsie opened it to let Mr Templeton in, showing him to the main parlour. Sarah hastened down from her room, where she had been refreshing her appearance. "Mr Templeton," she said, walking into the parlour. "I must thank you for your timely assistance today."

He stood and bowed over her hand. "No thanks are needed, I assure you."

She invited him to sit and took a seat opposite him. "Tell me sir, how is Mattie?"

"As well as can be," said Mr Templeton cheerfully. "With a bit of work, we were able to remove the trap from his foot. The good doctor re-set the fracture and bandaged it, but the poor boy will be on crutches for a good few weeks until it heals."

"Will he get into trouble over this?" wondered Sarah.

Mr Templeton shook his head. "The gamekeeper will no doubt discover the broken chain and see that the trap is missing, but there is no way for him to prove it was the boy that walked into it. Dr Benson is tight-lipped and will not speak of it to a soul, so as far as anyone is concerned, Mattie took an unfortunate tumble and fractured his foot."

"Good," said Sarah in relief. "I am glad, and very grateful to have come across you today, Mr Templeton."

"It was indeed providential that I decided to take this route on my way home, but I do believe you had the matter in hand. You strike me as a most capable sort, Miss Cranshaw." He got to his feet and Sarah did so too. "Well, I will not keep you. Please give my best to Mr Cranshaw." He walked to the door, and Sarah followed him. He bowed. "Good day, Miss Cranshaw."

"Good day, Mr Templeton."

He left, leaving a pleasant cloud of his cologne hovering in the air around her. She took a long sniff of it and sighed happily. The rest of the afternoon was spent in reminiscences of every word and gesture from Mr Templeton today. He had called her an intrepid female and a most capable sort. It was not exactly the most fulsome of compliments, but it was praise nonetheless.

It was not until early evening that Ambrose returned home. She had thought to regale him with tales of her adventures today, but all this was erased from her mind with a few simple words as he walked into the parlour. "Sarah, good news," he said quickly. "Daniel received a telegram from America today. Benjamin is back home from the war."

She rose to her feet and stared at him. "He's home? Really home?"

His face broke into a grin. "Safe and sound back in Ohio."

"Oh thank the Lord!" she cried and burst into tears.

With infinite patience, Ambrose took her into his arms and let her have her cry, patting her back comfortingly. When finally, she had herself in hand, he said, "There is more. Daniel is all set to sail to America as soon as possible with Isabella. He's going to see Benedict and Grace in the morning to ask if they wish to go too. It got me thinking. With all these letters you've received from Benjamin over the years, now might be your chance to send one to him in return."

She looked up at him with glistening eyes, a smile forming on her face. "I shall write tonight," she declared, "straight after supper."

Later that night, she indeed took pen to paper and wrote a very long letter to her dearest friend. It was past midnight when she finally put down her pen and sealed the missive. She tiptoed downstairs to leave it on the dining room table for Ambrose to take with him to Stanton Hall the following morning. With this mission accomplished, she returned to her room, undressed, dimmed the light and got into bed, though sleep was not quick to come.

The day had felt momentous. Benjamin was back home. He had kept his promise and returned from war. Her heart swelled in her chest at knowing he was safe. Now, they could resume a two-way correspondence—though for how long she did not know. Eventually, Benjamin would settle down in the bosom of his family and find himself a wife. That was the natural order of things. And once he did so, she did not think he would continue with the wonderfully frank correspondence they had shared up till now.

Then there was Mr Templeton. Today, she had spent more time in his company than she had done in years, when she was used to only receiving a smiling greeting from him at church. He had acted heroically, rising in her estimation, and more importantly, she had excited his admiration. Could it be that finally, after all these years, he was truly beginning to note her worth? She could not help but feel that her life, so long in stasis, was about to change.

CHAPTER 13

PHILIP TEMPLETON

"Happy the man, and happy he alone,
he who can call today his own:
he who, secure within, can say,
Tomorrow do thy worst, for I have lived today."
— Horace

HE HAD WOKEN this morning in a sombre mood, much as he had for the last week, ever since his return from London. He was usually of a cheerful and optimistic disposition, so he had expected that these gloomy reflections would be short-lived and that he would soon be back to his usual self. Not so. That thing that had happened at Tremayne's had caused a shift in his whole pattern of thinking. One could almost call it an epiphany.

Before that revelatory moment, there had been nothing to suggest his life was about to take a different turn. It had been running along its usual hedonistic course. Philip Templeton had determined early on in his life that he would devote his time to the pursuit of happiness. His own happiness, that is. Not for him the dutiful, self-sacrificing life. He was keen to spend his time indulging in the two things he enjoyed most — painting and women.

He had resolved on a simple rule to follow. Thirty per cent of his time would be devoted to the unenjoyable but essential tasks required to maintain his lifestyle. Under this he included scrutinising the accounts, reading the financial section of the newspapers, regular surveys of his property and tenants, exercise—to keep his physique in good shape—and last of all, going to church every Sunday. If he was going to engage in lewd behaviour behind closed doors, then it was fitting that he present a most Christian-like appearance in public.

The remaining seventy per cent of his time he decided would be spent in pleasurable pursuits. Over the years, he had been meticulous in maintaining that ratio of duty to pleasure, and he had lived well as a result. He had travelled extensively and painted all manner of exotic landscapes. He had seduced innumerable women, and painted them too. He had indulged in the most hedonistic of orgies at the exclusive club in London of which he was a dedicated member. Twice a month, he took himself to his townhouse in the great metropolis and spent happy hours frequenting Tremayne's, named after the lecherous nobleman who had established it some decades ago. There, he partook of every debauched entertainment imaginable. Then, replete on fine wine and even finer orgasms, he would return to Oxfordshire in time to attend church service on Sunday.

There was nothing to indicate that this latest trip to London would deviate from the usual. As per his usual, he had visited Tremayne's, partaken of a well-cooked meal served by a barely dressed and very comely maid—though that night he had not been minded to pay her attention—and then found his way to the room of pleasure. There, he had allowed a nubile young woman to undress him, watching dispassionately as she had unfastened buttons and pulled away material to reveal the magnificence of his naked form. Soon, he had been surrounded by a bevy of unclothed revellers wanting to touch and stroke and kiss him. A wonderfully buxom female had paid homage to his muscular chest with licks and nips. Another had presented him with her moist cunt and he had obligingly set his tongue to it. Below his waist, another eager female had taken his cock into her mouth.

He should have been in seventh heaven, his cock hard and ready to plunge into action. Instead he had felt by incremental degree, boredom, annoyance and then finally, profound disgust. He was not sure where this disgust had come from for what had once been a pleasurable pursuit. Maybe it was to do with that hollow feeling he had experienced in his chest last week at the christening of young Henry Sedgwick. He had stood and watched a radiant Grace Sedgwick smile at her newborn son, under the loving gaze of her husband, and he had felt a painful tug in his chest. Of course, he had dismissed the feeling as unimportant—it was probably just hunger as he had missed his breakfast. That was surely it. Whatever the true cause might be, at Tremayne's that night, he had felt a repugnance for the revelry around him. In one sudden move, he had pushed himself to his feet, shaking off the people worshipping his body, and stridden out of the room, uncaring of his nakedness.

"Fetch my clothes," he'd barked at the bemused, barely dressed serving maid, who had skurried off to do his bidding. A short time later, she had returned with them, and he had dressed quickly then taken his leave. On arrival at his townhouse, Philip had bid his servants to prepare him a hot bath, no matter that it was the middle of the night. Then, having cleansed the stench of perfume and incense from his skin, he had gone to bed to a troubled sleep. He had woken up the following morning, still troubled and despondent. And so it had been in the week since his return from London.

Philip stared absently at the painting of a sapphire Aegean seascape which hung above the mantlepiece in the dining room. What was it that had gone wrong with his perfectly ordered life that he was so cast down? None of the things that had once brought him joy seemed to appeal to him anymore. Just now, he had opened the post to find an invitation to a house party that would undoubtedly lead to sexual frolics, and his first instinct had been to decline. He had not been able to put brush to canvas all week. Artistic inspiration seemed to have vanished into the ether. The book he was reading, a titillating tale of a young man's sexual exploits, published privately by a friend of his, held no interest for him at all. And yesterday at Dr Benson's, he had felt not an ounce of desire for Mrs Benson, with whom he had conducted a salacious affair for several years. Nothing and no one held his interest anymore.

The only time he had not felt bored or despondent all week had been with Miss Cranshaw yesterday, when he had helped her rescue a small boy ensnared by a man trap in Squire Johnson's woods. He laughed to himself. Strange things indeed had come to pass when the best part of his week was spending time with an upstanding spinster, doing a good deed. Was he turning over a new leaf in his dotage?

Perhaps so, but there was more to it than that. In a rare burst of self-perception, he realised something else. Here he sat, alone in this great dining room. And confound it, he did not wish to be alone any longer. It would not be so bad if he could have a companion to share this life with. Someone sensible, for he could not stand female histrionics. His mind returned to Sarah Cranshaw, that oddly attractive and eccentric female whom he was quite sure harboured tender feelings for him. On an impulse, he stood and walked out of the dining room, leaving his luncheon uneaten.

"Jenkins," he said briskly, addressing his butler. "Send word to the stable to have the phaeton ready."

"Yes, sir," replied the old retainer who had served his family for two decades and more.

Philip donned his boots, coat and hat, then strode down the front steps of his great house to his waiting vehicle. His destination? Ivy Cottage.

CHAPTER 14

SARAH

"Love is all we have, the only way that each can help the other."
— Euripides

SARAH WOKE THAT morning in high spirits. Benjamin was home from the war, and Mr Templeton had given her compliments. It was enough to fill this spinster maiden's heart with joy. She could not ask for more.

Humming a jaunty tune under her breath, she went down to breakfast, a note on the table from Ambrose telling her that he had taken her letter to Benjamin with him to give to Daniel ahead of his departure for America. She wondered what Benjamin would make of the wanton revelations she had made about her nighttime activities. Something told her he would approve.

Breakfast over, she walked merrily to tutor her young charges at Gorston Manor, avoiding the shortcut through Squire Johnson's woods. In the course of the morning, it was remarked on more than one occasion by her pupils that she looked fine indeed and had a healthy bloom to her cheeks. That should not have been a surprise, for there is no greater beauty elixir than happiness.

On the return journey home, she stopped by a set of rundown cottages on the southern edge of the village and looked in on the Burrells and the Jacksons, two families whose ability to procreate numerous offspring was unequal to their capacity to earn an income. They were often in needful straits, especially at this time of the year when there were fewer casual farm jobs to be had. Sarah, with the full encouragement of Benedict Sedgwick, had made it a habit to check in on their wellbeing each week, taking along with her some donations of food and clothes.

A little urchin of a boy gave her a gap-toothed smile on arrival and ran inside to tell his ma that a lady was there to see her. Mrs Burrell appeared shortly after, a wailing child at her hip, a haggard look to her face.

"Miss Cranshaw, it's good of you to visit," she said softly.

Sarah smiled warmly. "Mrs Burrell, good day. I do not wish to intrude but was just stopping by to bring you these," she said, placing a straw basket on the table. "There are two dozen eggs there and a joint of ham. I've also spoken to Mr Timms. He says there are spare loaves to be had at the bakery at the end of the day. Perhaps you could send one of your older children there to ask for some each day."

"Bless you, miss. That is very kind."

"Not at all, this is the very least I can do. I pray Mr Burrell will have more success in finding employment this winter than he did last year. If all fails, do let him go see Ambrose, my brother, who may have some work for him on the Stanton estate. Please be sure to tell him."

"I will, miss, thanking you kindly."

Sarah turned to leave, "Good day, Mrs Burrell."

Having discharged this duty, Sarah continued on her way home, still in the sunniest of moods. At Ivy Cottage, she partook of a light luncheon then changed into her brown cambric gown. First, she looked in on an experiment she was conducting on the growth of mould on bread. Carefully, she checked each sample and noted down her observations. Having completed this task, she then went to work on her miniature railway, losing herself happily in the meticulous creation of the wheels and axles for her locomotive.

It was perhaps a half-hour later that her happy toil was interrupted by a knock at the door. Sarah heard the sound of a deep male voice speaking to Elsie, her maid. An instant later, the young girl came over to find her. "Mr Templeton is here to see you, Miss," said she. "I showed him in to the front parlour."

"Thank you, Elsie. I shall come along shortly."

Sarah glanced down at her gown. There was no time now to change. All she could do was pat a few wayward strands of hair behind her ear and hope for the best. She walked into the front parlour, cheeks flushed with happy excitement. "Mr Templeton, what a pleasant surprise," she said. "You will have to excuse me. I was not expecting any guests and have dressed in my oldest gown to work on my miniature railway."

He stood and bowed. "Good day, Miss Cranshaw. It is I who should beg for your pardon, arriving in such a way unannounced. Only, I thought you might like to check on our young patient, Mattie. I came in the phaeton to propose we pay him a visit, if you are free to do so now. I have no wish though, to interrupt your work on this miniature railway—which, by the by, I would be most interested to see."

"Oh," said Sarah, a little flustered. "That is a splendid idea! I would very much like to see how Mattie is getting along. Will you give me a few moments to change into something more appropriate for an outing?"

"Of course," Mr Templeton affirmed with a smile. "Perhaps in the meantime, you will allow me to admire your work on this miniature railway. That is, if you do not mind?"

"I do not mind at all," breathed Sarah, "though I should warn you that it is but a small hobby of mine. Do follow me, Mr Templeton, and I will show you."

Her heart still beating far more rapidly than it ought to, she led Mr Templeton to the back parlour room where she had set up her miniature railway. A waft of his cologne drifted her way, and she breathed it in euphorically.

Mr Templeton walked into the back parlour, looking about curiously. "Why Miss Cranshaw," he cried. "You have done yourself a disservice in describing this as merely a small hobby. What an impressive work of craftsmanship. Did you do this all yourself?"

"I had some help in starting it from Benjamin Stanton, but all the rest of the work is mine."

She felt him reach very carefully over her shoulder to take a small wagon into his hand and examine it. Such closeness to his body was overwhelming. She thrummed with awareness of his masculine presence. It was best to beat a hasty retreat before she embarrassed herself.

"If you will excuse me, Mr Templeton," she said in a shaky voice. "I will go and get myself ready."

She hurried out of the room and up the stairs. In the quiet haven of her bedchamber, she leaned against the door and tried to compose herself. She was a mature lady of thirty years, not a chit out of the schoolroom. She should remember to act accordingly. And she should also not read too much into this sudden and singular attention Mr Templeton was paying her, despite that strange feeling that had come over her last night that things were about to change.

Calm once again, she changed into a woollen gown in a shade of deep blue which, oh perfidious vanity, she knew complemented the grey of her eyes. At her mirror, she tidied her hair and added a discreet touch of rouge to her cheeks—and yes, perhaps also a dab of the expensive eau de cologne Daniel had given her as a thirtieth birthday gift. Not wishing to make Mr Templeton wait too long, she then stood and resolutely made her way down to the parlour again. There, she found the gentleman in rapt contemplation of her railway.

"This back panel," he said. "What will you do with it?"

She came to stand beside him, murmuring, "I have thought to have it painted as a backdrop to the railway, though I have not yet decided what scene to depict. It will have to be something simple, for I am no master at painting."

"Let me do it!" he proposed, then checked himself. "That is, if you will allow someone else's hand on your work."

"I–I did not know you painted, Mr Templeton," she stammered wonderingly.

"It is one of my active pursuits. However, of late, I must confess to not having had anything of interest to paint. But I would dearly love to have a go at this panel. I am thinking the northern approach to Hanborough station would be a perfect scene to depict. What think you?"

"Oh, Mr Templeton, it is exactly what I was thinking to do!" she exclaimed. "Except of course, I do not have the skills for it."

"Then let me do it, please."

"I would be honoured," Sarah let out on a fluttery breath.

Mr Templeton beamed. "Then it is agreed. Now, how about we pay young Mattie a visit?" He held out his arm and escorted her to the hallway where she collected her coat and bonnet. A moment later, they were on their way.

CHAPTER 15

BENJAMIN

*"One word frees us of all the weight and pain in life, that
word is Love."*
— Sophocles

October 1865
"PAPA!" BENJAMIN WATCHED as his brother, Daniel,
embraced their father. Beside them, Bella sobbed in her
mother's arms. His brother and sister, together with his cousin
Grace and her family, had arrived only a few moments ago,
having made the journey from England. Nearly five years had
passed since they had last seen each other, so the reunion was
an emotional one. All around him, people were embracing,
crying, exclaiming while he stood, a little removed from it all.

Just then, Daniel looked up and caught his eye. They
exchanged a long, silent stare. There was love in that stare, but
also anger and frustration. Daniel's eyes missed nothing as he
noted the changes in his brother, his lips pursing into a grim
line. His all-seeing gaze took in the scar, the lines of pain and
fatigue, the salt-and-pepper beard.

Benjamin's stare was no less angry. His lips curled as he
studied his immaculately dressed brother, hair fashionably
styled, face as handsome as ever. This was not the face of
someone who had witnessed the charge after a battle cry, the
howls of pain, the blood, the acrid smell of death. This was not
the face of someone who had shivered from cold under a flimsy

tent at night and woken to a miserable breakfast of hard tack and bitter coffee.

Next moment, Daniel stood before him. A moment later, he had clasped him in his arms, without a word. Benjamin accepted the embrace, even returned it with a clasp of his own arms around his brother. He breathed in Daniel's expensive cologne, and beneath that, the familiar scent of his childhood playmate. Memories flooded him of days spent tussling in the grass, playing pranks, riding their first horse, Daniel coaching him in the art of seduction. Though he still felt resentment, Benjamin gave in momentarily to the joy of being reunited with his brother again.

The next hours were a blur, as around him the Stantons tried to catch up on all that had happened during five years of separation. They sat together for a celebratory meal, talking rapidly, wiping the tears, smiling wide. Benjamin joined in as best he could, but by the early afternoon, he could take no more. Without a word, he slipped out of the house and went to the stable to saddle up his horse. Soon, he was galloping away, letting the wind brush his heated face.

He rode with a destination in mind, taking the south-eastern fork off the main road, then turning left and negotiating the muddy track a further mile south until he reached a copse of pine trees bordering a gently flowing stream. On the other side of the stream was a small meadow, in the middle of which stood a ramshackle cabin. He stopped and dismounted, tethering his horse to a nearby tree, then walked around the cabin, surveying the space. Eventually, he perched himself on the front steps, took out a pencil and sheet of paper, and began to sketch.

The sound of hooves had him look up from his work some minutes later. A lone rider approached on his horse, halted and jumped down, then walked over to him.

"I thought I would find you here," said Daniel conversationally. "Pa told me you had purchased old Jim Shaw's cabin with the money you inherited from Grandpa." He came to sit beside his brother, glancing at the drawing Benjamin had made. "What are you going to do with it? Live the hermit life like him?"

"The idea holds some appeal," responded Benjamin wryly.

Daniel pulled the sheet of paper towards him and examined it more closely. "Are these your plans for rebuilding the cabin?"

"Just some initial ideas."

His brother pointed to something on the drawing. "What's this?"

"A large rectangular barn," Benjamin replied. "I'm thinking of using it as an engineering workshop where I can design and tinker with machinery."

Daniel nodded, scrutinising the landscape around him. "It's good land. There's water, a steady supply of wood, green pasture for your cattle. I always thought old Jim could have made a lot more out of this place."

"We'll see if I can do any better. I've a great deal of work to do—knock the cabin down, dig the foundations and rebuild. I don't know how much I'll get done before the snow comes this winter."

Daniel turned his gaze towards his brother. "I can help you," he stated.

Benjamin snorted. "And ruin those perfectly groomed hands, viscount? I think not."

His brother's eyes narrowed. Without a word, he stood and walked along the porch to pick up the axe that was leaning against the wall of the cabin. "We better get started if we want to get anything done before dark," was all he said.

Two hours later, both brothers had worked up a fine sweat and demolished a good third of the cabin's structure. They would have continued, but a glance at the sun low on the horizon told them there was only a half-hour at most before it would get dark. Reluctantly, they put down their tools, wiped the sweat from their brows and returned to their horses. They rode home without a word, each of them deep in thought.

Back at the house, they were welcomed with a hot bath and a hearty meal, the rest of the family wisely refraining from questioning either brother about where they had been. Benjamin excused himself early and went up to his room, still not feeling up to the task of being sociable. He had just pulled off his shoes when there came a knock at the door. "Come in!" he called, suppressing a sigh of annoyance. The door swung open and in walked Daniel. "What now?" grumbled Benjamin.

Daniel bit out a laugh. "Don't worry, princess. I've not come to intrude on your sanctuary. I came to give you this." In his hand, he held a thick envelope. "It's from Sarah," he said, placing it on the bedside table, adding, "Do you know, Benjamin, how envious I felt every time letters came from you, a single sheet with sparse information addressed to me or Bella, and a bulging envelope for Sarah. I was reduced to begging her for news of you because my own brother shut me out of his confidence." He caught the momentary concern on Benjamin's face and huffed, "Fear not. She did not betray your confidence, though she did explain why you could not always be forthright with me. Steadfastly loyal, that girl. I like her."

A thrill had coursed through Benjamin's veins at the sight of Sarah's letter, but he replied coolly, "Hardly a girl. She's a mature woman of thirty." He paused, then asked the burning question, "Has she married?"

"No," Daniel said with a smirk. "Still very single and yours for the taking, only you'd have to come to England for her."

"It's not what you think, idiot. We are just friends." Though in his heart, Benjamin was not truly convinced of this statement. Daniel's words had lit a small spark of hope that perhaps there could be more to this friendship than an exchange of letters across the ocean.

"Of course," Daniel said with a mocking inclination of his head. "Just friends. Enjoy your letter." Then he turned around and left Benjamin alone in his room.

As soon as the door had shut, Benjamin pounced on the envelope. With hands that shook, he broke the seal and took out the folded sheets of paper. He went to sit by the fireplace and began to read.

16th September, 1865

My dearest friend Benjamin,

I cannot tell you with what joy I heard the news of your safe return to Ohio. It was like a weight that had pressed on my chest for so long was finally lifted and I could breathe again. For years I have lived through worry that the next communication from America would be the news I so dreaded hearing. And now the war is over and you are back home safe. Oh the sweet relief!

Dearest friend, I have read your letters and re-read them. They are among my most treasured possessions. I kept them all safe, apart from that one letter you asked me to burn, which I did. I have chafed at my inability to write to you in return, and now that I am finally able to, I do not know where to start. How do I summarise the four years since my last letter to you? I am well, in good health, though now an old maid, having passed the great age of thirty. I still live at Ivy Cottage with Ambrose, who continues to manage the Stanton estate. In many respects, not much has changed for me, except I have grown older.

I have deepened my acquaintance with your siblings, who have extended their friendship to me and Ambrose. I have grown close to Daniel and Isabella, enjoying their company, partly for their own sakes, but mostly because they are your family. Every time they quote their beloved classical philosophers, I think of you encouraging me to seize the day. Oftentimes, I catch a look or an expression on their faces that reminds me of you, and it makes my heart leap.

It is a strange thing, Benjamin, this friendship of ours. How can it be that we are so far apart, have spent so few hours in each other's company, and yet we know each other so well? Your words, dear friend, are seared into my soul. Through your eyes, I have seen the world beyond my small village of Stanton Harcourt and borne witness to this dreadful war. Through you, I have learned of what happens between men and women behind closed doors. I may be an old spinster maid with no experience of men, but through you I have lived.

Shall I tell you of the fevered imaginings I have at night, all from you, and the physical joy I feel as I touch myself, thinking of you? It is as if I live two lives. In the day, I am a prim and proper spinster maid. At night, I am a brazen hussy with craven desires. I lie naked in my bed and imagine myself with you. I am the whore who lets you use her body and comforts you when you are in pain. I am the comely maid you have a quick fumble with in a darkened alley. I am the sultry widow who splays her legs for your delectation of her cunt. I am all those things. Nobody seeing me at night or reading these words would ever believe they came from me, staid and proper Miss Cranshaw. It is only you that knows this, you that created this hungering need in me.

When I heard that Daniel and Bella were travelling to see you in America, I felt envy. I wished for a moment that it could be me, coming to see you. Will we ever meet again, do you think? Most likely we are not destined to. It would be strange and disconcerting to come face to face with you after all the intimacies we have shared. Maybe the very reason why we can be this honest with one another is that we are so far apart. Could we be so open with one another in person? Probably not. And yet I also long to see you in the flesh, to look into your dark eyes and hear your voice. I want to hold you in my embrace and whisper in your ear that you are not alone, dear friend. I am with you, no matter how far I am. I have felt your loneliness in the letters that you have sent. Now you have family and loved ones around you, I hope you are not so alone anymore. But whatever the case, know that I am always with you, your friend for eternity.

In time, dear Benjamin, you will meet a good woman and marry. You will have children of your own and a successful career as an engineer. I pray that you will have all these things, even if it will mean an end to this honest discourse between us — for your wife would not want you to share details of your intimate life with another. I will remain your friend throughout whatever the case may be. I pray for your happiness and an end to your sorrow.

As for me... well do not be surprised to hear that I continue to admire Mr Templeton from afar, although not so afar, as today I had an interesting contretemps with him. I was walking to Gorston Manor, where I tutor two young ladies, Misses Rosemary and Fanny Collins, and took a shortcut through the woods that belong to Squire Johnson. To my horror, I found a young boy caught in the snare of a man trap. It had snapped around his foot and imprisoned him to the chain tied around a tree trunk. The poor boy was in pain, having fractured a bone in his foot as he fell. Immediately, I rushed out onto the lane, intent on getting to Gorston Manor and seeking help there. Instead, I was accosted by Mr Templeton on his mount. I waved to him to stop and explained the situation. He went to the boy and rescued him heroically with me at his side.

Later in the day, he paid me a visit at Ivy Cottage to tell me how the boy, Mattie, had fared at Dr Benson's. I think Mr Templeton was quite impressed with my level headedness and quick thinking in the midst of an emergency. He called me an intrepid female and a most capable person. I wonder, perhaps, if he is finally beginning to notice me. He is still a bachelor, you know. Tonight, I do not think I will be able to sleep for all the excitement of the day. First, my encounter with Mr Templeton and then, the wondrous news of your return. My heart overflowed with happy relief, and I cried so long that poor Ambrose's jacket was quite soaked with my tears. And now, I have this strange feeling that all is about to change in my life, which so long has been the same. It is illogical, to be sure, but I cannot shake the feeling—and in some roundabout way, it is tied to you. Now you are back home and sure to resume the course of your life that was cruelly interrupted by war, it will not be long, I suspect, before you come into your own and marry. And this too may be my cue to end the years of spinsterhood and find conjugal felicity at last—with Mr Templeton perhaps? Maybe that is too far-fetched of a dream, but we shall have to see.

Life is good here. I have Ambrose, always a dear brother and friend. I have my dreams of Mr Templeton. I have my pursuits—I shall have you know that the miniature railway you started for me is coming along swimmingly. And of course, best of all, I have you, dearest Benjamin, my most intimate friend. I could not wish for more except to hear of your happiness. Write soon and tell me your news.

Your true friend,

Sarah

Benjamin read and re-read the letter. It brought about in him a feeling of elation, excitement and anxiety, this last as he read of Sarah's latest encounter with Mr Templeton. What if it was true and the cad had finally taken notice of his Sarah? That could not be borne.

He washed and undressed, then got under the covers in bed, his mind in disarray, a strange tight clutching at his chest. His Sarah. That was how he thought of her. She was his. Only he knew her trusted secrets. Only she was privy to every private facet of his life. He could not lose her, and certainly not to that rogue, Mr Templeton. In that instant, a certainty pierced his heart that Sarah was destined to marry no one but himself. What was it Daniel had said? *Still very single and yours for the taking, only you'd have to come to England for her.* Of course, that was what he had to do. Go fetch his girl before she was taken from him for good.

CHAPTER 16

BENJAMIN

"Man has no greater enemy than himself."
—Petrarch

OF COURSE, IT was not quite so easy a thing to make such a decision become a reality. His family would not thank him for leaving so soon after having returned from an absence of four and a half years. Isabella and Daniel had only just themselves arrived from England. He could hardly turn tail and leave them now. And yet he did not know if he had the patience to wait the several months they proposed to spend in America before joining them on their return journey to England.

And there was something else that gnawed away at his spirits. He was painfully aware of how little he had to offer Sarah. A scarred man, forever damaged by what he had seen and done in the war, he could not even provide her with a home of her own—not unless something worthy of her could be built over the ruins of old Jim's cabin. He could not leave now, not without having completed the work he had only just begun.

As he toiled side by side with Daniel the following morning, taking down every rotten joist from the old cabin, he tried to reason with himself. He had waited nearly five long years for Sarah. Surely he could have patience enough to wait a further few months. But then he recalled what she had written in her letter. Mr Templeton had called her an intrepid female and a most capable person, the first true compliments he had paid her. Of course she was that and much more besides. Benjamin had known it from the start. But now Mr Templeton had taken note of this. What else would he soon begin to notice? The excellence of her character? The craven sensuality she kept hidden beneath her prim exterior? The brilliance of her grey eyes that even an absence of five years and thousands of miles' distance could not dim?

He found himself becoming progressively more maddened and frustrated. That familiar anger began to engulf him, fuelling his rage. He wielded the axe like a man on a rampage, hacking furiously at the remains of old Jim's cabin. A red haze formed in his mind. He could not think straight. All he could feel was gut wrenching fear and rage.

"Benjamin!"

He barely heard his brother's voice through the haze engulfing him.

"Benjamin! Will you stop?"

This was said more sharply, this time penetrating his mind, but still he lifted the axe and lodged it in the wooden planks before him. He went to raise it aloft again.

"Benjamin, put it down!"

With a concerted effort, he stopped, his hands gripping the axe tightly. His brother's voice continued, more gently, "Let it go, Benjamin. Put the axe down and step away from it." Breathing heavily, he let it fall to the ground, then took a step back from it. He felt his brother's hand on his back, leading him firmly towards the front porch steps, as yet unmarked by his axe. The hand pressed gently, urging him to sit. Unable to offer resistance to such implacable calm, he did as he was bid, collapsing in a huddle on the top step, his face in his hands.

The brothers stayed there for some time, not talking. Benjamin's chest heaved with shallow breaths as slowly, he brought himself back to an awareness of where he was and what he was doing. Eventually, he straightened his back and took his face out of his hands, refusing to look at his brother. In a gritty voice, he said, "I apologise. It is the way with me these days. My temper gets the better of me."

There was no response, except for a sympathetic squeeze of his shoulder. Benjamin took a deep breath and turned to look behind him at the remains of the cabin. They had made good progress. Only about a last quarter of it was still standing. They could have the whole thing razed to the ground by the end of the day. "We have done well today," he said, sounding more composed.

"We work well together," agreed his brother.

"Think you we can make fast work of the new building?"

Daniel considered the matter. "It depends how long the dry weather holds up. I could get some more hands to help us—John, his cousin Robbie. Is it of great import that we finish this build quickly?"

"Yes," murmured Benjamin. He had used his axe in anger just now, but he also knew that every blow would lead him to finishing the cabin and reuniting with Sarah.

"Will you tell me now what it was that had you so upset?"

Benjamin did not answer at once. He could not find the words to explain. He heaved a breath. "Do you recall what you said when you handed me Sarah's letter yesterday?"

"About her still being unmarried?"

"Yes."

Daniel was quick to understand. "You want to build this house for her," he stated.

"Yes."

"And you mean to go to England."

"As soon as I possibly can," replied Benjamin.

Daniel regarded him humorously. "So, you are more than simply friends."

"There is something more," Benjamin chose his words carefully. "However, nothing has been declared."

Daniel gave an unamused laugh. "Believe me, I am well acquainted with such a thing."

Now finally, Benjamin turned to face his brother. "What do you mean? Who?"

Daniel shook his head, waving the questions away. "It is of no import, except in one respect. I have good reason to want to stay away from England for a considerable time—three months at least, perhaps more. It would make sense, Benjamin, if you were to step into my shoes and take over the reins at Stanton Hall while I remain here. It will not be too arduous a task, as the estate is well managed by Ambrose. And it should give you time to woo the delightful Sarah."

The idea did not displease Benjamin, but there was still a problem. He glanced at the ruined cabin behind him. "What of the house?"

Daniel held up his hands in front of him, saying mockingly, "Not so perfectly groomed any more. Will you trust me to build it for you? I am well capable of following a set of your drawings. With John and Robbie's help, I promise to have it ready for occupation by the time you have completed your courtship of Sarah and returned with her." He seemed to think about that last statement and amended it with, "As long as you give me until the new year. And of course, you will be able to put your own personal finish to the house on your return."

Benjamin hesitated. "She might not want me as a husband, or to live in America, so far from her family."

Daniel pressed the point. "And you'll only know for sure once you ask her. Go to England, Benjamin, and win her hand. I'll build your house."

No further convincing was required. "When?" asked Benjamin.

Daniel's smile spread across his face. "Tomorrow, dear brother. You leave tomorrow, and do not worry about Mama or Pa or anyone else. I will manage them for you."

To this, Benjamin could only respond with a brotherly embrace. The two men held each other tight, silently expressing their love and gratitude. As they returned to their travails shortly afterwards, it occurred to Benjamin that there were times when Daniel really was as strong, authoritative and accomplished as he had always thought him to be, and that it was a very useful thing to have indeed.

ON THEIR RETURN home later that afternoon, having finally razed the old cabin to the ground, Benjamin went straight up to his room to wash and change. Upon his appearance at the dinner table, it was apparent that Daniel had already set to work on managing the rest of the family into accepting his decision to leave for England. There were no remonstrances, only sorrowful acceptance that he would depart on the morrow.

After dinner, Benjamin and Daniel adjourned to their father's study where they sat for over an hour going through the plans Benjamin had drawn of his new home and making a few changes, such as adding a large dressing room to the main bedchamber and creating a private parlour upstairs for Sarah, large enough to accommodate a miniature railway.

Later that evening, Benjamin bethought himself to do one more thing. Walking the short distance to the neighbouring house that belonged to his uncle Jasper, he sought out his cousin Grace. He found her in the back parlour, nursing her small babe at her breast. Upon his entrance, she looked up in surprise. "Benjamin," she said softly.

"I can come back later," he muttered, feeling not quite at ease.

"No, it's alright. Do come and sit here with me. I hear you are leaving us tomorrow."

Benjamin settled himself on an armchair next to Grace. "Yes," he replied.

"And," went on Grace, "I have been told by Daniel on pain of being shunned that I am not to ask the reason for your hurried departure."

To this, Benjamin had no reply. Instead, he broached the subject of his visit. "Gracie, I have come to talk to you of a private matter. It concerns Jimmy."

Her eyes welled at the mention of his name. "I was so saddened to hear of his passing. Poor Jimmy," she murmured.

Benjamin cleared his throat. "I was with Jimmy in his last hours. He spoke of you, Grace, and your daughter. Pardon me, but he seemed under the impression that Anna was his child. He made me promise that one day, I would tell Anna about her father. Grace, is she his?"

"Poor, poor Jimmy," sighed Grace. "I had no thought that he believed she was his child." She shook her head at him. "No, Benjamin. He is not her father. Of that I am certain." She paused, thinking the matter over. "But I will speak of him to Anna when I tell her stories of my childhood here. I will tell her of my friend, Jimmy, and of the escapades we had. He will not be forgotten."

Benjamin let out a relieved breath. "Good. I am glad." He stood to go. With this duty discharged, he felt a weight leave his shoulders. He could say goodbye properly now to his friend, Jimmy.

Grace looked up at him, "I am sure I do not know the reason for your departure," she said, "but Benjamin, I wish you every success in your journey."

"Thank you, Gracie." He bent to kiss her cheek and to place a gentle hand on the baby's downy head. A generation of men had been lost in this war—Jimmy included—but a new generation would soon rise to take their place. He hoped they would not repeat the errors of their predecessors.

"He is precious," he said.

"I know," she murmured. "Goodbye, Benjamin."

With a last smile, Benjamin let himself out of the parlour. Next morning, with little fanfare or fuss—God bless Daniel— he set out on his long journey.

PART III

AFTER THE WAR

CHAPTER 17

SARAH

"Everything comes gradually and at its appointed hour."
— Ovid

November 1865

SARAH PRECEDED AMBROSE as they entered the church, her eyes searching for Mr Templeton as was her wont. She did not spy him in his usual pew or anywhere else, but her disappointment was not too great. Sundays had been quiet affairs these past several weeks, with both the Stantons and the Sedgwicks gone to America. This Sunday, however, would be different, for Mr Templeton had invited her and Ambrose to partake of luncheon with him at Graveley, his great mansion on the outskirts of the village.

The congregation rose to its feet as the service began, and it was at this moment that Mr Templeton hurried into the church. With remarkable precision, he weaved his way through the assembled people, smiling charmingly at acquaintances, until he reached her side, the first time he had sat so close to her. She felt the eyes of the congregation on her and blushed a rosy pink. Mr Templeton's marked attentions could not but be noticed. The gentleman, however, seemed oblivious to this, merely leaning towards her to whisper, "I am sorry to be so late. I was up early this morning putting the finishing touches to the panel and lost track of the time."

Her eyes shone as she spoke softly in response, "Is it finished?"

"It is, and you shall see it when you visit today."

"I cannot wait!"

"Shh!" a stern-looking matron chided from behind them as the organ began the first notes of a hymn. They reluctantly stopped their chatter and tried to pay attention to the service, with mixed success, at least on Sarah's part. Throughout it all, she was supremely conscious of Mr Templeton's fine form sitting beside her and his occasional flirtatious glances in her direction.

It had been five weeks since that day he took her in his phaeton to visit Mattie—five weeks in which Mr Templeton had been a regular caller at Ivy Cottage. He had taken an interest not just in her miniature railway but in the scientific experiments she was conducting. He had also volunteered to assist her in her charitable endeavours and paid her the most glorious of compliments. At first, she had been careful not to read anything into this strange state of affairs, but it was now becoming impossible to avoid the conclusion that he was indeed paying court to her. She, Sarah Cranshaw, prim spinster maiden was being courted by the deliciously handsome Mr Templeton. It was a long-awaited dream finally coming to fruition.

In these five weeks, Sarah had floated on a cloud of exultation. She woke each morning in excited anticipation of what the next day would bring. Change was definitely in the air. Her premonition had been right. It was exhilarating and terrifying all at once. She could not say where such marked attention from Mr Templeton would lead, but the hope that had been a tiny seedling for so long, was now sprouting the tallest of shoots. Could Mr Templeton mean to propose? Oh, it was too much! Too wondrous! It was best not to let her mind dwell on such an extraordinary prospect.

Such a surfeit of happiness was bound to have a beneficial effect on the countenance of any lady, and Sarah was no exception. She had noticed it when scrutinising herself in the mirror. Even Ambrose, never one to remark on such things, had told her the other day that she looked very fetching indeed. And of course, Mr Templeton had taken note, showering her with the most flattering of compliments. Sometimes, she thought all this good fortune was simply too good to be true, yet here she was, sitting right next to Mr Templeton in church for all to see.

The service over, they walked out of the church together, fielding curious glances and the occasional inquisitive remark from their neighbours. Mr Templeton bore it all with charming insouciance, though Sarah could not find the attention on her anything but disconcerting. Fortunately, Ambrose stepped in, closing down discussion and stating they should be on their way. The Stanton carriage had been put at their disposal, on Daniel's orders before his departure. Ambrose deftly led his sister to it and assisted her inside. Soon, they were trotting away from church and heading for Graveley, Mr Templeton riding there separately.

Once they had put some distance from the church, Ambrose fixed her with his gaze and spoke, "Sarah, love, you know that I do not like to interfere in your personal affairs. I have long known of your feelings for Mr Templeton, but I have refrained from speaking of them."

"I know," she murmured.

"However, the time has come for me to finally speak with you on the matter. Mr Templeton's attention to you has been so marked as to elicit gossip in the village. It has prompted me to wonder what his intentions are towards you, especially after we received this invitation to luncheon with him today."

"I have wondered on this matter too," began Sarah, but Ambrose raised a hand, asking her to let him finish.

"I went to see Mr Templeton yesterday," he went on. "You may think it is terribly old fashioned of me to do so, but I had to ask him of his intentions towards you. It was a most uncomfortable interview, I may add."

"Oh Ambrose," breathed Sarah. "And… what did he say?"

Ambrose let out a deep breath. "He assured me that his intentions were entirely honourable. That he had come to a stage in his life where he wished to settle down and marry, and that he had long admired your character."

"Oh!" Sarah put a hand to her palpitating heart.

Ambrose was quick to add, "He did not go as far as to ask for my permission to make his addresses to you, for which I am profoundly glad. Sarah, you must not take this to mean that he intends to propose, only that he is considering marriage. I would not want you to raise your hopes only to have them dashed."

"I–I do understand."

Her brother looked upon her kindly. "Do I take this to mean, Sarah, that you would welcome his suit, should he propose?"

"It is all I have dreamed of for many years," she replied tremulously.

"He has a reputation for being something of a rake," Ambrose reminded her gently.

"Then he is a reformed rake, for I have seen nothing but excellence of character from him these past few weeks."

"And what of Benjamin Stanton?" queried Ambrose.

Benjamin. How could she explain the jumbled feelings she had for him? Benjamin, who continued to find his way into her mind each night. Benjamin, whose letters she eagerly awaited and devoured. Calling him a friend could not begin to describe what he had come to mean to her. But he was far away in America, and it was quite possible that she may never see him again. At times, it almost felt as if he were a mirage or a figment of her imagination.

Her enduring silence had Ambrose frowning in concern. "I see it is not quite so simple as him being your friend. It is more, is it not?"

She sighed loudly. "I do not know. I cannot explain it. We have an unusually close friendship, despite the great distance between us."

"Sarah," he said. "You cannot keep your affections fixed on two gentlemen. There will come a time when you have to decide between them."

"What is there to decide," replied Sarah hotly, "when Benjamin is far away in America and unlikely ever to return? I would not be surprised if in one of his letters soon, he announces that he is engaged to marry some worthy American lady. He has been so lonely and will want to seek loving companionship which I am unable to give him, since I am here and he is over there. You ask me to decide, but it is not as if I am the one to make the choice; it is being made for me. Mr Templeton is right here and talking marriage. Whatever affection I have for Benjamin is of the impossible kind, and are you not the one who has always advocated for being sensible and rational about one's situation?"

Ambrose looked away, as if these words pained him. Gruffly, he replied, "I am, and do believe one must always be clear-sighted about the facts. But do have a care for your heart, Sarah, for it is the one part of us that does not act rationally."

Just then, the carriage turned into the scenic avenue that led to Graveley. The conversation came to an end, and Sarah gazed out of the window with interest, never before having been to Mr Templeton's house. They came to a stop in front of a majestic set of steps which led to an imposing brick building with tall arched windows. As she emerged from the carriage, Sarah studied the magnificent aspect before her and could not help but think, "*Of this one day, I could be mistress.*" She immediately tried to quell this worldly thought, with little success, for she was a mere human and not infallible. The whole idea seemed unbelievable.

Striding rapidly towards them was Mr Templeton, having arrived moments before and dismounted his horse. He beamed his charming smile as he said, "Welcome Miss Cranshaw, Mr Cranshaw. It delights me at last to play host. Do come in." He led them inside, took her coat and bonnet then ushered them through to the drawing room. There, they were served some light refreshments and engaged in desultory conversation for a short time. It was not long, however, before Mr Templeton broached the subject of the back panel he had painted for her miniature railway. With twinkling eyes, he drawled, "Miss Cranshaw, would you care to see the finished work?"

"Oh yes, I would very much like to!"

"Then let me show you. Mr Cranshaw, do you come with us?"

Ambrose, who had been busy examining a volume that had been left on the table beside him, looked up. His eyes met with Sarah's in understanding and resignation. "If you will excuse me," he said, "I would look through this latest work by Dickens. Do go ahead without me."

Mr Templeton stood. "Then, Miss Cranshaw, shall we?"

With pulse racing, Sarah got to her feet. She was cognisant of Ambrose's trust in her judgement, that he had left her to be alone with Mr Templeton. What a rare and excellent brother he was! She placed a hand on Mr Templeton's proffered arm and let him lead her out of the room.

He took her through another room and then down a corridor to the back of the house, from which double doors opened onto a brightly lit semi-circular shaped room. Various canvases, some complete, others only partly begun, rested against one wall. A large table stood in the middle, covered with a cornucopia of paint bottles, brushes and cloths. And in the far end of the room, there it was. Her panel.

She walked eagerly towards it and let her eyes travel the length of it from one end to the other. "Oh my," she breathed. "Such fine detail." She turned to Mr Templeton, brimming with joy. "It is perfect! How can I ever thank you?"

His eyes had stayed glued to her the whole time she was examining his painting. Now, they gleamed as he muttered, "Like this." Next moment, he had taken her in his arms and planted his lips on hers. Sarah froze in shock. Mr Templeton was kissing her! *Oh my gracious Lord!* Could this really be? Her hands flew up to clutch at the lapels of his jacket. She kissed him back inexpertly, trying to recall what Benjamin had told her in one of his letters about the art of kissing. He had written of kissing with an open mouth so that both tongues could join. Perhaps that was what she ought to be doing now.

Hesitantly, she parted her lips. No sooner had she done so than she felt Mr Templeton's invasion. How bizarre. It was an odd sensation but not too unpleasant. She felt the stroke of his tongue against hers. Was she doing it right? She very much hoped so. Mr Templeton's murmurs of encouragement certainly made it seem as if she were acquitting herself well in this new, foreign endeavour.

He pulled back a fraction to smile against her mouth. "Sweet Sarah. I knew you would taste so deliciously sweet."

"I–I…" She could not utter anything intelligible.

He chuckled. "I have been too hasty. I meant to declare myself before ravishing you, my dearest."

"Declare yourself?"

His expression sobered. "Sarah, you cannot be unaware of my intentions towards you. I wish you to be my wife, sweet girl. Will you marry me?"

She stared into his handsome face, feeling overwhelmed. Was this really happening to her? It was the culmination of every dream she had ever had, yet none of it felt real. A niggle of doubt crept into her mind, but she pushed it firmly away. The end of her spinsterhood was in sight. "Yes," she squeaked, unable to say anything more.

He kissed her again, then pulled back with a fond smile. "Let us return to the drawing room and share the good news with your brother."

It was with little surprise that Ambrose received the news of his sister's engagement. He congratulated Philip and Sarah, though perhaps not effusively so. Luncheon was a pleasant affair, as possible dates for the nuptials were discussed. Sarah favoured a spring wedding, when the blossoms would be in full bloom. Philip had no objection to the idea, and Ambrose very little to say on the matter.

Later that evening, as Sarah lay in bed in search of slumber, her hand strayed down to her mound as it usually did at night. Her mind began to conjure a favourite of her imaginings—that of Benjamin coming up to find her naked on a bed and then diving between her legs to feast on her cunt. But she paused. It was not right that she think of Benjamin this way anymore, not now that she was engaged to Philip Templeton. Her core throbbed and was needy for attention, but she resisted, turning to her side instead and resolutely trying to get to sleep. It was a very long time before her scattered thoughts settled down enough to finally let her slumber.

CHAPTER 18

BENJAMIN

"Let me rage before I die."
— Virgil

EVERY DAY OF his long journey to England, Benjamin chafed at the delay in reaching Sarah while at the same time fretting about what would happen upon his arrival there. Would she welcome his return? What would he say to her? How quickly would they overcome the awkwardness of seeing each other in person after all the intimacies they had shared in writing? How would he go about changing their relationship from friends to something more?

All these questions ran through his mind with increasing frequency the closer he got to his destination. Late on a Saturday afternoon, his ship docked in Liverpool and he disembarked, walking on English soil for the first time in nearly five years. He caught the last train to London, but he was too late on arrival there to get a connection to Oxford, so he reluctantly retired to the Stanton townhouse for the night.

He woke the following morning, having barely slept, intent on reaching his destination at the soonest opportunity that day. Some instinct told him that there was no time to be lost in reaching Sarah. Finally, at ten o'clock, his train entered Oxford Station. From there, he procured a carriage to take him the remaining distance to Stanton Hall. There had been no time to send word beforehand that he was arriving, so it was with some surprise that he was greeted by Siddons, the family butler.

"Mr Stanton," he said. "We had not been expecting your arrival. If I had known, I would have sent the carriage to await you at the station."

"That is quite alright, Siddons. I am here now."

"And may I say, sir," continued the butler, "how good it is to see you safely returned from the war."

"Thank you. I need to wash straight away. Can you send up some hot water?"

"Of course, sir." Siddons continued uncertainly, "Had we known of your arrival, sir, cook would have made luncheon, but I am sure she can prepare something suitable."

"No need, Siddons. Just have some bread and slices of cold meat with a pot of tea, and that will be more than sufficient for my needs."

"But sir—" protested the butler.

"No, I insist. Now let me wash off all this grime from my travels." Benjamin bounded up the grand staircase and headed towards the room he had occupied all those years ago. It wasn't long before he had washed and dressed in a fresh set of clothes. As he stood before the mirror, combing his hair and tidying his beard, he wondered despairingly for the hundred's time whether he was enough to win the heart of Sarah Cranshaw. He ran his finger along the jagged scar on his cheek. It had healed to a pale pink but was still prominent. His palm slipped down to his hard chest. He had grown thin during his time at war, but three weeks of eating well had begun to put flesh back on his bones. The mirror showed, at least, that he was tall, and he had certainly grown strong over the years—that was something in his favour, was it not? He hoped he would be enough.

He went down to the dining room where the light repast he had requested had been laid out for him. He ate quickly, not wanting to waste any more time. He had to get to Sarah. He was not sure what he would say upon seeing her, but see her he must. The meal over, he stood and went to fetch his coat, speaking to the butler as he shrugged it on. "I am going out for a walk, Siddons, and do not know when I shall return."

"Yes, sir."

Next moment, he was out the door, descending the front steps of Stanton Hall, then walking quickly in the direction of Ivy Cottage. His heart swelled; his chest tightened. He had to get to Sarah before it was too late. Too late for what, he did not exactly know. He simply felt it.

He unlatched the gate to Ivy Cottage and walked up to the door, pounding on it nearly as fast as his heart pounded in his chest. He waited. There was no answer. He pounded again, and again there was no response. No one was inside the cottage. He stepped back in intense frustration. It was Sunday. Sarah would have gone to church with her brother. Perhaps they were lingering, talking to acquaintances and would soon be on their way back. He took out his pocket watch. It was just after twelve o'clock. He would go for a walk and return in an hour. That was what he would do.

He set off, walking a circuitous route around the Stanton Hall grounds, a route he had once taken with Sarah on one of their walks. At one o'clock precisely, he knocked again on the door of Ivy Cottage. Again, his knock went unanswered. Where was she? He tried to think rationally. It was one o'clock, a time to eat luncheon. She must be out for luncheon, perhaps with those young ladies that she tutored at Gorston Manor. Yes, that must be it. Unless…

What if she were somewhere else? By now, the pain in his chest was transforming into frustration and the beginnings of that familiar rage. He had come all the way from America, damn it to hell and back! Could she not have the decency to be there when he needed her so desperately? Where had she gone? *Not there. Please God not there.*

Unable to bear the suspense, he set off once again, this time in the direction of Graveley. Mr Templeton's stately home had been pointed out to him during his last visit to England. He knew precisely where to go. He walked quickly, anxiety and anger in every step he took. When he neared the house, he darted furtively behind a set of trees and brought his gaze towards it. There, just beyond the front steps, stood a carriage. And if he was not much mistaken, it was the Stanton carriage.

He needed to be sure that what he was seeing was not what he suspected. Using all the skills he had honed as a scout during the war, he circled round to the back of the house and edged closer. There, before him, was a circular shaped room with floor to ceiling windows, one of which was ajar. He would take a look through there, then work his way around the house. He dashed quickly towards it, keeping down and his body flat to the wall, the way he had learned to do during his many scouting missions.

Once he reached the edge of the window, he leaned forward slowly to peer inside. He saw a large space that looked to being used as an art room. Some canvases were stacked against the far wall. In the middle of the room was a table covered with an artist's materials—paint pots and brushes—and beyond that table stood an easel with a panoramic painting which he could not see clearly from where he stood. Other than that, the room was empty.

He was about to circle back towards the front of the house when he spied some movement at the door. Two persons had entered the room. His heart nearly stopped, then began to hammer in his chest. It was Sarah. And with her was Mr Templeton. She came forward to inspect the painting on the easel, a look of wonder on her face. Then she turned to Mr Templeton, and straining his ears, Benjamin heard her say, "It's perfect!" Then he made out the words, "Thank you." The next moment, that rogue had taken her into his arms and captured her lips.

No! Please God no! Helplessly, Benjamin watched Sarah experience her first kiss. He knew it was her first time from the clumsy way in which she attempted to return Mr Templeton's embrace. He recalled how he had once described to her in detail the art of kissing. It was as if she were remembering his words too, for after bumping lips several times with the man, he saw her hesitantly open her mouth to accept the invasion of his tongue. *No! No! No!* A piercing pain stabbed his chest. It should have been him, not Templeton, to give Sarah her first kiss.

He watched, his body and mind screaming in agony, as Templeton broke the kiss and spoke soft words to her. Benjamin did not catch all he said, except for the last sentence: "Will you marry me?" Then in despair he heard Sarah's brief response, "Yes." Engulfed in pain, he turned away then, unable to watch anymore.

He ran back to the cover of the trees then continued running, wanting to put as much distance as possible between himself and that agonising scene. He had known he was going to be too late. He had felt it all yesterday and this morning. *Too damnably late!* He had come all this way on a fool's errand. He was a damned, pathetic fool. On and on he ran, each pounding step sounding the words fool, fool, fool in his fevered brain. The roads were empty on this Sunday afternoon. He passed no one, save for a bemused-looking farmer walking through his fields.

He did not stop running until he reached the parkland of Stanton Hall, slowing to a walk as he caught his breath. All the while, he berated himself. Why on earth would Sarah wait for him? He had never given her any reason to. He should have told her what she meant to him rather than hide behind the word "friend". Or maybe he had been a fool to think the intimacy of their correspondence had meant something more to her. She was not his girl and never had been—just a mirage, a figment of his imagination, a sap to his fractured soul, helping him endure the madness of war. None of it was real except in his diseased mind.

In a fit of self-loathing, he punched his hand to the trunk of a wide oak tree, welcoming the pain. He punched again and again, until both his hands were a bleeding mess. Then, falling to his knees, he collapsed in a huddle on the muddy ground, his body shaking with uncontrollable sobs. He was nothing. Always second best. He should have been the one to die at Gettysburg, not Jimmy. What worth his miserable life? He did not even have the courage to end it right here and save everyone the trouble of pretending to want to be around his pathetic, shameful self.

He did not know how long he stayed like this. The cold seeping into his bones eventually brought him back to an awareness of his surroundings. He sat up and took out a handkerchief to staunch the blood still trickling from his hands. It was an ineffective bandage, but it would have to do until he got home and dressed the wounds properly. Then, slowly, he rose to his feet and resumed the walk back to Stanton Hall. He glanced down at his best suit, which he had put on earlier today, full of hope. It was splattered with mud and blood now, a fitting reflection of his bruised and battered spirit.

Siddons exclaimed in dismay upon catching sight of him at the door, but Benjamin waved him away and continued his journey up the stairs to his room. There, he discarded the ruined suit jacket and washed his bloodied hands. He withdrew bandages from his trunk and dressed his wounds with the efficiency of long practice. His wartime wounds were nothing though to the wounds of the heart he had just now received. Finally, he changed into a clean set of clothes and made his way down to find Siddons again.

"Sir, are you quite alright?" asked the distressed butler.

Benjamin waved a hand. "Do not fuss, Siddons, but bring me a bottle of the viscount's finest whisky to the library. I shall spend the evening there."

Siddons looked doubtful as to the sagacity of such a move, but he was too well-trained a servant to voice his disapproval. Instead, he bid a footman go light the fire in the library and went to fetch a bottle of whisky, as had been requested.

Benjamin retraced his steps up the stairs, this time heading to the library. He entered the room where he had first encountered Sarah. She had been sitting in that chair over there, shoulders shaking with sobs. How fitting that today, it would be him sitting on that chair and drowning his sorrows.

Siddons came in a few minutes later and laid before him a tray with a whisky bottle and a glass. "Is there anything else I can get you, sir? Something to eat perhaps?" he asked worriedly.

"Nothing," Benjamin replied. "This is all I need, thank you, Siddons."

The butler withdrew, casting one last concerned glance at him. Alone, Benjamin poured a first shot of the amber drink into the glass and knocked it back in one swallow. He welcomed the burn at the back of his throat. Yes, that was all he needed tonight. Solitude and whisky to lick his wounds. He poured another measure in the cup and drank it down.

Slowly, each sip of the alcohol began to numb his pain. He set to thinking about what he would do next. Go back to America? No, he could not endure the looks of pity he would get from his family. So, here he would stay and play lord of the manor in Daniel's stead. Perhaps in the days and weeks ahead, he would find some path forward, some way out of the mire he was in. He poured some more whisky into the glass, his hand not quite steady. In the meantime, he would get wonderfully, gloriously drunk.

CHAPTER 19

◄ — ♥ — ►

SARAH

"And yet, no joy is ever unalloyed,
and worry worms its way into delight."
— Ovid

SARAH AWOKE EARLY on her first day as a betrothed lady. She stretched luxuriantly and smiled to herself remembering Philip's proposal. He wanted to marry her, Sarah Cranshaw, a thirty-year old spinster—not some pretty young debutante. She hugged that happy thought to herself.

But an instant later, a shadow flitted over her. She could not say why she felt a moment of unease. Something felt not quite right. It was silly really. She shook the feeling away and got out of bed determinedly. It was early enough that she might just catch Ambrose before he left for the day. She dressed quickly and hurried down the stairs to the dining room.

She found Ambrose at the table, finishing off his morning cup of coffee. In a rush of affection, she went to him and kissed his cheek. "Good morning, Ambrose," she said gaily.

He had been staring absently at his cup when she came in, a sombre look on his face. At her show of affection, he glanced up, his expression clearing. "Good morning, love," he replied. "You are up early. Exhilaration got your sleep?"

She laughed. "Something like that. You must own that it is a most unusual and unlikely state of affairs for me, being engaged. It is taking time to become accustomed to it."

He smiled humorously. "Well, my dear, you have several months to become used to it, after which you will require several months more to accustom yourself to being a married lady."

She put an elbow on the table inelegantly and cradled her cheek with the palm of her hand. "Such big changes to my life," she mused. "I shall be living in that grand house with a butler and a host of servants at my disposal. How strange that will be."

"And the most important change of all, is that you shall have a husband to share your life with for better or worse. Are you sure, Sarah, that it is Mr Templeton you wish to spend the rest of your days with?"

She was about to assure him that this was so, then remembered the shadow that had passed over her spirit a few moments ago. "I think so," she said uncertainly. "For so many years, he has been the person I yearned for, thinking it was hopeless. To have him propose feels like a dream."

"Sometimes, dreams are better left in the realm of imagination."

"You do not sound as if you approve of the match," she parried with a frown.

"It is not for me to approve or disapprove," he stated equably. "I have nothing against the man."

"Yet still you have doubts," she remarked.

"It is just that I find his sudden courtship of you after so many years' acquaintance a trifle strange. Why now?"

"It could be that after so many years of determined bachelorhood, he now feels an urge for more stability and companionship," Sarah suggested, her brow furrowed. "He implied as much to me in one of our conversations."

"And is that enough for you?" Ambrose asked with a frown.

"It is a sound base upon which we can build something more in time," replied Sarah, sounding more confident than she was. She smiled at her brother reassuringly. "I do not expect, at this stage in my life, to experience the mad throes of romantic love.

That is the stuff of young dreams. I will take his admiration and regard, and all the privileges that will come to me as his wife, and embrace all these gifts with gratitude." It was almost as if she were trying to convince herself, as well as her brother. She reached a hand to his. "I think I will be very happy with Philip."

"Your happiness is all I have ever wanted."

"I know," smiled Sarah. "You dear, excellent man."

He rose to his feet and kissed her cheek. "And now, I must be away."

"Do you go to Stanton Hall?" she enquired.

"Not at first. I have business at the home farm, after which I shall stop by at the main house. Why do you ask?"

"Oh, nothing much," replied Sarah. "I meant to go to the library there for some books and thought I would walk with you."

"We can walk part of the way there together. Hurry though."

Quickly, Sarah wolfed down a slice of buttered bread and drank her coffee. Then she went to fetch her coat and bonnet, going to meet her brother at the door not two minutes later. Together, they set off for Stanton Hall in positive spirits, Ambrose turning right towards the home farm while she continued straight on to the main house. She went to the servants' entrance, not wanting to bother Siddons, whose rheumatism had flared up lately. On nimble feet, she headed up the stairs and along the galleried corridor towards the library.

As she stepped over the threshold, she knew at once that something was amiss. A strong aroma of liquor wafted towards her. She closed the library door behind her and carefully walked a few steps more into the room. There, across from her on the armchair on which she had once sat crying many years ago, rested a man, fast asleep.

She tiptoed forward, her pulse suddenly racing. Who was he? She examined him from the soles of his feet to the greying beard on his face, the skin of which was tanned a deep brown. A long, pink scar slashed across the top of his left cheek. Even in sleep, he exuded a sense of danger, as if he could rise in an instant, place his large, rough hands around her neck and squeeze the life out of her. She shivered and stopped a few feet from him, the skin on her arms prickling. She did not recognise this man, though there was the hint of something familiar about his form. He could not be an intruder, for surely his presence would have been known by the servants. Who was he and why was he here?

She was about to tiptoe back out of the library when, as if sensing her presence, his eyelids lifted. Brilliant dark eyes stared at her. She knew those eyes. Could it be? No! But yes. It was him! A rush of elation swept through her.

"Benjamin," she whispered.

In an instant, he was on his feet and striding towards her. The reek of alcohol, as well as the fierce look on his face, had her stepping away in fear. Her back hit the door, and her hands scrambled frantically for the handle.

"Don't go," he cried, his voice gravelly and deep. "I will not harm you, Sarah."

He stopped two feet from her and raised his arms in surrender. She paused too and stared, bewildered.

"I am sorry to scare you so," he continued in that raspy voice. "My appearance is much changed, I know, but it is me, Benjamin, and I would never harm you."

There was nothing to fear. It was Benjamin, her dear friend. Though why he was here and stinking of alcohol, she did not know. Of course he would be changed. It had been five years, during which time he had been at war. When last she had seen him, he had been a young man of twenty-two, a mere boy. Standing before her was a grown man who had seen and done things no man ever should.

She expelled a breath. "Benjamin, I did not expect to see you here. Pardon my poor manners. This has come as a shock."

He ran a bandaged hand through his dishevelled hair, looking shamefaced. "Again, I apologise. If I had known that you would be coming here this morning, I would not have exposed you to any of this… unpleasantness." His eyes pierced through her then shifted to the floor. He said in a softer voice, "I shall go presently to my room and make myself presentable. Perhaps then, you will agree to meet me in the parlour, if you have not grown a disgust of me."

She nodded vigorously. "Yes, yes, that is a good idea." She needed time away from him to regain her composure. She had never expected to see him again, and yet here he was, looking so changed. Her heart tripped over in her chest. With a bright smile that did not quite reach her eyes, she stepped aside to let him pass.

"If you will excuse me," he said gruffly, and hurried out of the room.

As soon as she was alone, she sighed in relief. She closed her eyes and rested her head against the door, willing her heartbeats to slow. Benjamin was here. How could it be? And what was the matter with him? What had happened? She snorted derisively. Of course, she knew. That dreadful, miserable war was what had happened. But still, she had questions aplenty. Why was he here now? What had happened to his hand and why had he apparently drunk a bottle of whiskey and fallen asleep in the library? In the midst of her joy at seeing him was the conviction that something was very wrong.

She opened her eyes and straightened her posture, wrinkling her nose delicately at the strong aroma of whisky that emanated from the discarded bottle on the tray. With a shake of her head, she hurried out of the room and went to search for Siddons. She found him polishing silver in the dining room.

"Good morning, Siddons," she said, putting some cheer into her voice. "I see we have a visitor."

He turned to her in alarm. "Miss Cranshaw, do not tell me you went up to the library!"

"I did, and I saw," she said grimly. "He is gone now to his room to fix his appearance and shall come down shortly. I suggest we have a pot of ginger tea at the ready for him, to help with the after-effects of intoxication. A generous breakfast too."

"Yes, miss."

"And Siddons, do tell me why it is I find Benjamin with bandaged hands and reeking of liquor in the library."

The old butler grew agitated. "Miss Cranshaw, I do not know. Mr Stanton arrived unannounced yesterday morning in a rented carriage and seemed in good spirits, if preoccupied. He went to wash and change, then told me he was going out for a walk. Several hours later, he returned with mud spatters on his clothes and blood on his hands. He refused any offer of help and gave no explanation as to what had occurred. Once he had changed and dressed his wounds, he asked for a bottle of whisky to be brought to him in the library, and there he has remained ever since."

Sarah frowned in consternation. "Do you have any idea where he went?"

"None, miss."

"I see. Well, let us get some food and tea into him, and perhaps then he will give *me* an explanation."

She turned and headed to the parlour where she sat impatiently, waiting for Benjamin's reappearance. It took him a quarter of an hour before he walked into the room. He came straight towards her and bowed, saying, "Sarah, I must apologise again. I never envisaged our reunion would turn out like it did. Let me start over, please. It is good to see you again."

She curtsied. "It is good to see you too, Benjamin," she said, sounding formal even to her own ears. "It troubles me though that you have injured your hands and seemingly spent the night in the library inebriated."

He hung his head and sighed, but before he could respond, she spoke again, "No, do not attempt an explanation until you have had something to eat and drink. Come along, breakfast has been laid for you in the dining room." She turned to go, and he followed her obediently, taking a seat across from her at the dining table. She poured a hot infusion of ginger tea into a cup and passed it to him, so saying, "This will help with your woolly head."

He sniffed it and scowled but drank uncomplainingly. When he had emptied his cup, she poured him another, then busied herself loading a plate of eggs and sausages. This too she passed to him. As she went to butter some slices of bread, he demurred. "I am not an invalid, Sarah. I am well capable of buttering my own bread."

She ignored him and continued buttering the bread without a word. She placed the plate beside him and nodded towards the food, making it clear she expected him to eat. With a resigned sigh, he did as he was bid. She watched him, her eyes missing nothing as he ate every morsel. When he was done, she handed him a cup of coffee, which he accepted with a muttered, "Thank you." He sipped from it, not looking at her.

She waited a moment longer, then spoke, "Now, will you explain, Benjamin. What happened to your hands? Did you get into a fight?" She wondered who on earth he could have fought with. Nothing made sense.

He stared at the bandages on both hands. "Of a sort," he muttered, then was silent.

Sarah's impatience grew. She huffed in annoyance, "What sort of answer is that? Tell me what happened."

The eyes he raised to hers were bleak. "I got into a fight with a tree," he said gruffly. "It is what I do sometimes when I get into a rage. These days, I am quick to anger. Better I punch a tree than another human being."

"And even better if you punched nothing," she replied tartly. "Why were you angry? Tell me." What was he keeping from her? What could send him into such a rage that he would hurt himself so? Her heart bled in pain for him, but she felt frustration too at her inability to understand what was happening.

He looked away in irritation. "Never you mind. Let us change the subject matter for it begins to fatigue me. Tell me of your news."

"You still have not told me why you are here," she continued, as if he had not spoken.

"Am I under obligation then to explain my every move?" he drawled derisively.

"No, of course not," she replied, stung, "though as your friend, I would think it within my rights to ask why you have made the journey to England all alone when you have only recently reunited with your family."

He sighed dramatically. "This interrogation is getting to be tedious. Why should I not come here? This is my home too, in case you had forgotten."

"I–I did not mean it that way," she stammered. "Only that it is an odd thing to do."

"Well, I am an odd person, so perhaps not such an odd thing to do."

She saw he was not going to give her any more of an answer, so she changed course. "How long do you propose to stay?"

He shrugged, looking unconcerned. "A few months, maybe more. It depends on Daniel and when he decides to return. He does not seem to be in any hurry to do so."

"Are you here to fill his shoes while he is away?" she asked, perplexed.

He inclined his head mockingly. "I am to take over the reins here during his absence. So you see, I get to play lord of the manor. Quite an improvement, don't you think, for someone who only a few weeks ago was hunkering down in a tent at night. I think so, at any rate, and I intend to make the best of it. What better way to start than with a bottle of Daniel's finest whisky?"

Sarah stared at Benjamin in consternation. This was not the friend who had written her all those heartfelt letters. This Benjamin was a stranger to her. "Indeed," she said dryly. "Well, I wish you joy as lord of the manor."

He began to tap his fingers impatiently on the table, as if he wanted to end the conversation. She too was not in any mood for further discourse. She stood, readying to leave. "It was good to see you again, Benjamin. No doubt we will see more of you in the days to come." She walked to the door, and he stood too. She put up a hand to stay him, "No, there is no need to see me out." She opened the dining room door, then paused and looked over her shoulder. "Oh, I nearly forgot. You asked me for my news. Well, I am happy to say that as of yesterday, I am engaged to be married to Mr Templeton." She threw him one final cross look and left the room, making her way quickly out of the house.

CHAPTER 20

BENJAMIN

"Be patient and tough; one day this pain will be useful to you."
— Ovid

BENJAMIN FOLLOWED SARAH with his eyes as she left the dining room. He was a fool! A damned stupid fool. He would be well served if she never spoke to him again. He got to his feet in disgust at himself. Why could he not have been warm and charming like he used to be, and tried to put her at ease? Was it not enough that the sight of him had instilled fear in her? He would not quickly forget that look she gave, like a frightened deer, as she tried to unlatch the library door to escape from him. Dear God, was he that much of a monster?

His head still hurt, feeling the effects of last night's overindulgence in whisky. He ran an agitated hand through his hair. What he needed was some fresh air. On impulse, he strode out of the dining room, past a flustered Siddons and up the stairs, walking along the corridor that led to the library. At the end of it was a large sash window which he opened with one, strong push upwards. Without hesitation, he climbed over the sill and dropped his feet on the ledge below. Walking sideways on the ledge, he reached the flat part of the roof and went to sit on his old, familiar perch.

He sat and breathed the fresh winter air, looking out towards the vast expanse of green fields dotted with trees. For a long time, he stared blankly ahead, breathing in and out deeply, and willing himself to return to some semblance of calm. What was he to do now? He could not return to America just yet, but the purpose of his journey was ruined. He had come for Sarah, and now she was lost to him.

She had looked so fine just now at the breakfast table. The years had been kind to her, unlike how they had ravaged him. Keen intelligence shone from the grey eyes he had never forgotten. And the way she had chivvied him into eating his meal? He smiled in recollection. That was so very like her—persistent in her kindly concern. Seeing her again had put him in no doubt that he wanted her very much. He had always wanted her, even that first time in the library when he had found her crying over another man.

Of course, he had pretended to himself and to her that he was merely a friend. What else could he have done when she was so enamoured of a man who seemed to possess so many qualities he himself did not have? So, he had returned to America and proceeded to chase other women, intent on proving that indeed, he did not want Sarah. He had been young and foolish. At his very core though, he had always known it was more than friendship, at least on his part. He had thought, from the tenor of her letters, that it was something more for her too, but he had been wrong.

She was engaged now to Philip Templeton. Benjamin could not have her, at least not in the way he wanted. Pain gripped his chest again, and it took him several moments more to tamp down his agitation. Over and over in his head, he asked himself the same question. What was he to do? That question had plagued him ever since Sergeant Stevens had informed him he would be mustered out of the army.

He thought of home and of Daniel, toiling to build a house for him. What an extraordinary act of kindness. He did not deserve such a brother. It had been wrong of him to put up a wall between them all these years, all because of his feelings of inadequacy—more proof, if ever it was needed, that he, Benjamin, was the lesser man. For reasons of his own, Daniel needed to be away from England, and he had asked Benjamin to take over the reins here on his behalf. That was what he would do. Not so that he could play lord of the manor, as he had mocked earlier, but to discharge his debt and duty to his brother. As for Sarah… it seemed as if all hope was lost, but he would see her again in due course. Maybe then, he would find an opportunity to apologise for the way he had acted just now. And after that, he would have to take it day by day.

He took a steadying breath and stood, then negotiated his way to the window, climbing back inside to the shocked stare of a passing house servant. "There is nothing here to see," he said curtly. "Keep on with your duties." With that, he strode along the corridor to the library. Daniel had told him that Ambrose kept a ledger there of all the rents collected and expenses paid on the Stanton estate. He would start by studying it and getting acquainted with estate business.

He walked into the library to find seated at the desk none other than Ambrose Cranshaw. The latter came to his feet instantly. "Mr Stanton," he said with a smile. "I was told you had arrived yesterday from America. May I say how pleased I am to see you." He strode towards Benjamin and held out his hand.

Benjamin took it, replying brusquely, "Ambrose, good to see you. For the love of all that's holy, let us dispense with any formality. I abhor it. Call me Benjamin from here on, not Mr Stanton."

Ambrose's smile widened. "Of course, my mistake. I see you are cut from the same cloth as Daniel."

Benjamin raised a brow. "He is my brother," he pointed out.

"And what news of Daniel. Is all well?" Ambrose asked, his eyes scrutinising Benjamin.

"All is quite well. For reasons I am sure you will understand, Daniel wishes to prolong his stay in Ohio."

At this, Ambrose's face paled. If Benjamin had been in the mood to examine this response, he might have done so with more curiosity, but his head was still full of Sarah. "So," he continued, "I have volunteered to come and keep an eye on things here in his absence."

"I see," murmured Ambrose.

"I have a letter for you with his instructions." Benjamin pulled Daniel's letter out of his pocket and handed it to Ambrose.

"Do you mind if I read it now?"

"Not at all," replied Benjamin.

He watched, his mind still in turmoil, as Ambrose cut the seal on the envelope and unfolded the single sheet it contained. The estate manager read the contents and re-read them before looking up. "It is as you say, Benjamin," he said. "Daniel wishes me to report to you as I did to him on all matters relating to the Stanton estate. We were in the habit of meeting here in the library every Monday morning, at which time I kept him apprised of the latest developments on the estate and we went through the ledger together. Would you be happy to continue with such an arrangement?"

"I have no objection to that," said Benjamin. "In which case, perhaps we could start now. I had come here meaning to peruse the ledger, but it will be much more sensible to do so with your guidance."

"Of course," concurred Ambrose. "Then might I suggest we seat ourselves over here."

The two men settled themselves either side of the ledger on the desk, and Ambrose began to go through the figures in each column with Benjamin, who was relieved to find that the months he had spent working for his father prior to the war had not been in vain, for he was able to quickly understand the workings of the accounts. He found the work, prosaic as it was, stopped him from thinking of the woman he had lost through accident and his own foolishness.

The two men occupied themselves with this task for the next half-hour, after which Ambrose gave Benjamin a summary of the latest happenings on the estate. "We are having issues with one of the two steam ploughs we bought recently at great expense," he said. "It was against my advice, but Daniel was most insistent on it, cheered on by my sister, I might add. And now, less than two weeks after delivery, the accursed machine has broken down. I went to the home farm this morning to see it for myself. It is something to do with the boiler, but beyond that, I am not knowledgeable enough to say. I shall write today to the manufacturer and request they send an engineer to repair it."

Benjamin, who had been staring morosely into space as Ambrose spoke, now became more alert at the mention of a steam plough. "Before you do that," he suggested, "let me go take a look at it."

Ambrose regarded him doubtfully. "I have heard from Daniel that you have an interest in machinery, but I am not sure that is sufficient expertise for such an undertaking."

"Do you have the schematics for the machine?" asked Benjamin, ignoring this last remark.

"Yes, let me get them out." Ambrose retrieved a document box from one of the shelves and set it on the desk. After a minute or two of rummaging through the papers, he took out a set of documents and handed them to Benjamin. They contained detailed drawings of the steam plough as well as documentation regarding its maintenance.

Benjamin examined this for some time then addressed Ambrose with a confident expression. "I think I can work with this. Do let me have a try." Perhaps this would help take his mind off his present distress.

"Very well," said Ambrose resignedly. "But if the plough is still not up and running by the end of the week, I shall send for the engineer."

"That seems fair," responded Benjamin, a sense of purpose awakening in his breast. A short time later, the meeting concluded and Benjamin sat down to compose a letter to his brother.

November 14th, 1865

Dear Daniel,

I have arrived safely in England, the sea crossing uneventful except for one very stormy night that had me confined to my quarters. The ship docked at Liverpool harbour mid-afternoon on Saturday, and I was able to catch a train to London that very same day. However, I was too late for the connection to Oxford and had to bed down for the night at the town house. Perhaps had I been a little earlier, events might have taken a different turn, or maybe not. For on Sunday after church service, Sarah and Ambrose took themselves to luncheon with Mr Templeton, and it was then that this gentleman proposed marriage to Sarah, a proposal that she accepted. So you see, my journey here has been in vain.

There is little need to describe the depth of my disappointment though I will confess to imbibing a great deal of your best whiskey, dear brother, as a salve for my sorrows. I have spent much of this morning nursing my aching head and contemplating what I should do next. I do not feel quite ready to return home, and I know you wish for more time with the family. For now, I shall remain here, at least until the new year, and keep an eye on things for you. I may be of more use than you think, for I hear your new steam plough has broken down, and I have volunteered my services to take a look at it. I make no guarantee of repairing the machine, but I shall give it my best try.

Dear brother, I wish I had been more honest with you all these years, rather than putting up this barrier between us. I would wish to remedy this now, and in that spirit of greater confidence, I will tell you this. On finding out about Sarah and Mr Templeton, my pain and rage were so great that I punched one of your oak trees repeatedly until both my hands were bleeding profusely. It is something I have learned to do when I am under one of my ungovernable rages, for it is best I hurt myself than someone else. I came back to the house in a fine state, and poor Siddons was quite in a tizzy about it. It was then, after I had dressed the wound, that I asked him to bring me a bottle of your best whiskey to the library and proceeded to get stupidly drunk.

Let me tell you also that I met with Sarah today–she it was that unfortunately discovered me in a drunken sleep in the library — and being the fool that I am, I frightened her with my fierce manner and grizzly appearance, then compounded the error by being quite rude. It was that rather than show my pain, for a man has his pride after all. Needless to say, I am drowning in regret. Daniel, how am I to bear seeing Sarah on the arm of another man? I wish you could be here to counsel me, for I have never felt more alone. What am I to do now?

Your loving brother,

Benjamin Stanton

CHAPTER 21

SARAH

"Friends show their love in times of trouble."
— Euripides

SARAH'S WRATH LASTED no longer than it took to walk back to Ivy Cottage. By the time she had reached her home, her ire had been tempered by worry for her friend. Why had he hurt himself? What could have happened yesterday to upset him so? It was quite clear to her that Benjamin was going through a difficult and painful time. The horrors he had seen in the war were unfathomable. A man as gentle and sensitive as Benjamin was never going to come back from four and a half years of such torment unchanged. It was bound to leave a mark on him, not just in the physical form of his scar.

As his friend, she would do everything in her power to help him. But how? What could she do to undo years of hurt and misery? She did not know for sure, but she would start by going to see him on the morrow and spending time in his company.

Her musings were interrupted by the arrival of Philip Templeton, bringing with him the scenic panel he had painted for her miniature railway. She stifled a sigh and went to greet him as Elsie opened the front door. "Philip, good morning."

He set his fond gaze on her. "Good morning, sweet Sarah," he called out cheerfully. "Look what I have brought for you."

She smiled, "I cannot wait to see it set in place. Let us do it now." She led him into the back parlour, where he proceeded to remove the paper wrapped around the panel for protection. Then, very carefully, he lowered it onto the table, slotting it into the grooves at each end to secure it in place. They both took a step back to admire the view. "It is just the thing," praised Sarah.

"I am glad you like it," he said, placing an arm around her waist and pulling her to his side.

She nestled into his body, subduing a feeling of unease, and inhaled his manly cologne—was the scent of it always this cloying? Aloud, she asked, "What next for you, now that you have completed this painting?"

He grinned with boyish excitement. "Thanks to you, Sarah, I have discovered a new muse, that of transportation. I have thoughts to complete a series of tableaus documenting the changes from old to modern, from horse-drawn coaches to steam-powered locomotives. I propose to entitle the series 'Locomotion through the Ages'. What think you?"

"I think it a splendid idea," she replied with a smile.

"In which case, my dear," he said, dropping a kiss to the top of her head, "I hope you will not mind if I absent myself for a few days to go to London and make some preliminary sketches. I am impatient to get started on this endeavour. It is this way with me when I am struck by inspiration."

"No, of course not," she said. A part of Sarah wondered if he was more enthusiastic about the project than spending time with his betrothed.

"That is one of the things I like about you, Sarah," he said, turning her body to face his. "You abound with good sense. I know you will not cling and beg for attention like a young, simpering miss."

"I would never do so," she replied hollowly.

"You, my dear, are a treasure," he murmured, swooping his lips down to hers. "Now, how about a kiss for your betrothed before he leaves?"

His lips brushed hers coaxingly, and knowing now what was expected, she parted her own to allow him in. She felt his tongue sweep into her mouth and caress hers. It still felt rather odd to her, but not unpleasant. Her hands slid up his broad chest as he drew her close and kissed her repeatedly, open mouth to open mouth. This business of kissing was slick and messy, she thought, as she let one hand travel higher to settle on his smooth jaw. She stroked it, absently wondering how it would feel if it were covered in a beard she could run her fingers through. A vivid image came to her mind of one such beard, brown hair laced with silver. She shivered and clenched deep in her core, releasing a flood of her arousal.

It was then that Philip broke the kiss, pulling back with a rueful expression. "If I am not careful, Sarah, I will get carried away and behave most improperly when I so very much want to do things the right way with you."

"It was quite delightful," she panted, trying to catch her breath.

Philip's eyes gleamed with satisfaction as he dropped his hands from around her. "But for now, it is best I take my leave," he said. "Goodbye, sweet Sarah. I shall send word when I return."

"Goodbye Philip, God be with you."

With one last smile, Philip bowed, picked up his hat and departed. Sarah stood listening to the closure of the door behind him as he left. A moment later, she was hurrying up the stairs to her room. Once there, she latched the door and began to unbutton her dress, removing it carelessly and throwing it over a chair. Next came off her shoes and damp drawers. Still in her shift, petticoat and corset, she threw herself on the bed and brought her fingers to her wet core. Oh the need she felt! She pressed her legs together, trying to sate the longing. When that was not enough, she took two folds of the blanket and pressed it to her aching core. Face down on the bed, she buried her face in the pillow, imagining someone kissing her madly, the scratch of his beard on her soft skin. All the while she pressed her core to the folded blanket between her legs, seeking that blessed release. With a muffled cry, she felt the contractions of a powerful orgasm pulse through her body, over and over until she lay spent.

Eventually, she turned to lie on her back and stared at the ceiling, a sense of guilt and dismay seeping into her chest. In the mad throes of her passion just now, it had not been her betrothed that she had imagined, but Benjamin Stanton.

CHAPTER 22

BENJAMIN

"Love is no assignment for cowards."
— Ovid

BENJAMIN SET OUT the following morning for the large shed which housed both sets of steam ploughs on the home farm. He had been there the previous afternoon and spent several hours inspecting the faulty machine, trying to ascertain the cause of the problem. He believed he had found the answer. There was a leakage from the boiler valve that controlled the flow of steam to the main cylinder.

Yesterday, he had spent the day draining the boiler and beginning to de-assemble the parts that needed repair. By that point, however, it had turned too dark—even with the lamps he had lit—to keep on with his work. Reluctantly, he had headed back to Stanton Hall, determined to return at first light the following morning and continue his task.

It was a relief to have something to do that required his full attention. It prevented him from dwelling too much on his heartbreak and from spiralling into despondency. Work was his salve, he realised. Was it not Horace that had once said, *'Life grants nothing to us mortals without hard work'*? That was what he would do, work hard and discharge his duty to his brother as best he could. Perhaps then, he would begin to feel a lessening of the burden in his mind and in his heart.

As soon as he arrived at the shed, he set to work, removing his outer coat and rolling up his sleeves. Time passed as he toiled, his mind concentrated on the challenge before him. It was not going to be an easy task to repair the valve with the limited tools at his disposal. He had to ensure that it fit perfectly on the boiler dome and stopped excess steam from escaping once the boiler was in operation. He worked away at the various metal parts before him, using his chisel and hammer to forge them into the right shape.

The noise from the hammer masked her approach, so it was with a start that he heard her voice speak from behind him, "Is it the boiler valve then that is at fault?"

He dropped the hammer with a loud clang and turned abruptly. Sarah stood a few feet from the shed door, observing his efforts with interest. He tried to speak, but no words came at first. "Ah, erm…"

She moved towards him, a hesitant smile on her face. "I suspected as much when Ambrose spoke of it to me last night at supper. He said you had volunteered to help repair the fault. Do you think you will manage?"

His voice finally returned, "I believe so, though it will take time. I am attempting to tighten the valve fitting through the primitive means at my disposal, then I shall have to put my repair to the test by filling the boiler and heating it to see if the steam still leaks out. If it does not work, and in all probability it will not on the first try, I shall have to empty it and remove the parts all over again."

She came to kneel at his side, looking closely at the boiler parts he was working on. "Is there anything I can do to help?"

His gaze flew to hers in surprise. "This is no work for a gentlewoman," he said tersely.

"Nor is it work for a gentleman, yet here we are," she pointed out.

His mouth curved in the beginnings of a smile. "I am not sure I could be called a gentleman. I have long worked with my hands and so has my father before me." He held up his hands, still bandaged, and showed her the tips of his calloused fingers which were slightly blackened from the work he had been doing.

In response, she stripped off her gloves and raised her hands for his inspection. The fingers were long and elegant, the nails neatly trimmed. Benjamin's gaze took in creamy skin that looked soft and inviting. For a brief instant, he entertained the idea of burying his face in those hands, but the thought was quickly replaced by bafflement. What was she trying to do, showing him her beautiful hands?

Then she turned her hands palm up and he noticed that the ball of her fingers bore thickened skin with a few faint scars from where she must have cut herself on more than one occasion in the past. She saw the question in his gaze and explained, "The same goes for me. These are not the hands of an idle gentlewoman. I have spent far too many hours making use of them on crafting the parts for my miniature railway."

He inclined his head in acknowledgement. "I take your point, Sarah, but this is messy work, even for you."

"That is why I came in my oldest gown today," she challenged. "Oh, do please let me help."

He was no match for her insistence. He wondered also about her motives. Was she here to reconcile with him after their sharp words yesterday, or did she simply want to get involved in this task because engineering was her passion? "Alright," he replied, "but you must keep away from the engine when I heat up the boiler."

She looked as if she were about to dispute this matter but changed her mind on seeing his uncompromising expression. "Very well," she muttered. She spied a wooden stool in one corner of the shed and went to fetch it, settling herself down beside him.

It occurred to him that now would be an opportune time to make amends for his behaviour the previous day. He cleared his throat. "Sarah," he said, "my manner with you yesterday was unforgivable. It is difficult for me to speak about the things that ail me, and so I tried to deflect your questions with unwarranted mockery. Please forgive me."

"Oh my dear friend, you have long been forgiven," she said softly.

"Is that what I am, your friend?"

"Of course," she responded indignantly. "How could there be any doubt?"

He looked away, unable to meet her eyes. "I have often wondered what it would be like between us when we met after the forthright nature of our correspondence."

She bent her head, studying the scuffed floor at her feet. In a low voice, she said, "When I wrote the things I did to you, it was never with the expectation that one day, we would meet face-to-face again. There are things you know about me, shameful things, that I would not have dreamed of revealing to anyone."

"There is nothing shameful about the things you did!" he rasped angrily. "Do not, I beg, feel shame for knowing your true sensual nature."

She laughed lightly even as a rosy flush came over her face. "That is what I admire about you, Benjamin," she said. "You are unapologetically honest about yourself. Would that I could be the same as you, but I am afraid I have had too many of our society's values instilled in me to be unashamed of such things. And besides this, you also know all the details of my foolish infatuation for Mr Templeton these many years."

"Not so foolish," he rumbled low in his throat, "given you are now betrothed to him. I have been remiss in not offering you my congratulations. I know this is what you have dreamed of all these years, and I… I am happy for you." That last statement was hard to say, but he forced it out nevertheless.

"Yes," she murmured, clasping her hands together in her lap. "It is still difficult to believe that this has come to pass. It is as if I am living in a dream."

"*And I in a nightmare,*" he thought. He expelled a breath. It was best to get back to work. He bent to pick up the metal part he had been working on, saying, "I have been trying to shear the edges over here in an attempt to seal the valve more securely."

She leaned closer to see, and as she did so, he was engulfed in her feminine, slightly floral scent. He breathed in deeply. "Yes, I see," she murmured, observing him at work as he continued stoically with his task.

Time passed. It was spent in companiable silence, interspersed with the occasional instruction or query as they worked together. Towards the middle of the afternoon, Benjamin deemed the parts ready for re-assembly. Once that was done, he and Sarah went back and forth with buckets to the nearby well, filling up the boiler with water. Then, adjuring Sarah to maintain a proper distance, he lit the coals in the firebox and waited for the water to heat in the boiler. It took several minutes as they waited on tenterhooks to see if the repair was successful.

The engine chugged and hissed, and a surge of steam flowed through to engage the cylinder. They both held their breath. The rotor, around which was attached the steel cable that pulled the plough, began slowly to turn. Then it stopped. They heard a loud hiss of steam as it escaped from the valve in the boiler dome. Benjamin sighed in disappointment. He had known it was too much to hope that the repair would be successful first time around, yet still he had hoped. There was nothing for it now but to wait for the boiler to cool and tomorrow, he would drain it and start over again. He banked the fire in the firebox then stepped back, wiping his hands on a rag.

He turned to face Sarah, lips downturned. "Well, that is that," he said.

"I shall come by again tomorrow," she responded calmly, "after I have finished my tutoring duties in the morning. Perhaps we shall have more luck then."

He smiled wryly. "Perhaps. And thank you, Sarah, you have been invaluable today."

She laughed, "Hardly that, but I hope to have helped a little." She pulled her coat on, which she had discarded earlier, together with her bonnet and gloves. He too donned his jacket and searched for his hat. Retrieving it from a dusty corner, he gave it a quick swipe with his hand before placing it on his head.

"Let me walk you back to Ivy Cottage," he said as they stepped out of the shed. He locked the door securely and pocketed the key.

"There is no need, but I shall accompany you part of the way towards Stanton Hall," she retorted.

He had no intention of parting company with her until she had been escorted back to her home, but he refrained from saying so. He was not quite ready yet for his time with her today to be over. Together, they began their walk. There was a light drizzle and a fresh breeze, but he did not mind. It helped cool his heated body, which had been supremely aware of Sarah's proximity all this time—and besides, he was well used to being out in the cold.

Sarah broke the silence between them with a question. "When you return to America, what do you propose to do? Work for your father again?"

Looking ahead of him, he replied softly, "Papa and I spoke of it when I first returned home. He saw how weary and wretched I was, for he told me there was no rush for me to do so. Perhaps that was what gave me the courage to tell him that I had no wish to be a gentleman farmer at all."

"But how marvellous!" Sarah clasped his arm in excitement. "Remember how you dithered about it before the war? And now it is all out in the open, as it should be."

"Yes," he said, taking the hand she had placed on his arm and slipping it through his.

She did not remark on this but kept smiling, then thought to ask, "So, if you are not to be a farmer, what is your plan for the future?"

"Must I have a plan?" he countered, only to be argumentative.

"Well of course you must. You cannot simply sit at home and do nothing. Idleness is not good for the soul, you know."

He grunted in amusement, "And now you sound like a puritan."

"This is a universal Christian value too," she huffed. "And not just Christian but also a precept from classical times. Was it not Horace that once said, *'Life grants nothing to us mortals without hard work'*?"

He smiled to himself but contented himself with saying, "You have been reading Horace now, have you?"

She spoke so quietly he had to strain to hear her words, "After you left that last time, I picked up a volume of Horace's odes and verses from the Stanton library, and Daniel generously let me keep it. It served as a reminder of you."

His grip on her arm tightened imperceptibly. They had come to the avenue which led to Stanton Hall on one side, and to Ivy Cottage on the other. Sarah slowed her steps, as if to bid him goodbye, but he turned left purposefully and continued towards her home. They walked on in charged silence, the air between them buzzing with the unspoken electricity of their emotions. Benjamin could feel it as if it were a tangible thing in the air. In this instant, he thought he could discern the sentiments beating in her heart. He could swear that this chemistry between them was not one-sided, and for the first time since his arrival in England, it gave him hope.

After a while, he decided to humour her and answer the question she had posed about his future. "Papa then wanted to know what I wished to do," he said in a voice that sounded hoarse to his own ears, "and I told him I was not fit anymore to work with others. I need to be alone, at least until I have figured out how to put a stop to the rages that overpower me."

He saw her gaze fall to his bandaged hand that held her arm, and he knew where her thoughts had flown. "You were quite right yesterday," he said. "Punching nothing would be infinitely better than punching a tree, if only for the health of my poor hands. I have yet to learn how to do it."

"And is that why you were sent here all alone? To enclose yourself in the protection of the fortress that is Stanton Hall?"

It could have salvaged his pride to respond affirmatively. This was a plausible reason for coming to England rather than the real purpose he was at first unable to enunciate. But he would not lie to Sarah. The truthfulness between them was a thing of rare beauty that he could not desecrate. "No, Papa had nothing to do with the decision to come here. I did want to be alone, but more than that, I wanted to be of use to Daniel. I think he wishes to assuage some guilt he may feel at living in the lap of luxury all these years while I fought in the war. It is his way of saying, 'Now it is your turn to enjoy the material pleasures I have so long been privileged to have'."

"I would have thought he would want to spend time with you rather than send you away," remarked Sarah, not quite convinced of this argument.

"We may not have spent a great deal of time together, but it was valuable nonetheless. Daniel and I… we have reached an understanding. If you like, we had a clearing of the air between us. It had been poisoning our relationship for far too long, much of it my own fault, I may add. But being with him again, and being faced with his unfailing kindness—added to which my time at war had built an understanding that life is too short to keep family at a distance—the walls I had built to shield him from my envy fell away, and I remembered just how much it is that I love my brother."

"Oh Benjamin," murmured Sarah, much moved. "I am so glad to hear it." They walked on, each lost in their own thoughts until she spoke again. "And then, having come here searching for solitude, you had to endure my badgering of you yesterday morning. I am so sorry."

"Do not be!" he ground out. In a gentler voice he went on, "I have spent one of the happiest days I can remember for a long time today, and much of it was due to you, so you have nothing to be sorry for."

"Being productively engaged more likely is the cause of your greater happiness," she said sagely, but he saw that she had blushed slightly at his words. "So you see how important good, honest work is to one's wellbeing."

"I do see it, but I also see how one's wellbeing is augmented by the company of a true friend," he responded, a trifle huskily.

She smiled. "On this then, we are agreed. And so, my good friend, I shall come to assist you again tomorrow after I have had my lunch."

They had come to a stop in front of Ivy Cottage, but Benjamin was loath to let her go. On an impulse, he said, "Speaking of lunch, I thought perhaps you and Ambrose would wish to join me for luncheon on Sunday after church, much as you have been in the habit of doing with Daniel and Bella." He paused. "Mr Templeton too, of course."

"We would be glad to," said Sarah warmly. "As for Philip, I cannot say for sure. He is away in London to do some sketches for his next painting, and I do not know when he shall return."

What kind of man proposes marriage and then leaves his betrothed not a day after, and for such a trifling reason? The thought was quickly followed by another. *If it were me betrothed to Sarah, I would keep her close. I would not let a day pass without my being by her side.* And then another thought came to sour his mood. *But it is not I who is betrothed to her. It is Philip Templeton who has that privilege—at least for now.* Brusquely, he bowed, "Good day,

Sarah," he said. A moment later, he had turned tail and walked briskly away.

CHAPTER 23

SARAH

*"There is only a finger's difference between a wise man and
a fool."*
— Diogenes

SARAH EASED HERSELF into the church pew with Ambrose at her side and Philip on the other. He had returned from London yesterday afternoon and paid her a call at Ivy Cottage. Her handsome betrothed had kissed her and declared himself over the moon at being reunited with his sweet Sarah. Such a charming turn of phrase he had used, though strangely, she had felt more vexed than flattered by the attention.

As Ambrose was present with them, there had been no repeat of the frolics that had occurred on their last meeting — nor of the shameful behaviour she had engaged in afterwards in the privacy of her room. Philip had merely contented himself with a light peck of her lips, then expounded on the success of his visit to the great metropolis and his eagerness to get started on his next painting. "I know how I am once the muse takes me," he had explained, "and thought it best to come see you before I get lost in my new painting. I would not want you to think I am neglecting you, my dear."

She had conveyed the proper disclaimers. Of course she thought no such thing and of course he must paint when the muse was upon him, at which he had once again expressed his great admiration of her good sense. Then she had proceeded to tell him of Benjamin's arrival and of the invitation to luncheon at Stanton Hall the following day.

"Well I never," had declared Philip. "One brother leaves for America only for the other to turn up unexpectedly. How peculiar! I must call on him straight after I leave here and pay my respects."

He had stayed a further half-hour, catching up on his dear Sarah's news but mostly talking animatedly about the sketches he had made and the wonderful subject matter to be had for his tableaus on transportation through the ages. Then he had excused himself, saying he really must be on his way. Another quick embrace and he had gone, leaving Sarah feeling curiously relieved. Philip's manner was very charming, but for some reason she was growing tired of it. Throughout the visit, Ambrose had said little, though he had observed them with a keen eye. Once Philip had gone, her brother had refrained from making any commentary, for which she had been thankful. He had simply given her shoulder a gentle squeeze and kissed her cheek, before retiring to his study.

Now here they were, side by side in church, and attracting no small degree of attention from the gathered congregation. Although there had yet to be an official announcement of their engagement in the paper, rumours of it had travelled like wildfire through the village. It was all everybody could talk about. Fancy Mr Templeton wanting to marry staid old Miss Cranshaw! What a turn up for the books! There had also been a few less kind words spoken, mostly from the disappointed young ladies who had set their caps at the handsome Mr Templeton.

Such had been the level of prurient curiosity that Sarah had been glad to avoid all visits to the village this past week. Once her tutoring duties were fulfilled, she had hastened to the shed where Benjamin had worked steadily on repairing the steam plough. They had refilled the boiler and heated it a further two times before they finally achieved success late on Friday afternoon. The steam had powered the cylinder without escaping from the valve. The leak had been repaired.

They had watched the engine with baited breath, bracing themselves for a sudden hiss of steam leaking from the boiler, but none had come. Finally, they had turned to each other with jubilant smiles. "You did it!" cried Sarah.

"We did it," he corrected her.

Then she had flown into his arms, and he had held her tight for an instant or two before abruptly letting her go. "Let me bank the fire," he'd said, "and we can go find Ambrose to share the good news with him." The embrace had been brief, but it had felt so right. Of course, she reasoned, there was nothing more natural than embracing a dear friend. It could not mean anything more. After all, she was engaged to Philip now.

Sarah was brought back to the present by the sounds of the organ heralding the beginning of the service. All the assembled people rose to their feet. As she did so, she cast a glance around the hall, wondering if Benjamin had elected to stay home today, knowing as she did about his need for solitude. The Stanton carriage had come to take them to church this morning, as was usual, but Benjamin had not been on board. She doubted therefore that she would see him in the congregation, but she had to make sure.

At first, she did not glimpse him. Then her eyes landed on a tall figure standing to the side, at the far end of the hall. It was Benjamin. Her heart thrilled at the sight of him. She was glad he felt able to join them, but this gladness was mixed with worry. She hoped this was not too much of an ordeal for him, being in the midst of a large group of people. Throughout the service, her eyes kept straying to him in concern, while she wondered to herself why his wellbeing occupied so much of her mind. It was what good friends did, she told herself firmly. They showed care and concern for each other.

Around halfway through the proceedings, he tilted his head and from across the great room, their eyes met. He smiled then in acknowledgment. It was a sweet, gentle smile, so in keeping with his sweet, gentle nature. No beard or scar or hard lines of suffering on his face could hide anymore what he truly was from her. It shone from his soulful brown eyes. As she bowed her head, she said a silent prayer for her friend. *Most gracious Lord, ease his pain and suffering. Bring light to his fractured soul.*

As she raised her head, this time it was Philip whose eyes met hers. He smiled warmly and placed his hand on hers. She knew that this simple gesture had been observed by those around them. And while she was not altogether comfortable with the attention, a small, very human part of her felt a degree of smug pride at being claimed so publicly by this most coveted of men.

When next her eyes sought Benjamin, it was to find him wearing a fierce scowl on his face. *"Oh dear Lord,"* she thought. It was as she had feared. Her friend was finding difficulty in being among a crowd of people. It could not be anything else causing his anger, or could it? Surely it could not be jealousy of Philip that had him scowling. Her heart skipped a beat at the errant thought. No, of course not, she reminded herself. That was absurd. Why on earth would Benjamin feel jealous? It was not as if he wanted her for himself. Why, all his philandering adventures with the ladies, so detailed in his letters, was proof of it.

No, her friend was here in England to find solitude and now, surrounded by a crush of people, he was struggling to contain his emotions. Was this the start of one of his rages? Would he storm out and find a tree to punch? Abruptly, he turned away from her and fixed his scowling gaze on the stained glass of the window to his right. She watched him in an agony of worry and had a sudden realisation. Could this be what had set him off last Sunday? Could it be he had gone to church and had been unable to stand being surrounded by so many people, and then stormed away in a rage at himself? *Oh, Benjamin.* Her heart constricted in pain for him.

The service came to an end, and she stood, intent on finding her friend. It was next to impossible to do, however, as she was swarmed by well-wishers congratulating her and Philip on their betrothal. She smiled woodenly while trying to catch a glimpse of Benjamin, without success. Eventually, it was her brother who, sensing her distress, extricated her from the crowd, stating firmly that they must be on their way. Ambrose led her to their carriage while Philip went to find his horse. They would all reconvene at Stanton Hall. But where was Benjamin?

Ambrose opened the carriage door and helped her inside. To her great surprise, the carriage was not empty, for there, sitting with his head between his hands, was none other than Benjamin. She went straight to his side and called his name. He looked up instantly, his voice composed as he spoke, "Sarah, Ambrose, good day."

"Good day, Benjamin," replied Ambrose in much the same tone.

But Sarah was in no mood for social niceties. "Benjamin!" she exclaimed. "Are you well?"

He raised a brow. "Perfectly."

"Oh," she said, feeling deflated. "You looked so angry just now, that I thought perhaps…" She could not go on.

"You thought I was getting into a rage?"

She nodded mutely, wondering at his calm manner.

"Well as you can see," he replied with a touch of ironic humour, "I am quite well and not about to engage in a fist fight with any of Daniel's trees."

"This is no laughing matter," she said crossly. "You had me sincerely troubled on your behalf."

"I can see that, and I appreciate your concern, Sarah, but it was unfounded," he responded smoothly.

"I thought that maybe you had found it intolerable to sit among a large crowd of people."

He sighed. "It was not the most pleasant of things, that is true. But it was not intolerable."

"I see. Then why did you look so angry?"

At this, Ambrose intervened, "Sarah, enough interrogation. Do leave the poor man alone."

"But I—" she spluttered, then stopped. One look from Ambrose was enough to convince her she should not go on. Here she was again, badgering her friend with questions. It was only because she wanted to know what it was that had caused him to look so furious just now, and what it was that had led to his drunken rage last week. If it was not because he had found it intolerable to be in church, surrounded by people when he craved solitude, then what was it? She wished he would tell her.

"Is Mr Templeton not joining us?" asked Benjamin blandly.

It was Ambrose who answered. "He is riding to Stanton Hall separately and will meet us there." Then he decided to change the subject matter. "So, Benjamin, now that the steam plough is back in operation, I had thoughts to put it to work tomorrow. I do hope you will come and see."

"You could not keep me away. Of course I shall be there," he responded warmly.

"And you, Sarah?" queried Ambrose.

"After the many hours I have spent on that machine, I hope you do not think I will ignore its first adventure," she retorted.

"I did not think you would," said her brother evenly. "Well then, that is settled. We shall go to the home farm after we conclude our morning meeting."

The carriage drew up at the front steps of Stanton Hall, and the two men descended first. It was Benjamin who then handed Sarah down from the carriage. A few moments later, Philip cantered towards them on his horse, his carriage and bearing impeccable, and came to a stop a few feet from them. With athletic grace, he dismounted and handed the reins to the groom that had hurried over from the stable.

Philip strode towards Benjamin with a smile, "Mr Stanton, how do you do?" he said.

Benjamin inclined his head regally, "I am well, thank you, Mr Templeton. Please do come in." He escorted his guests inside where coats, bonnets and hats were duly discarded, then invited them into the drawing room. His manner was everything that was proper for a host. Throughout the next few hours, as he plied his guests with refreshments then offered them an elaborate luncheon, Benjamin engaged them in polite conversation and proved himself to be the epitome of a polished gentleman, despite his earlier protestations that he was no such thing.

It was a novel aspect to Benjamin that Sarah had never seen before. He was gracious, punctilious in his manner, acting in every way the proud scion of a noble family, the son of an earl no less. And yet Sarah could not quite like this Benjamin. Although he was charming and displayed a great deal of wit, he spoke in generalities, never letting himself be drawn into any serious discourse. It was as though he were hiding his true self behind a mask of civility. She much preferred the Benjamin who toiled at her side while they tried to repair the steam plough or the Benjamin who wrote her forthright and heartfelt letters.

She ought to have enjoyed this lunch. Her betrothed was at her side, paying her the warmest of attention. They were served a fine meal of poached trout with a delicate sauce, followed by roast guinea fowl and some aromatically spiced mince pies. Benjamin, her friend, was a splendid host and looked as if he had not a care in the world, while Ambrose was his usual good-humoured self. Yes, she ought to have enjoyed this occasion, but she did not. She could not put her finger on why this was. Philip was as charming as ever, so what was wrong?

At last, it was over. On the front steps of Stanton Hall, Philip said a fond farewell to Sarah. Raising her hand to his lips, he smiled engagingly and drawled, "Until our next meeting, sweet Sarah. What a pleasure it has been to spend time in your delightful company. But now, let me hasten and begin work on my new creation. Goodbye, my dear." With another flourish, he kissed her hand once more — she wished he would not do so — bowed elegantly and took his leave.

She turned to Benjamin then and for a fleeting second, detected a look of fury on his face. It was quickly gone, so quickly in fact that she almost believed she had imagined it. The next instant, Benjamin walked down the steps to bid them goodbye, playing the gracious host to the end. "Good day, Sarah and Ambrose," he said. "I look forward to seeing you both on the morrow."

They said their goodbyes and began the walk back to Ivy Cottage, having elected to walk the short distance rather than take the carriage. With her hand neatly tucked in Ambrose's arm, she heard him sigh gently, "Well thank the Lord that is over and done with."

"You did not enjoy this lunch?"

"Did you?" countered her brother.

"The trout was beautifully done and most flavoursome," she said.

"Oh, I had no trouble with any of the fine repast on the table, but Sarah, you know full well that was not what I was talking about."

"Then what was it you did not like?" she asked, wanting to understand.

"Surely you must have noticed?" He looked at her with a trace of pity.

Sarah felt a rise in her discomfort again. No, she had not enjoyed that luncheon either, but why? A troubling thought was seeping in at the fringes of her mind, but she stubbornly pushed it away. "I am sure I do not know what you mean," she said crossly.

"Then it is not for me to say," he replied. "However, I will say one thing. If ever you have a change of heart about this marriage to Mr Templeton, you must tell me and I will extricate you from the engagement at once."

"Ambrose, why do you bring this up now?" asked Sarah, feeling more and more vexed.

He sighed in exasperation. "Sarah, you are a grown woman, and I pay you the respect to know your own mind and make your own decisions, but sometimes, I do wonder at you and your inability to see what is right beneath your nose. However, I will not involve myself any further in your affairs. What you do is up to you."

Sarah regarded her brother with annoyance. "I do despise that way you have of not telling me what I most particularly wish to know."

"And I am sorry for it, but there are some things, Sarah, that you shall have to work out for yourself, and that is all that I will say on the matter." He would not be drawn out any further, and so they completed their walk home in tense silence, neither of them feeling well disposed towards the other.

Alone in her room, Sarah paced the floor, wondering why it was that at this time when she should have been at her happiest, she felt so woefully dejected. The man she had worshipped for years from afar had finally come to appreciate her qualities and wanted to marry her. Why then was she so troubled? An image came to her mind of Benjamin, and the anger he had tried to mask. What was it that was right beneath her nose that she could not see?

It could not be, surely, that Benjamin was jealous! What signs had he given her that he wanted her? He had once said to her that if a man was interested in a lady, then it was usually evident in his marked attentions or warm looks. Well, such marked attentions and warm looks she had received in abundance from Philip, and lo and behold, he had proposed to her. She struggled to think of occasions when Benjamin had paid her similar attention. With a sharp stab to her heart, she realised it could only mean one thing. Benjamin was not interested in being anything more than a friend to her. And why should that hurt so? Could she not be satisfied with the great fortune she had in being betrothed to Philip? She set her lips in a firm line. She should and would make the best of what she had been given. With this last thought, she changed into an old gown and went down to lose herself in work on her miniature railway.

CHAPTER 24

BENJAMIN

"It is easy to go down into Hell, but to climb back again, to retrace one's steps to the upper air—there's the rub."
— Virgil

LUNCHEON HAD BEEN a torturous affair. Benjamin had been forced to play the genial host while that handsome rogue made cloying love to Sarah. He had kissed her hand and said sweet nothings to her throughout the proceedings. What made it even worse in Benjamin's view was that these words of affection were meaningless to Templeton. The man was not in love with Sarah. That much was clear. He was using his charm and his knowledge of her long-held affections to spin a web around her, dazzling her with his momentary attention. All for what purpose, Benjamin could not say.

Sitting in church earlier that day, Benjamin had seen from afar Templeton's overt display of affection. He had been hit with pain and fury all at once. That was when Sarah had caught his stare, and he had been forced to look away. As the priest intoned the words of a prayer, it had taken all of Benjamin's strength to bank the fire of his anger. He would not make a spectacle of himself. There, in the hallowed space of the church, he had sent a plea—or more accurately a pledge—to God that he would take himself and his anger in hand. He would become a better man, worthy of Sarah even if she was not meant to be his.

Help had come from a surprising quarter, as it often does with divine intervention. As he had stared at a stained glass window and battled the emotions roaring in his breast, it was as though he saw the face of his long lost friend, Jimmy, smiling at him through the window pane. Jimmy had looked down at him with his habitual carefree smile. His face had seemed to say, "Do not feel any sadness on my account. I am where I am supposed to be and perfectly happy."

The longer that Benjamin had stared at his friend, the more the tightness in his chest had eased. He had found himself smiling back at Jimmy. And then, just as he had been about to wonder if he was going mad after all, he had heard the priest's voice in his ear, sounding peculiarly like Jimmy's, reciting the words of Saint Paul, "We are afflicted in every way, but not crushed; perplexed, but not driven to despair; persecuted, but not forsaken; struck down, but not destroyed."

The vision of Jimmy had faded and he had looked ahead to the benevolent face of the priest at the pulpit and listened to his parting words to the congregation. "As you leave this church today, remember this. Our lives are ridden with pain and difficulty, but through it all we are being made more into the image of God. Jesus is greater than every misery, every calamity and every adversity. He is victorious over every pain. So I say to you this. Do not dwell on your afflictions. Do not mire yourselves in self-pity. Do not bring forth to your minds every injustice done to you. Today, I ask you to rejoice in God's love and feel gratitude for His eternal grace, for only through gratitude will you forge a path out of despair."

It was as though the priest had spoken directly to him. Benjamin had stood then and made a hurried exit from the church. He had found his way to the waiting carriage and sat there with his head in his hands, feeling a wondrous sense of release. It was not quite a moment of epiphany, for he knew as sure as he would take his next breath, that there would still be pain to bear and challenges to overcome on the road ahead. Side by side with this pain, however, there was new hope that something worthwhile could be salvaged out of the wreck of his life. He recalled a saying from Virgil that his mother often liked to repeat, *"Come what may, all bad fortune is to be conquered by endurance."* He felt a new wave of determination settle upon him. He would persevere; he would endure.

And so it was that when Sarah had come upon him in the carriage, he had been able to speak to her with a newfound equanimity, and to maintain a sense of calm throughout the rest of that torturous meal. Now, he bid Sarah and Ambrose goodbye and watched them as they walked down the avenue towards Ivy Cottage. He frowned, thinking again about Templeton and the man's obvious lack of true feelings for Sarah. She did not deserve to be bound for life to a man such as he. Why was it she did not see this?

He had sensed her melancholy just now. Though her mind refused to tell her the truth, she felt it in her heart. It saw through Templeton's sweet nothings, but she was too dazzled by the sudden reversal in her fortunes, by the victory of having won this much coveted prize, to listen to what her heart told her.

Benjamin consoled himself with the thought that there were still several more months to go before her nuptials to Templeton. All hope was not yet lost that between now and then, she would see sense and put an end to the betrothal. He would cling to that hope, and in the meantime, show her in all the ways he could, what true love truly looked like. Had he not come to England to woo her? Then woo her he would, though it would have to be more subtly done than he had anticipated.

With a vigour in his step, he went up to the library and searched the large collection of books for words of inspiration from his mother's beloved classical philosophers. After a browse through the shelves, he pulled out a volume of Ovid's Metamorphoses, then he settled himself in an armchair and began to read.

CHAPTER 25

SARAH

"The greatest pleasure of life is love."
— Euripides

December 1865

"SO YOU SEE," said Philip, "I shall need to travel north to Stamford to sketch Lord Colgan's ancient barouche, which dates back to the 1760s, and then continue my travels to Mansfield, where I understand there is an 18th century landau in excellent condition among Mr Brenham's collection of vehicles."

"Yes," murmured Sarah. "I can see quite how important it would be to include such historic vehicles in your series on transportation through the ages."

"I knew you would understand!" exclaimed Philip. "My dear, much as I hate to leave you, I must depart tomorrow and shall be gone for about a week."

"Yes, I see." Sarah smiled valiantly. "I do hope your journey prospers, Philip."

They were out for a stroll in the beautiful parkland of Graveley, and Philip had spent most of that time recounting his efforts at locating historic carriages to document in his tableaus on transportation. Over the course of their month-long betrothal, Sarah had discovered a few things she had not known about Philip. First, that he was passionate about his painting, and second, that when he embarked on a new artistic endeavour, he did so with single-minded dedication. She admired that dedication, truly she did, yet she found to her dismay that it narrowed the scope of their conversation to one single subject. She could not say that she was fatigued with the topic of Philip's paintings, but she would have liked to talk of other things—perhaps things that were of interest to her.

Whenever such heretical thoughts crossed her mind, she banished them quickly with a stern talking to herself. Marriage was a partnership, one in which there needed to be give and take. What Philip took in terms of wanting to discuss the paintings that mattered to him greatly, he gave back in affection and praise. He was always so charming and complimentary with her. Never a cross word passed his lips. He was all complaisance. She should never forget just how fortunate she was to have won his devotion.

Then there was the matter of his absences. There had been that first trip to London, the day after their betrothal. That had been followed by a trip to Bath, and now this latest proposed journey north. It was all for a worthy cause, she reminded herself. Such a venture as Philip had embarked upon would produce an important historical testimony of the different methods of transportation used through the ages. She admired his vision and application in bringing such a project to fruition. And yet she also could not help feeling that he thought more of the project than of her. Was this a taste of how married life would be between them?

Their walk had taken them on a circular journey around Graveley's parkland. They stopped now, in the shadow of a thick tree, as Philip pulled her into his arms, avowing, "You, my dear, are a diamond of the first water." He swooped his head to capture her lips in a kiss.

Sarah was used to his kisses by now, so she wrapped her arms around him and accepted the embrace dutifully. Such was her familiarity now with his touch and scent, that she did not feel the thrill that used to take hold of her at his proximity. His kisses were pleasant and she enjoyed them, though she did not crave his touch as once she thought she might. Philip lingered a few moments more, as if savouring the taste of her lips, then withdrew gently and smiled, "There now, I must not let myself get carried away. There are times, Sarah, where I would wish propriety to the wind and sweep you into my bed."

"Oh," she breathed, flattered despite herself. She attempted a seductive smile. "It is not much longer to go now until we are wed. Then you may seduce me to your heart's content."

His laugh rumbled against her breast. "What a minx you are turning out to be, my sweet and prim Sarah. I shall hold you to that promise, never fear." He let go of her and took a step back. "Come now, it is getting cold, and it is past time I should be taking you home." He led her to the phaeton that awaited them at the front steps of the house and handed her up into the carriage. Then he climbed on next to her, took the reins and began their journey to Ivy Cottage. Once there, he bid her another fond farewell, before turning the carriage around and heading back to Graveley.

NEXT DAY, AFTER she had completed her tutoring duties at Gorston Manor then visited the Burrells and the Jacksons with donations of food and clothes, Sarah made her way back to Ivy Cottage. There, she had a light luncheon and changed into an old gown before retiring to her back parlour and picking up the latest copy of Bradshaw's *Monthly Railway Guide* which had arrived in the post that very morning.

It was a particular habit of hers to peruse this eponymous guide to train timetables across the country. She had a long-standing game with her old friend, Benedict Sedgwick, in which they would compete to find the fastest train route from one destination to another, all from memory. Since Benedict and his family had now returned from their visit to America, she was sure it would not be long before he invoked the game and put her to the test. She was determined not to be bested by her friend again in this activity.

Her rapt attention was interrupted by an energetic knock at the door. Elsie went to open it, and a short time later, Benjamin was shown to her parlour. Sarah stood to welcome him, a delighted smile on her face. "Benjamin! To what do I owe the honour of this visit?" she asked teasingly.

He smiled gently back at her. "I have brought you something for your railway," he said. So saying, he took out a small package from his pocket and handed it to her. She took it from him and tore at the paper wrapping. Inside, was a small model of a steam locomotive.

"Oh my!" she exclaimed in excitement. On further examination, she added, "I see it is a 2-4-0 wheel arrangement. Is that one of the Great Western Chancellor locomotives?"

"It is," he said proudly.

She gazed at him wonderingly. "Where did you get this, Benjamin?"

He gave her an affronted look. "Why I made it, of course."

"You did? But you never said a word of this."

He shrugged, a little bashful. "I meant it to be a surprise. Ever since I saw your magnificent model of the Iron Duke, I have wanted to have a go at making a model of my own. I started work on it soon after I arrived here—it has kept me fine company on my days and nights of solitude."

She eyed it admiringly. "Well, I must congratulate you on the excellent workmanship. Just look at the detail on the two leading wheels." She looked up at him. "And you are giving it to me?"

His voice was deep and throaty. "Yes, Sarah. I made it for you."

"But this is too much. I could not accept," she burst out, holding it out to him.

He grasped her hand gently and pushed it back towards her. "It is yours, Sarah, and nothing is too much for a friend as dear as you."

Her throat went dry, and she had to battle to stop her eyes from welling. She took a deep breath in and let it out, then murmured quietly, "Thank you." She turned away quickly then, and to give herself time to regain her composure, busied herself with the careful placement of the locomotive on the tracks of her miniature railway. After a while, she stepped back to observe the panorama before her. "Now all it needs is a set of carriages in Great Western Railway livery," she said, thankfully sounding more composed.

Benjamin came to stand beside her. "I agree, and I am pleased to say I have already started work on the first carriage."

She curved her lips into a smile. "Then I shall begin work on a second one, and we shall compare each other's efforts."

"It sounds to me, Sarah, as if you are setting up a competition between us. Will there be a prize for the winner?"

She cocked her head to one side, considering the matter. "Possibly," she said thoughtfully. "But what would be the prize?"

"I know what prize I would want were I to win," he said huskily.

"And that would be?"

"A kiss from you," he said quietly.

She laughed awkwardly. "Benjamin, I am betrothed. That would not be right."

She saw that he tried to look unconcerned. "No, I suppose not. In that case, Sarah, you had better win this bet by completing your passenger car before mine."

"Very well," she breathed. "And what do I get as a prize if I win?"

"Whatever it is you wish from me, I will grant it. That will be your prize."

She laughed shakily. "We have an agreement then. I shall have to think carefully about my wish."

He made for the door, putting on his hat. "Think carefully on it," he said, "and whatever it is you want, I will give it gladly."

Feeling the colour high in her cheeks, she accompanied him to the main vestibule. He bowed. "Good day, Sarah. I shall see you at church tomorrow. And I believe we are all invited to luncheon at Mulverley Grange afterwards."

"Yes," she murmured. "I shall see you there. Good day, Benjamin."

Without another word, he turned and took his leave. As the door shut behind him, Sarah put a hand to the heart that was beating loudly in her chest. Good Lord what was happening? Why was Benjamin flirting with her? What could be his intention? And lest she forget it, she was engaged to marry someone else. Whatever this was, it was wrong. She would have to put a stop to it forthwith.

LUNCHEON ON SUNDAY was a boisterous affair. Grace and Benedict regaled them with stories of their adventures in America and of how little Anna had won the hearts of all, and most particularly her grandpa, whom she had wrapped firmly around her finger. Much was made of Sarah's betrothal, with Grace wanting to know how it had all come about and the details of Mr Templeton's proposal.

In a lull in the conversation, Ambrose, who had said little till now, suddenly asked, "And what news of Daniel? I was surprised that he and Bella did not return with you."

"Oh Daniel," Grace smiled fondly. "He is far too busy with his building project to have come home with us."

"Building project?" wondered Ambrose.

"Yes, he is building Benjamin's new house."

All eyes turned to Benjamin. Sarah could not help but ask, "Did you know of this?"

Benjamin nodded. "Yes, it was agreed between us before I left. I would take his place over here while he built the house on the land where Old Jim's cabin used to be."

At Sarah's confused look, he went on to explain, "Old Jim was an eccentric character who owned a large plot of land some three miles from our house, in a secluded meadow bordered by a stream on the eastern side and a forest of fir trees on the western boundary. He built a ramshackle cabin on that land and lived the life of a hermit, so we didn't see much of him at all. However, not long after my return home, I happened to hear him speaking at the tavern that he meant to sell up and go back east. I decided to make him an offer for it on the spot. Next day, we went to a notary and did the deed."

Sarah stared at Benjamin in admiration. "How decisive you were in making him an offer."

Benjamin made a self-deprecating gesture. "It is good land, and the price was right. I had the funds from Grandpa's inheritance, and so I took the opportunity that was presented to me."

"Uncle Frank was very impressed with your initiative," interjected Grace. "Then when we arrived from England, we found Benjamin busy knocking down the old cabin, and Daniel of course went straight to work to assist him." She laughed, "I think he needed to prove to everyone that he was not just a pampered viscount but a real man who could work by the toil of his hands, just like his pa. And then he got the bit between his teeth that Benjamin urgently needed this house for his bride. He has been working on it every day from dawn till dusk. He even commandeered my brother John and my cousin Robbie to help him with the work, several other men from the village too."

"I went to see it the day before our departure," added Benedict. "He has done a fine job on it. It is still not quite finished, but I think you will like it very much, Benjamin—and so will your bride."

"Your bride?" asked Sarah, a queasy feeling forming in her stomach. "Do you mean to get married, Benjamin?"

"Yes," he said simply. "If one day she will have me."

Who was she? Why did Sarah not know of her? And why did the idea of Benjamin getting married fill her with dread when she herself was also to wed? She should not feel jealousy. After all, Benjamin was her friend, not her lover. She was going to marry Philip. She should be happy for her friend. But who was this mystery bride? She itched to know, and at the same time did not want to know at all. The thought of Benjamin getting married suddenly seemed to throw all her plans, all her certainties into the air. She put her fork down, unable to take another bite of food, such was the turmoil in her breast.

By the time she was able to follow the conversation again, it had moved on to other matters. Benjamin was speaking, "So it is all agreed then. We shall have a gathering of family and friends for New Year's Eve at Stanton Hall."

Grace giggled. "Remember that first time we got together to celebrate the new year, and we all played a game of questions and commands?"

"How could I forget?" said Benjamin humorously. "I learned quite a few surprising things about my family that day."

"We shall have to play it again," she said with a wicked smile.

Benedict placed a hand on his wife's. "Gracie, last time we played the game, it was with a very intimate circle of family members. Remember we shall have Ambrose and Sarah, together with Mr Templeton, celebrating the new year with us. It would not do to play the game and ask of them the sort of questions that were asked last time."

Grace made a little moue of disappointment but took her husband's words to heart. "You are right, Benedict. What a shame though." She cheered in an instant though as another thought came to her. "Then perhaps we can play a guessing game as to who Benjamin's bride might be. I put my money on it being Chastity Hewitt. She showed an uncommon interest in the news that we were building your house, Benjamin. Am I right?"

Benjamin, however, would not be drawn. "Maybe you are right, Gracie, and maybe you are not."

The rest of the luncheon proceeded in a blur for Sarah. All she could think about was that Benjamin planned to marry and that Daniel was "urgently" building a house for his bride, who may or may not be his old flame, Chastity Hewitt. At the same time, she could not help but think, if the matter were so urgent, then why had Benjamin come to England instead of working on his new home? It did not make sense. And that was not all. That same thought she had had before kept intruding at the edges of her mind, though she anxiously tried to sweep it away. Could there be a connection between Benjamin's recent flirting, this bride and the thing that Ambrose claimed was right beneath her nose? No, it was too wild a thought. And she should not forget. She was betrothed to Philip Templeton.

CHAPTER 26

BENJAMIN

"Come what may, all bad fortune is to be conquered by endurance."
— Virgil

New Year's Eve, 1865
BENJAMIN WITHDREW SOME folded sheets of paper from his desk drawer and set to read the letter again. It had come from Daniel, delivered by Benedict upon his return from America a week ago. Since then, Benjamin had kept going back to it, wanting the guidance of his brother's wise, kind words.

He had now been in England for nearly two months. In that time, much had changed, but the most important matter still lay unresolved. Sarah had not broken off her engagement to Templeton. She was still lost to him, despite his surreptitious efforts to woo her.

In the guise of a mere friend, he had kept her company on walks, lunches and dinners. He had made an offering to her of the locomotive he had painstakingly built for her miniature railway. She knew he desired a kiss from her and that there was a lady he wished to marry, if only she would have him. He had hoped by now that Sarah would have started making sense of the many clues he had dropped about his feelings and intentions. Unfortunately, his beloved was proving to be obtuse in her thinking. Surely by now, she would have seen through the sham of Templeton's charmingly false courtship? But no, she still clung to the notion that she was destined for that rake.

It was enough to drive a man as violently in love as was Benjamin to drown his sorrows in drink. Except he had not. And there was the great change that had occurred in the past two months. Benjamin had remained steadfast in his determination to become a better person. There had been only one further episode of punching a tree in anger, and that had been on the day the announcement had been made in *The Times* of Sarah's betrothal. That had been followed by a proud showing off of the family heirloom ring that Templeton had put on Sarah's finger as a symbol of their engagement. This had been too much for Benjamin to bear, and he had escaped to the wooded park to let his pain and frustration rip through him.

However, he had not let that one lapse send him into a spiral of despair. On his return to the house with bloodied hands, he had not instructed Siddons to bring out the whiskey. Instead, he had dressed the wounds, taken out the volume of Ovid's Metamorphoses, and sought solace in the words of an ancient poet.

There had been one other positive development in the time he had spent in England, and that had been his blossoming friendship with Ambrose Cranshaw. Benjamin felt an affinity for the man on several levels. Firstly, he was Sarah's only sibling and the person closest to her. Then, of course, there was the curious rapport that seemed to have grown between Ambrose and Daniel, which also strengthened the connection Benjamin felt for the man. And quite apart from all that, Benjamin had found Ambrose's tranquil disposition to be the perfect balm for his battered spirits.

The two men met every week to discuss the business of the Stanton estate, but they also got into the habit of conversing on other matters. Over time, Benjamin had opened up to Ambrose about his personal struggles, the pain he felt and how it turned into rage at himself. Ambrose would hear him out, then provide a grain of wisdom in his quietly lucid way. This friendship with Ambrose helped sustain Benjamin in his time of need. And so too did his brother's love, felt across the ocean and expressed in the letter that he now held in his hands.

December 1ˢᵗ, 1865

Dear Benjamin,

I was sorry to hear of your disappointment about Sarah. I was saddened both on your account and on Sarah's, for I have come to care for her as a brother, and I do not like the idea of her marrying a man such as Philip Templeton.

Your house is almost done. In another two weeks or so, it should be ready for habitation. I have put all my effort and dedication into making it a fine house for you. It may not welcome your bride just yet, but someday, I believe there will be a deserving woman who will share that home with you. Do not despair, dear brother.

As to your question on what to do now, I have two things to say. Firstly, are you sure all hope is lost with regards to Sarah? Perhaps she will change her mind now you are there and break off her engagement to Philip Templeton, though admittedly, the chances of her doing that are slim. I have come to know her as being rather stubborn, a trait she shares with Ambrose. She will cling stubbornly to her commitment to Templeton, even in the face of his undoubted unsuitability for her. I may be biased, but I believe she would be mad to choose Templeton over you. You, Benjamin, are the very best of men. You have a caring gentleness in your soul, just like Mama. I would hope Sarah will soon see past the scary appearance to who you are beneath, though I must say I envy you that raffish scar and luxuriant grey beard.

The second thing I have to say is this. Come home! We long to have you back, dear brother, and though you may return without a bride, you will be surrounded by the people who love you. You will have your own house and as much seclusion as you crave, and you can set to work on building that large shed for your engineering work. I have no doubt you managed to repair that steam plough and put it to good use. Am I correct? If you come home, I am sure there will be plenty of similar contraptions you can fix! Labour to do what you love, Benjamin, and soon you will experience the satisfaction of success. After that, perhaps romantic love will follow with someone new. Who knows what God has planned for each of us?

So, come home. We do miss you.

Your loving brother,

Daniel Stanton

Benjamin sighed and put the letter away once more. These past months, he had persisted in the hope that Sarah would come to change her mind about Philip Templeton, but the time was coming close when Benjamin would have to admit defeat and cede all hope of winning the woman he loved. He would give it one more try before giving up and going home. With that thought, he stood and adjusted his neckcloth. All the guests had arrived an hour earlier—Ambrose, Sarah, Templeton, Benedict and Grace. It was time for him to show his face and play the benevolent host.

CHAPTER 27

SARAH

"But still she flees him, swifter than the wind."
— Ovid

SARAH SCREWED A pair of drop pearl earrings into her ears, one of the few items of jewellery left to her from her late mother. She gazed at her reflection in the glass mirror. A pale face with clear grey eyes, a wide forehead and a stubborn mouth stared back at her.

A year was coming to an end and another one was about to begin, one in which she too would begin a new chapter of her life—that of a married woman. Yet most of the excitement she had felt at the prospect of marriage had dissipated. Here, in the privacy of her room, she admitted to herself that the reality of being with Philip Templeton did not accord with the dreams she had harboured of him for so many years. He was still handsome and charming to her eyes, but the mysterious hold he had on her had waned.

She supposed that was true of life. As the old saying went, familiarity breeds contempt, but she had not expected it would happen even before the wedding. In truth, the business of marriage was a far more prosaic undertaking than the romantic imaginings of young women. And she was no chit in the schoolroom but a mature woman of thirty. She should not be surprised, therefore, that the magical appeal of Philip Templeton had disappeared on closer acquaintance. That did not mean their marriage would be an unhappy one. It simply meant that she would have to approach the venture with sober practicality. Yes, for too long, she had let herself be carried away on girlish dreams. Now was the time to put those fanciful dreams to bed. This included any thoughts she may have had of Benjamin.

Tonight, she was staying at Stanton Hall, and had been given this pleasingly furnished bedchamber two doors down from the library. All the other guests were also sojourning here for the night. Philip, she knew, had been put up in a room at the farthest end of the house, well away from hers. She wondered if this was something to do with Ambrose—his brotherly way of protecting her virtue. She laughed to herself. If so, he needn't have worried, for apart from a few embraces that she had endured rather than enjoyed, Philip had been chivalrously correct in his behaviour with her. She stood briskly and patted down the folds of her evening gown. With one last glance at herself, she turned and made her way down the stairs.

Dinner was an elaborate meal of ten glorious courses. Cook had excelled herself and the finest wines had been sent for from Stanton Hall's cellar. Looking dashing in a well cut dinner jacket and elegant neckcloth, Benjamin presided over dinner with the graciousness of a man born to such a life. Not that he was any more dashing and handsome than her own Philip, she hastened to remind herself. Her glance flew to her betrothed. He sat across from her, a twinkle in his eyes, brimming with cheerful bonhomie.

With dinner over, the gathering reconvened in the drawing room, the men having elected to forego their port and cigars rather than leave the two ladies on their own. Soon, the clamour went up for some music and dancing. Ambrose, a skilled pianist, was called upon to play a waltz. Tables and chairs were moved to one side to make space. Benedict offered his hand to Grace while Philip hurried to Sarah's side to ask for a dance.

This left Benjamin, as the odd man out, to sit and watch the dancers.

"You shall have the next dance," promised Grace consolingly.

Benjamin shook his head and smiled. "Do not concern yourself with me, Gracie. I am quite content to sit here and admire the view."

Then, Ambrose struck up the first note, and soon, Philip had Sarah in his arms, his hand to the small of her back, his smile adoring. Sarah let him take the lead in the waltz, though she noticed that with the copious wine he had imbibed tonight, he had grown decidedly more amorous than usual. He held her close to his muscular body, his lips hovering an inch from hers, and even sneaked in a quick kiss as he twirled her around the room. When the dance came to an end, he pulled her to him tight and kissed her again, uncaring of the proper decorum. She wished he would not do so.

Observing them, Grace clapped her hands in delight. "So romantic! Look how in love they are," she said to Benedict.

Her husband, however, only had eyes for her. He gazed down lovingly at his wife and pronounced, "Almost as much in love as we are," then kissed her soundly.

All this kissing really was not appropriate conduct. Sarah took an awkward step back from Philip, and as she did so, she spied Benjamin watching them, a pained expression on his face. He hid it quickly with a sardonic smile. "Yes indeed," he remarked. "Romance is in the air tonight. I suggest, Ambrose, you play another waltz for our four lovers."

Ambrose pursed his lips but did as he was bid, starting up another waltz. Philip pulled her towards him again, "Shall we, my dear?" He did not wait for her to answer, leading her into a dance once more.

Afterwards, the couples sat down to catch their breaths and drink champagne from their refilled glasses. As the evening progressed inexorably towards midnight, the company became ever more gay, ever more carefree. Sarah tried to enjoy herself as much as the others around her seemed to be, but a heavy weight had descended into the pit of her stomach. Every so often, she brought her gaze to Benjamin and despite the jovial smile on his face, she could sense that he too was in poor spirits. One time she did so, their gazes met. His eyes burned a deep, rich brown, transmitting a potent message. The moment was over quickly, as Benjamin turned to address a remark to Ambrose.

On the approach of midnight, all present went quiet, listening to the chimes of the clock. Then, there were cheers and applause as the party gathered congratulated one another. "Happy New Year, my darling," purred Philip, pulling her into his embrace. His lips descended on hers, and his tongue probed, demanding entry. Reluctantly, she parted her own lips. He tasted of wine and sin. She let him kiss her, but a moment later, pushed him gently back, conscious of her surroundings. Her eyes searched for Benjamin, but his back was turned to her.

Ambrose came over next, and she went willingly into his arms. "Happy New Year, Sarah," he said. "May it bless you with joy."

"Happy New Year, Ambrose, the best brother in the world." He laughed at that and kissed her cheek.

Embraces were exchanged with Benedict and Grace, and finally, she faced Benjamin. "Happy New Year, dear friend," she murmured.

"Happy New Year, Sarah," he responded gently and pulled her all too briefly into his arms.

After that, the evening wound down very quickly. Grace yawned, pronouncing herself well ready for her bed. Soon, everyone present was bidding the other goodnight and retiring to their beds. Philip drew her to him one more time, smiling fondly into her eyes. "Sweet dreams, darling Sarah," he said, giving her one last kiss. She was relieved when he released and escorted her to the foot of the stairs.

She went up the steps, then along the corridor, past the library to her bedchamber door. In she went and placed her lamp on the dressing table. She sat once again before the glass mirror and carefully removed the drop earrings, placing them inside her small jewellery case. Pin by pin, she released her hair from its knot atop her head and painstakingly brushed its length.

Only then did she stand to divest herself of her evening gown, corset and petticoats. She folded them neatly into her travelling case in readiness for her return home tomorrow, and shook out the grey wool gown she proposed to wear in the morning. Finally, she removed her shift and drawers, and with a shiver, swiftly sponged her body clean with the water she had poured into the wash bowl. Still shivering, she pulled her nightgown over her head and slipped on the thick woollen robe she wore in the evenings to keep herself warm. Despite the lateness of the hour, she was not quite ready for sleep. She would tiptoe in her slippers to the library nearby and find herself something to read.

Picking up the lamp once more, she went to her door and opened it quietly. As she took her first steps towards the library, she felt a sudden gust of chilled air sweep over her and paused, mystified. Looking behind her to the end of the corridor, she identified the source of the chill. The large sash window was wide open. She immediately knew why. She stood outside the library door, uncertain, then came to a decision. Quickly, she returned to her bedchamber, deposited the lamp on the dressing table and picked up her thick woollen shawl, which she wrapped securely around her shoulders. Then, she made her way out again, shutting the door quietly behind her.

At the end of the corridor, she reached the open window and without hesitation, climbed over the sill to stand on the wide ledge outside, letting the moonlight illuminate her path. Taking two very careful steps sideways, she negotiated her way to the flat part of the roof, spying the dark figure seated a few feet from her, his knees tucked into his chest. He did not hear her approach until she had dropped to the seat beside him. "I thought I would find you here," she said nonchalantly.

He raised his head in surprise. "Sarah!" came his startled voice.

She nudged his elbow playfully. "Any meteors?" she enquired.

"None, I'm afraid."

"Hmm," she murmured, looking up to the sky. "However, it is a clear night and I can see several constellations. Do you see that bright red star over there? That is part of the Orion constellation. It forms the shape of a triangle with two other stars. And the bright star below? That is Sirius and over to the left is Procyon."

He looked towards where she was pointing. "Yes, I see them," he whispered.

They sat side by side observing the stars for a long time. "So, my friend," Sarah said eventually. "What brings you out here in the late hours of a winter's night?"

He kept his eyes on the sky. "It is where I go when I want to think," he replied quietly.

"What is it you were thinking of?"

He turned his head abruptly towards her. "You," he said.

"Me?"

"Or rather, the hopelessness of you," he continued. "I came to the decision that nothing I can do will stop you from making the biggest mistake of your life, so I might as well go back home."

She frowned. "You are speaking in riddles, Benjamin."

"Am I? I would think I had spoken quite clearly." He stared meaningfully into her eyes. She trembled, and it was only partly due to the cold. But she was not yet ready for the message that was being conveyed, clear though it was, so she looked away, breathing deeply to calm her agitation. She heard a rustle and then he said, "I have something for you. Here."

He placed an object into her hands. She looked down at it— a small-scale railway carriage, exquisitely built. Picking it up, she examined it as best she could in the moonlight. "You have completed it," she said superfluously.

"Yes." And then into the silent void, he added, "I recall we had an agreement if I should complete my carriage first."

An excitement gripped her chest. "Hmm," she murmured incoherently.

"Time to pay up, Sarah. Give me something to remember you by once I am gone." He pried the miniature carriage gently from her nerveless fingers and tucked it back into his pocket. "Come here," he mumbled gruffly. The flat of his hand was on her back, pulling her towards him. She did not put up any resistance. In fact, as he angled her body against his, her hands flew up to clutch at his shoulders. She felt like she could not speak, only tremble in his arms. "Sarah," he muttered one more time. Then he brought his face close to hers. "Kiss me."

With a mumbled cry, she did just that. Her lips travelled the remaining distance, unerringly finding his. They fit together as if they had been made to be like this. His lips felt warm and soft, and suddenly, she was frantic to know their taste. Without thinking, she parted her lips and swiped her tongue across the seam of his mouth. A moment later, he had taken over the kiss, and in that moment, she was lost.

Like a person starved, he devoured her, but she was just as ravenous, taking every drop of his essence greedily, hungering for more. She was consumed. She could not think, only feel. She felt him, his overpowering need of her, matched only by her need of him. They came at each other's lips like feral creatures lost to civilisation, joining their tongues in an elemental dance of longing and passion. Her hands tore through his hair, needing to hold him close. His own hands were buried in her thick strands, pulling her wildly to him. This was what it felt when two hearts came together in a kiss of deep, desperate love.

She knew it as clearly as she knew day from night. This. This. This.

Benjamin moaned against her mouth, "Oh love, oh love, oh my sweet darling love."

"Benjamin," she sobbed.

"Yes, darling. Believe it."

"Benjamin," she said again, reality crashing down around her ears. She tore herself from him, filled with disgust at herself. What was she thinking of? She was promised to another. She stared at him in shock, unable to believe what she had just done.

"Sarah, do not look so," he pleaded. "It is me, the man who loves you, who would go to the ends of the earth for you."

But she was beyond listening. With lips that trembled, she could barely get the words out, "This was wrong. We should not have done this." She came to her feet, and his hands came out quickly to steady her. Once she had gained her balance, high up on the rooftop, she batted his hands away. She faced him and said again, this time her voice stronger, "This was wrong!" She turned to leave, walking on shaky legs towards the window, ignoring his pleas.

"Sarah, don't go. Please listen. That new house in Ohio was built for you. I came to England for you. It is you, always has been you I love."

She continued on her way, climbing over the window sill back into the house. She would not be party to a deception against the man she had agreed to marry. There was right and there was wrong. She heard Benjamin follow her and turned to him, placing a staying hand to his chest. "No, Benjamin. We must not. Goodnight." She hurried away, conscious of his eyes following her, and did not stop until she was in the safety of her own room.

CHAPTER 28

— ♥ —

BENJAMIN

"Remember when life's path is steep to keep your mind even."
— Horace

"NO, WE MUST not," she had said. "This was wrong." The words echoed inside his head as he lay on his bed, not bothering to undress. It had felt so right to him, but she had said no. He had put aside his pride and pleaded for her, told her of his love. To this she had turned her back and said no.

He pressed a hand to the hollow ache in his chest. It was time to accept the cards that fate had dealt him. He and Sarah… it was not to be. Despite the rightness of them together, she would not change her mind. He had done all he could to win her, but it had not been enough. He did not think he could bear to be here a moment longer. He had to go home, hide in his new house and lick his wounds.

When morning came, he washed and dressed, going down to the breakfast table looking, he knew, pale and haggard. It did not mark him out for attention as his fellow guests were similarly indisposed, though perhaps for different reasons. Benedict clutched his head and bemoaned his overindulgence in alcohol the night before. A pale-looking Grace rested her head on her husband's shoulders and refused any food, contenting herself with a cup of tea. Even Philip Templeton looked to be under the weather. Sarah sat furthest away from

Benjamin, avoiding his gaze as best she could. She looked wan, dark smudges under her eyes betraying her lack of sleep.

By mutual consent, all the guests departed soon after, most probably to go rest at their homes and recover. Benjamin bid them farewell, and again, Sarah refused to meet his eyes. Benjamin drank in his last look of her as she climbed aboard the carriage that was to take her and Ambrose back to Ivy Cottage. He stood watching it go. Once it was out of sight, he turned and with heavy steps, climbed back up to the house. He called to Siddons with a set of instructions, then went up to the library and sat at his desk to compose letters to Ambrose, Benedict and Sarah. To the first, he was brief, merely explaining that he had decided it was time to return home to America and that he was leaving the running of the estate in Ambrose's capable hands. To Benedict and Grace, he conveyed apologies for his abrupt departure and sent his good wishes. And finally, he began to write to Sarah.

January 1st, 1866

Dearest Sarah,

I wish I could say I was sorry for what happened last night, but I am not. I have loved you for years and I hope you will not begrudge me that one and only kiss, one that I will remember to my dying day. Do you recall the words you once wrote about such a kiss? You said it is quite one thing to embrace someone you love and another to embrace one you are simply dallying with. Last night, I saw the truth of those words. No kiss has ever consumed me or felt so right as when your lips met mine. So, I cannot be sorry for it, despite what occurred afterwards.

I came to England with one purpose only, Sarah. It was to win you. Imagine my distress when I discovered I had arrived a day too late and that you had pledged yourself to Philip Templeton. You see, I came straight to see you, but you were not home, so then I went to Graveley. I was concerned that you might be there, and my fears were realised. Through a window, I observed that man give you your first kiss, and I heard as you accepted his proposal of marriage. My heart cried that it should have been me! Oh the pain of seeing you with him that day. I ran back to Stanton Hall and vented my anger. That was the reason for my bandaged hands that day you found me in the library, and for the empty bottle of whiskey.

And so I endured. I went from day to day, trying to make myself a better person, one that would be worthy of you. I hoped, you see, that you might change your mind and end your betrothal to Templeton. It was clear to me the man did not love you as he should. He said sweet words of affection, but his actions were not the ones of a man in love. I was determined to show you in all the ways I could how much you mean to me. I bided my time patiently and kept on hoping. But last night, all hope was lost. I will not importune you with my presence any longer, nor can I endure the sight of you with him another day. So, it is time for me to leave. By the time you receive this letter, I will be long gone.

Goodbye, dearest Sarah, and God bless you. I wish you every happiness even though you will not be mine. If ever you wish to write and resume our correspondence, then I will respond, though of course with the right degree of propriety. No longer will I share descriptions of my indiscretions — not that there will be any, not now that I know what it is to kiss the person I love. My heart is yours, always.

Your loving friend,

Benjamin Stanton

Benjamin put the pen down, assailed by a memory of how in this very room, on first meeting Sarah, he had thought it odd that she should persevere in harbouring a passion for someone in the face of evidence that it was hopeless. And now, it was him that was doing it. Grimly amused, he folded the sheets into an envelope and sealed it. He addressed it to Sarah in his neatest writing and left it on the desk for Ambrose to find, along with the other missives. Then, he went to his room and put together his meagre belongings. Less than an hour later, he was on his way to the station.

CHAPTER 29

SARAH

"Cleverness is not wisdom."
— Euripides

BACK AT IVY Cottage, Sarah unpacked the belongings from her travel case and put it away at the top of her wardrobe. Once that chore was done, she went down to the back parlour, taking with her the small passenger carriage that had been left outside her bedchamber door this morning. She coupled it with the locomotive Benjamin had made for her and placed them carefully on the rails.

She had been such a fool! She had let herself be beguiled by Philip, by his handsomeness and his charm, and convinced herself that she loved him when it had not really been love that she felt. And as for her feelings for Benjamin, she had been doubly a fool.

Over and over, she had told herself that what she felt for Benjamin was a delusional fantasy, made up in her head, the product of her fevered imagination at night. How could it be real when they had barely known each other? It was just a correspondence across the ocean sustained over many years, but it could not be real love. Philip, on the other hand, was flesh and blood right here, and he had wanted to marry her. She had thought herself so sensible in accepting his offer, but she had been mistaken.

The door behind her opened, and she heard Ambrose come to stand a short distance from her. "That is a fine piece of craftsmanship," he remarked. "Benjamin's work I take it."

"Yes," she said quietly.

She heard him sigh and turned to face him. He studied her for a moment, then asked gently, "Do you wish to talk about it?"

She shook her head then changed her mind and nodded. He laughed and pulled her into his embrace. He held her comfortingly for a moment, then said, "Come to my study. We shall get Elsie to make us a pot of tea, and then we will talk this out."

This they did, settling themselves comfortably on two frayed armchairs. Ambrose started the thread of the conversation, coming straight to the point. "So, it is Benjamin," he said.

"Yes," she replied softly. "I have been very foolish."

He observed her wryly and concurred, "Yes, you have, but we all have it in us to be extremely foolish at times."

She glanced at him. "You knew, didn't you?"

He looked back at her sadly. "It was not my place to tell you, Sarah. You had to find it out for yourself."

"And so I have," she murmured under her breath.

He smiled. "So you have. What is it that happened last night? Will you tell me?"

"After we all went to bed, I could not sleep and decided to go to the library. I will not go into the details, but I saw Benjamin. We kissed and he declared his love for me."

Ambrose stretched out his legs before him and regarded her thoughtfully. "So why the long face?" he asked.

Sarah looked at him crossly. "It was an immoral thing to do, Ambrose, as long as I am betrothed to Philip."

"Yes," he agreed, "it was, but you can do something about it."

She was quiet for a moment. "I shall have to go see Philip," she said finally.

Ambrose sat up and refilled his cup of tea. He took a long sip and put it down. "The poor man was not looking quite the thing this morning," he said casually. "I suggest you wait until later this afternoon to speak to him. Do you wish me to come with you?"

Sarah stood and came over to him, placing her arms around his shoulders. "I do not deserve you, Ambrose," she said. "But no, thank you. This is something I should do myself."

SO IT WAS, later that afternoon, that Sarah set out for Graveley, walking briskly. On arrival there, she was ushered into the drawing room by the butler, who promised to fetch Mr Templeton. A few minutes later, that gentleman entered the room, a puzzled frown on his face. "Sarah, my dear, this is a surprise," he exclaimed. "Did I promise you an outing today? I do not recall."

Sarah rose to her feet and faced him bravely. "Philip, good day to you too. No, we did not have a prior engagement arranged, but I wish to speak to you. It is about our betrothal."

Philip scrutinised her, his expression hardening. "What is it you wish to say?"

This interview was never going to be an easy one, but she had to be strong and do what was right. "Philip," she began. "No one could have been more surprised and flattered than I was when you began to pay your addresses to me. I have long been besotted with you, of which you were no doubt aware, and so when you proposed, I did not hesitate to accept. But I have come to see that we would not suit."

She paused and glanced at him uncertainly. Philip stood still as a statue, his arms crossed as his eyes stared at her wordlessly. She took her courage into her hands and went on, "You do not love me, Philip, and I think in time you would become bored with my company. And also, I have come to understand that the feelings I had for you were a girlish infatuation and not built on true regard. So, I have come today to beg your forgiveness and ask that you release me from our engagement."

Philip continued to stare, looking thunderstruck. Eventually, he muttered, "Well, I'll be damned. So you mean to turn me down."

"I am sorry, Philip, so very sorry."

He sank down into a chair and rubbed a thoughtful hand to his cheek. Then he gave a snort. "This is a turn up for the books. I, Philip Templeton, am being jilted."

"Please do not think of it that way. Perhaps it would be more correct to say that we are both coming to our senses and realising that we would not suit."

He gave her a long look. "I am going to be a laughing stock, you do realise."

"I think perhaps it will be me that will be the laughing stock." She hesitated then, unsure whether she should tell him. But it occurred to her that he would find out soon enough from the village gossips, and it would be best if the revelation came from her lips. "There is more, Philip. I do not know how to say this to you." She took a deep breath in and gathered her courage. "I have also come to realise that there is someone else who holds my affections very deeply."

He pinned her with his stare, then slowly, a look of understanding came into his eyes. "Benjamin Stanton," he said, resolving the mystery.

"Yes, it is him. We have been friends for a very long time, but it has developed into something more."

"I see," he said in glacial tones.

There was nothing more to say. He observed her in silence, his mouth set in a hard line. Finally, he stood. "Well, that is the end of that. I will send word to *The Times* that our engagement has been called off."

Sarah nodded, pulling off his ring from her finger. "I was very honoured to receive this," she said, "but now I must return it to you." He took it without a word and placed it in his pocket. Then he walked her to the door, the interview over.

"I am sorry it had to come to this," said Sarah stiffly.

"No sorrier than I am, I assure you." Then Philip Templeton bowed. "Good day to you, Miss Cranshaw."

"Good day, Mr Templeton." Sarah took her leave, buttoning up her coat to ward against the chill December air. "*It is done,*" she thought, with a sense of relief. She took the steps down from the house and began to walk away briskly. With each step that she took, she felt renewed hope and determination. She was free! She quickened her steps. There was somewhere she urgently needed to be. Her heart singing, she almost ran in her haste to reach Stanton Hall.

Some minutes later, Sarah arrived at her destination. She hurried up the steps and pulled the heavy doorbell, panting with her exertion. Now that the moment had come, she felt lightheaded with excitement and dread. It took an unseemly long amount of time before the door was opened by a distracted looking Siddons.

"Good day to you, Siddons," said Sarah, smiling widely.

"Good day, miss," replied the butler.

"I have come to see Mr Stanton."

"Miss Cranshaw," said Siddons, a perturbed expression on his face. "It is the strangest thing, but Mr Stanton has gone."

"Gone?" questioned Sarah sharply. "What on earth do you mean?"

"I mean miss, that he has gone. Back to America. After you all left this morning, he informed me that he would be departing within the hour. He came down with his travelling case and took the carriage to the station."

"Did he say why?"

"No, miss," replied Siddons. "It came as quite a shock to us, to be sure. I believe he has left some correspondence for you up in the library."

"Thank you, Siddons."

Sarah was already racing up the stairs to the library. She ran into the room and looked around wildly for such letters. She found three missives stacked neatly on the desk, one of which was addressed to her. With hands that shook, she took it and ripped the seal open, taking out the sheets of paper. She read his letter then, her eyes widening in shock, followed by anguish and then despair.

When she was done, she collapsed on the armchair—that same armchair on which Benjamin had first found her crying. This time, her tears were not for Philip Templeton but for Benjamin. Her heart convulsed in her chest. Benjamin had come for her that day. He had seen her with Mr Templeton. That was the reason for his drunken rage and his bandaged hands. Oh, what wicked fate! Had he arrived even a day sooner, things could have turned out so differently. And now he was gone.

Suddenly, she stood, determination blazing in her eyes. She would go to him. Perhaps she could catch him up before he boarded the ship to America. There was not a moment to be lost. Clutching the letter in her hand, she flew down the stairs, past a bemused Siddons, and out the door. She rushed down the front steps of the house and began to run, all the way along the avenue that led to Ivy Cottage. At times, she had to stop to catch her breath, but then she quickly resumed her journey, wanting to reach her home as soon as possible. It was taking too long to get there, and she did not have any time to lose.

Finally, after what seemed like an age, she reached the front gate of Ivy Cottage. With hands that shook, she unlatched it and pounded at the door. It was opened a moment later by a bewildered looking Elsie.

"Miss—"

"There is no time, Elsie," puffed Sarah. "Get my travel case down from the wardrobe. I need to pack for a journey."

"Miss?" her maid asked doubtfully.

"Do it now!" insisted Sarah, brushing past her and going to Ambrose's study. He was already at his door, gazing at her in concern.

"Sarah, what is it?"

She went to him, but could not speak at first, as she tried to regain her breath. Benjamin's letter was still clutched in her hand, and wordlessly, she handed it to her brother. He took it, perusing the contents quickly. Then he looked up. "Oh, my dear. I am so sorry."

"I must go to him," Sarah said, having finally regained the power of speech.

"Sarah, my love, consider. All this can be resolved in time. Write to him now and explain."

"No!" cried Sarah sharply. "There is no time to be lost. I am going after him, Ambrose, whether you like it or not."

He looked at her in alarm. "I cannot let you go chasing after him all on your own. It would not be right. In any case, how on earth would you catch him up? I believe he already has quite a head start on us."

Sarah's eyes burned with fierce determination. "There is a way. I have it memorised from *Bradshaw's Guide*. If we use the Great Western route to Birmingham, then we could get a mail train connection to Liverpool and get there by morning."

"The mail train! Sarah!"

But Sarah was beyond listening. "How much money do we have? I will need funds for the journey."

"Sarah!" Ambrose remonstrated again. He stared at her a few moments, then a resigned expression came over his face. "Very well, if that is what you mean to do, we shall both go. Be quick now and pack a travel case for yourself and me with enough clothes for a few days' travel. I will go unlock the safe and take out some funds for our journey."

They each set to their task, Ambrose stopping on his way to find Elsie and ask her to send word to Stanton Hall for the carriage to be fetched. Not a half-hour later, they were ready, their cases safely stowed in the carriage, and on their way to the station.

CHAPTER 30

SARAH

"Fortune... and love favour the brave."
— Ovid

THE TRAIN JOURNEY was accomplished in weary silence interspersed with the occasional fraught questions from Sarah. "What if we are too late and his ship has already sailed?" "How will we find him?" "Is there another port from which ships sail to America?" "What if we are going to the wrong place?"

To all these, Ambrose gave calm and reasoned replies. "If he has already sailed, then you can write to him and wait for his response." *No, I could not wait that long.* "We will go to the docks and enquire about ships sailing to America." *Yes, that is what we shall do.* "There are other ports, but Liverpool is the most likely one to embark from." *I hope you are right.*

In this fretful state, Sarah and Ambrose arrived in Birmingham. They were in luck. A mail train was indeed due to leave overnight for Liverpool in two hours' time. However, there were no passenger carriages available on the train. This was not going to dissuade Sarah. If there were no passenger seats, then they would sit in the carriage with the mailbags, such was her determination to be on that train. Even Ambrose and all his reasoning was no match for this fierce resolve. After paying a small fee to the coachman, they were allowed aboard the mail carriage. With her enterprising nature coming to the fore, Sarah moved a few of the mailbags so as to create makeshift seats from them. And then, they both settled themselves as best they could for the overnight journey to Liverpool.

So it was that, tired and rumpled, they arrived at Liverpool station just after eight o'clock the following morning. From the station, they took a hackney carriage to the docks, where Sarah made enquiries from a helpful dock worker about ships sailing to New York that day. "The *Scotia* yonder, miss," said the dock worker. "It be leaving for New York." He pointed to where a long, paddle-wheeled steamship was docked several yards to their right.

Arm in arm with Ambrose, Sarah walked quickly towards the ship. The dock was busy with trunks being loaded and passengers boarding. Ambrose guided Sarah towards a ship steward who was checking a group of passengers' tickets. They waited, trying to keep their impatience in check, until he waved the passengers aboard and looked in their direction. "You will let me do the talking, Sarah, if you please," Ambrose admonished as they approached the steward.

The man in question looked at them enquiringly. "Good morning, sir. May I please see your tickets?" he asked.

Ambrose spoke in his gentle, cultured voice. "I wonder, sir, if you could help me on a matter of some delicacy. I believe a Mr Benjamin Stanton of Stanton Hall in Oxfordshire, is travelling on this ship. I am manager of his estates and there is a matter of grave urgency on which I must speak with him before he departs. Would it be possible to let me on board so that I may find him?"

The steward frowned in irritation. "I am sorry, sir, but only passengers with tickets may go aboard now. The ship is leaving imminently. Perhaps, if you have papers for the gentleman in question, I may arrange to have them delivered to him. Let me see the manifest to find his cabin. A Mr Stanton, you say?"

"Yes, that is correct," said Ambrose.

The steward leafed through a large sheaf of papers in his hand, looking for the Stanton name. "Ah, here it is. I see Mr Stanton is booked into cabin 216." He looked up at them. "Do you have documents for him? If so, I can ensure he receives them."

Sarah had been listening to this exchange with growing frustration. Now, she clutched Ambrose's arm tightly and spoke up, "If I may ask sir, is it possible to purchase a ticket to get on board? You see, it is a matter of the utmost urgency that I speak to Mr Stanton."

The steward turned to her in astonishment. "This is highly irregular—" he began.

"It is most irregular," she agreed hurriedly, "but it is a matter of the greatest importance. I would be immeasurably grateful if you could see your way to assisting us."

The steward hesitated then shrugged. "The ship leaves in just under an hour, madam," he said. "If you make your way to the offices of MacIver and Co on Water Street over there, you may possibly have time to purchase a ticket, but you must make haste."

"Thank you, sir, we will. Please do wait for us."

"We run to a tight schedule, madam." He took out his pocket watch and inspected it. "In exactly thirty-two minutes, we shall be shutting the doors."

"Very well." This time it was Ambrose that spoke. "We shall make haste and return within that time. Come, Sarah." With that, he began to walk her quickly in the direction of Water Street. As they walked, he said under his breath. "If you mean to go on the ship, Sarah, then I shall have to come with you. I cannot let you travel alone."

A thought suddenly occurred to her, heightening her distress. "Do we have the funds for it?" she asked breathlessly.

"That we do," he said grimly.

After that, they were silent, Sarah's whole being intent on reaching their destination as quickly as possible. Ten minutes later, they entered the imposing white stone building on Water Street and were directed to the ticket office on the third floor. Breaths puffing, they took the stairs up, urgency in their every step. At last, on the third floor, they found a clerk seated at a desk and as quickly as they could, gave him to understand that they required tickets for passage on the *Scotia* today. Again, they were met with astonishment, but Ambrose spoke so persuasively and calmly that soon the clerk drew up the contract papers to write out the tickets.

"That will be £60, Mr Cranshaw, for two first class cabins on board the *Scotia*, leaving today for New York."

Sarah stifled a gasp. Sixty pounds was an exorbitant sum. "Is there nothing cheaper? A second class cabin perhaps?" she asked hopefully, but the clerk was apologetic.

"I am sorry, madam. The *Scotia* only has first class accommodation."

Sarah's heart sank deep into her chest. There was no possible way they could afford such a steep sum of money, even half of it for just one ticket. A feeling of doom came over her. This journey had been in vain. She would not be getting on board the ship that carried Benjamin away from her.

All this time, Ambrose had remained silent. She looked to him now in consternation, knowing what he was about to say. Her brother stared into her eyes, a look of compassion on his face. Dear Ambrose, trying to find a way to let her down lightly. "It's alright," she mumbled. "I understand."

But then, Ambrose turned to face the clerk. "That will be fine," he said firmly. "Two first class tickets please, and could we make haste?" Under Sarah's astonished gaze, he took out a pouch and counted the requisite coins, handing them over to the clerk.

Quietly, she hissed into her brother's ear, "How on earth can we afford this expense?"

He huffed out a laugh. "Sarah, ever since the late earl left me some funds in his will, I have put away a hundred pounds as a dowry for you, in case it was ever needed. Just know that you have now made inroads into that sum."

She stared at him, speechless. Truly, he was the very best of brothers. But then, there was no further time for speech as the clerk returned with their tickets. He looked at the clock anxiously, saying, "There is only a quarter of an hour remaining before the doors are shut. I would advise great speed in making your way to the ship."

"Thank you, sir," replied Ambrose. "We shall make haste. Good day." And with that, they began another hurried journey, this time back to the ship. They had left their travel cases at the dock, and now, panting with the exertion, they returned to the steward and placed their newly purchased tickets into his hand. He smiled, more friendly now, and directed them to cabins 288 and 289. Their cases were handed over to an attendant, and a short time later, they found themselves boarding the *Scotia*.

CHAPTER 31

BENJAMIN

"There is in the worst of fortune the best of chances for a happy change."
— Euripides

BENJAMIN LAY ON his berth staring at the ornate decorations on the ceiling. The call had gone out some time ago for "all ashore who are going ashore", and soon, the ship would begin its journey across the Atlantic. He supposed he should be going out on the main deck to watch England's shore recede from view, but he could not find the strength to do so. He was bone-deep weary.

He closed his eyes, wanting to drift into the blessed nothingness of sleep. The gentle rocking of the ship told him they were finally on their way. He was going home. There was some comfort to be found in that thought. Darkness swirled around him as sleep claimed him, if only for a short time.

A sharp set of knocks on his cabin door jolted him out of his slumber. Who could be disturbing him at this time? Perhaps if he ignored whoever it was, they would go away. A pause. He reposed and began to float away into reverie once more. Another sharp knock. Good God, was there no peace to be had? Thoroughly disgruntled, he came to his feet and, rubbing his eyes angrily, went to open his cabin door.

A steward stood outside, holding a folded sheet of paper in his hand.

"What is it?" asked Benjamin curtly.

"Sir, I have a message for you from a Mr Ambrose Cranshaw. He said I was to make sure you received it straight away." So saying, the steward handed the folded sheet to him.

Baffled, Benjamin took it, thanking the steward absently before shutting the door. What on earth could this mean? He unfolded the sheet and cast his eyes on the brief note.

Benjamin,

Both Sarah and I are aboard the ship. All will be explained shortly if you make your way to cabin number 288.

Ambrose Cranshaw

Benjamin could not believe it. He rubbed his eyes and read the note again. His heart jolted. This could not be true. Sarah was on the ship? Why? How? It was beyond belief. Crumpling the note in his hand, he opened his cabin door and hurried down the long corridor, reading the numbers on the doors until he reached 288. There, he gave three sharp knocks.

The cabin door opened instantly, and there before him stood Ambrose Cranshaw, unbelievable as it was. Benjamin narrowed his eyes and barked, "Ambrose, what is this? Where is Sarah?"

Ambrose smiled and pulled the cabin door back. "Do come inside," he said softly, "as I do not wish the entire deck of this ship to listen to our discourse."

Benjamin strode inside and turned to face him. "Now answer me, please," he demanded.

Ambrose inclined his head. "It is simple really. Sarah read the letter you left for her and decided she had to come find you. And as it is not quite the thing for a gently bred lady to go gallivanting after a man, I of course accompanied her, as was only proper. I think for the rest, it is best if she explains herself to you." He pointed towards an internal door. "She is waiting in the adjoining cabin."

Benjamin was already striding towards the door, but was arrested by Ambrose's next words. "Benjamin! Stop a moment."

At Benjamin's impatient look, Ambrose continued, giving him a meaningful look, "Please do not be too long alone. And though I will give you some time for private discourse, do remember that I am here, on the other side of the door."

Benjamin nodded in acquiescence, only half listening, for by now, he had opened the door and was staring at the wondrous sight of Sarah standing mere feet away from him.

CHAPTER 32

SARAH

"One of the most beautiful qualities of true friendship is to understand and to be understood."
—Seneca the Younger

SARAH WAITED IN her cabin in a state of febrile tension. She would have wished to have gone straight to Benjamin, but Ambrose objected to this plan, insisting she wait here for him. Reluctantly, she had agreed. For the last ten minutes, she had been pacing the narrow confines of her cabin impatiently. What could be taking him so long?

The door behind her clicked open, and she whirled to face the person who had come in. It was Benjamin. His hair was mussed and there were tired lines around his eyes, but to her ardent gaze, he was the most beautiful sight she had ever seen. Slowly, he shut the door behind him and prowled towards her. He came to a stop a mere foot away and whispered, his voice hoarse, "Sarah."

Next instant, his hands cupped her face and he brought his lips to hers. Her arms flew to clasp him to her body, opening herself up for his urgent kiss, feeling once more that inimitable joy that comes with being embraced by a loved one. Their breaths became one, so too did the rhythm of their hearts. For a long, long time, they held each other, speaking of their love in the language of their bodies, letting each touch, each caress express what was in their hearts.

"Oh darling," Benjamin groaned, when finally he could free his lips enough to speak. "Does this mean what I think it does?"

"Yes, I came for you as soon as I could." She pulled back then, eyes full of rebuke. "Benjamin, you were too hasty in making your departure yesterday. Had you stopped to think, perhaps you would have realised that I could not entertain any sort of romantic relationship with you until I had extricated myself from my engagement to Philip."

"And have you?" he barked.

"Yes, my dearest, I have. While you were packing your belongings in haste to be gone, I was paying a visit to Graveley. It is done, and I have been released from my betrothal to Philip."

"Thank the Lord!" Benjamin sighed, bringing his forehead to hers.

But Sarah was not finished with her tale. "And then," she continued, "as soon as my business with Philip was concluded, I rushed to Stanton Hall. I could not wait to tell you that I was free and that I returned the sentiments you had expressed on the rooftop to me that night."

Benjamin kissed her again then, and she marvelled once more at how right it felt. She did not think she would ever get enough of his kisses. He nibbled at her bottom lip and growled, "Tell me how it is you feel. I need to hear the words."

"I love you, my dearest, darling one," she breathed, eyes shining with joy. "It was always you, never Philip." She put a hand to his face, caressing his soft beard as she had forever longed to do. Then, she resumed her tale. "My heart shattered when I got to Stanton Hall and found you gone. Then I read your letter and knew I had to get to you before it was too late. Only when we reached the *Scotia*, we were told in no uncertain terms that we could not board the ship to speak to you unless we were ticketed passengers." She frowned at him. "I will have you know that this escapade has cost Ambrose sixty pounds."

He laughed, dropping another kiss on her lips. "I will pay him back, with interest. The important thing is that you are here now and that we are together. Sarah, will you be my wife, please, just as soon as it can be arranged?"

"Yes, I will."

He held her to him once more, rocking her in his arms as if to soothe her, or was it to soothe himself? After a while, he spoke softly in her ear. "Why did you not tell me that night? Why did you let me think that all hope was lost?"

She nestled against his hard chest. "I am sorry, Benjamin. I was not thinking clearly. I was suddenly consumed with the knowledge that I had acted dishonourably, kissing you when I was promised to another. If I had stayed a moment longer in your arms, I do not know what else I would have done, what other sin would have compounded my original misdeed. I had to take flight."

"Well," he said, "it is over and done now. Will you live with me in Ohio, Sarah?"

"I will go wherever you are."

"And the same goes for me, my love," he murmured.

"Then we shall settle the matter in due course. Benjamin, how soon may we marry?"

He laughed merrily, his heart carefree for the first time in a very long time. "As soon as we arrive in New York, we can apply for a license and find a minister. Although..." He paused, lost in thought.

"Although what?" she asked impatiently.

"There is another possibility, but I would have to make enquiries first."

"Then please, darling, make those enquiries," she pleaded.

He smiled into the top of her head that was tucked under his chin. "I see you are just as keen to become Mrs Stanton as I am to put a ring on your finger and call you mine."

"Benjamin," she whimpered, "you have excited me for years with tales of your seductions. It is well past time I experienced those delights for myself."

"And so you will, my sweet vixen." He thought for a minute then added, "Do you know, I believe I wrote to you of these seductions because deep down, I wished it was you I was seducing. All these things I wrote of, I wanted to do with you. It sounds so depraved, I know, but that is how it was with me."

She trembled, whispering, "No less depraved than I was, imagining it was me you were doing those things to. Benjamin, I have to tell you, I am… I am… wet… down there."

"Agh!" he groaned. "What you are doing to me, Sarah!" He kissed the top of her head. "I promised Ambrose nothing untoward would happen between us." He took a deep breath to try to calm himself. And then came to a decision. "Take your drawers off and go lie on the bed, Sarah. I will not approach or do anything untoward, only watch you. I want you to touch yourself, darling, and bring yourself to a sweet orgasm."

She gasped, then hurried to do his bidding. Slipping her hands under the petticoats of her gown, she removed the drawers and threw them over a chair. Then she spread herself on the bed and brought a hand under her petticoats until her fingers reached the soft, wet folds of her cunt. Her breath hitched as she began to touch herself, and as she saw what Benjamin had done. Her discarded drawers were in his hands. He raised them to his nose and sniffed, breathing in her most intimate scent. All the while he followed her movements with his dark eyes. Her fingers rubbed that special place, over and over again, while she stared into the eyes of the man she loved.

"Benjamin," she panted.

"Yes, darling. Let yourself go."

"Ah!" With a muffled gasp, she claimed her blessed release, her core convulsing in waves of blissful pleasure. She looked to him, face flushed, yet feeling wonderfully content.

"Good girl," he praised. "You did so well. And look what you have done to me." He pointed down at himself. The crotch of his trousers had swelled. He dropped his hand there and held himself through the fabric.

She raised herself on her elbows to look more closely. "Your turn, Benjamin," she said. "Show me how you touch yourself."

He threw her an agonised glance, but he could not hold himself back any longer. With frantic hands, he loosened the top of his trousers and pulled out his engorged male shaft. It was as he had described to her—red, stiff and angry looking. He took hold of the drawers he had been so ardently sniffing and wrapped them around his hard length. Then with jerky movements, he began to rub himself up and down, an intense look of concentration in his eyes, which were glued to hers. All too soon, he reached his climax, his eyes drifting shut on an involuntary moan.

For a few moments, he stood there, breathing heavily. Then quickly, he re-arranged his clothes, crumpling the soiled drawers in his hand. She came to him and took them gently from his grasp. As she did so, he leaned forward and kissed her forehead. "This," he promised, "is just the beginning. I cannot wait, Sarah, to make you mine."

EPILOGUE

SARAH

"Love is composed of a single soul inhabiting two bodies."
—Aristotle

Three days later

"SHALL WE?" ASKED Ambrose. They stood outside the fore saloon, where a small number of people were gathered awaiting their arrival. Sarah had dressed for the occasion in the best gown she had brought with her, one in a shade of dark blue. Her hair was arranged in as elegant a coiffure as she could manage. On her ears were her mother's pearl earrings. That was the best she could do to make herself presentable for her wedding.

Two days ago, Benjamin, with Ambrose for company, had sought out Captain Fraser and spoken to him at length about what he proposed. At first, the captain had demurred, but Benjamin had persevered in his arguments. There was a pastor on board the ship, a Reverend Arnold, who could bless the ceremony. And then Ambrose spoke up. Did not the Merchant Shipping's Act of 1854 have a section which provided that every master of a ship carrying an official log-book should enter in it marriages that took place on board? It was a known fact that a marriage solemnised at sea by the master of the ship was as legal and valid as though celebrated on shore.

In the end, Captain Fraser had agreed, on the proviso that the Reverend should give his blessing to the marriage.

Reverend Arnold, when consulted, had been delighted to oblige. And his wife, a sprightly lady of three score years and more, had volunteered her services on the pianoforte for the occasion. So here now stood Sarah, about to be wed. Her heart fluttering excitedly, she breathed, "Yes, let us go in."

She placed her hand on his arm and let him lead her inside the saloon. Upon their entrance, the opening notes of Mendelssohn's Wedding March were heard, as Mrs Arnold smilingly played the well-known tune. And there, right before her, stood Benjamin, his beard neatly groomed, dressed in his best jacket, and gazing fervently in her direction. Slowly, she made her way towards him, then Ambrose took the hand she had placed on his arm and gave it to Benjamin. The Reverend cleared his throat and began the service.

She could not remember afterwards, the full details of the occasion. She spoke when requested to, and made her solemn pledge. And once it was all done, Captain Fraser took out his log-book with a flourish and wrote:

"10.30 A.M.—Solemnised the nuptials of Benjamin Stanton, Esquire, gentleman, and Sarah Cranshaw, spinster. Present, Mr Ambrose Cranshaw, Reverend Joseph Arnold, Mrs Arnold, and James Brentley, Chief Officer. This marriage thus celebrated was conducted according to the rites and ceremonies of the Church of England."

After which Captain Fraser produced a sheet of paper and wrote out a certificate of their marriage, which was signed by himself and the Reverend as witnesses. The certificate was duly handed to Benjamin with great ceremony. "And here you are, sir," said Captain Fraser. "Legally wed, all right and tight."

Lunch that day was a more elaborate affair than usual. The ship's main cook had been persuaded to bake a cake and deck it with white icing. It was brought out with much fanfare at the end of the meal, and the happy couple cut the first slice hand-in-hand. It was all wonderfully merry, with many a well-wisher congratulating them on their nuptials. Sarah smiled, and smiled some more, but what she truly wanted was for them all to be gone and to be alone with her husband.

Benjamin whispered into her ear, "Patience, Mrs Stanton," and she flushed with pleasure at hearing her new name. The rest of the afternoon passed by painfully slow until at last, they retired to their joint cabins—for Ambrose had very kindly agreed to exchange accommodation with Benjamin. They reached the door of number 288 and Benjamin stopped, turning to her with a grin. "I believe tradition dictates I do this," he said, swooping her into his arms and carrying her across the threshold. He set her down inside and locked the cabin door.

"So, Mrs Stanton," he drawled. "Are you ready to be ravished?"

"You will have to give me time to prepare myself, sir," she replied coquettishly. "Take out your pocket watch and count exactly ten minutes, then you may enter my bedchamber," she added with an impudent smile.

"Very well, but not a minute more," said Benjamin with a raspy voice. He kissed her gently on the lips. "Go then, dear wife, and prepare yourself."

She hurried into her cabin and began to discard her clothing until she was dressed in nothing but her shift. She loosened the pins from her hair and brushed it out. Then at last, she removed the shift and sponged her body clean with a wet cloth. And once she was clean, wearing not a stitch of clothing, she went to lie on the bed in as seductive a pose as she could think. She waited a minute, then two.

The door opened slowly, and there was her husband. His gaze took in the sight of her, reposing naked on the bed. "Mr Stanton," Sarah murmured invitingly. "What took you so long? I have great need of you." She splayed open her legs, as she had often imagined herself doing, revealing herself to her husband.

His eyes flared with desire. And then he was on the bed, leaning over her. "Mrs Stanton," he said softly. "Did you wish me to worship your cunt?"

"Yes, sir," she breathed.

He gave a wolfish smile. "Then that is what I shall do." He shifted down the bed until he was level with that most intimate part of her, and gazed his fill. "Mrs Stanton," he murmured. "You are a delight to behold." Then his lips were on her, as she had dreamed on so many nights for so many years. But the feel of his tongue on her sensitive folds was more blissful than she had ever dared imagine. She moaned, her eyelids shutting as she lost herself to this indescribable new sensation.

Benjamin savoured her, licking delicately and making sounds of approval deep in his throat, "Mmm." Gradually, his sensual touch gained pace, licking back and forth, fluttering over her flesh like the wings of a butterfly. It was too much; it was not enough.

"More," she panted. And he gave her more. She felt that familiar throb in her core, the tightening that signalled the coming waves about to crash on a shore. Another lick and she was engulfed in wave upon wave of pleasure. She made a desperate cry and rode out this blissful release until she could move no more.

When next she opened her eyes, Benjamin lay next to her, unclothed, his head so close she could count the long lashes of his eyes. "That was marvellous," she said in wonderment.

"It is you that is marvellous," he said in a deep, throaty voice. "Come here, darling." He took her into his arms and joined his lips to hers. They kissed long and lingeringly.

At last he pulled back with a tender smile. She took his dear face in her hands, raking her fingers through the softness of his beard, and asked, "Will you make me yours now, Benjamin?"

"You are mine, dearest love, just as much as I am yours," he murmured.

"Do not play games, Benjamin. You know what it is I mean," she said with a hint of impatience.

He laughed. "Patience, Mrs Stanton, all in good time," but he heeded her instructions. He parted her legs and settled himself above her, guiding his length to her opening. "It may hurt this first time," he warned.

"It does not matter if it does. I want you inside me, please, Benjamin. I have dreamed of this so long."

He kissed her again and with his lips on hers, thrust once, then a second time, and pushed past the barrier of her maidenhead. She felt a sharp pain but held on to him tight, her lips never leaving the softness of his. She felt a fullness as he pressed into her and a sense of victorious possession. *He is mine!*

Next moment he was moving inside her, plunging back and forth, his elbows bracketing her and his eyes never leaving hers. In a short time, the pain was replaced by a sensual pleasure. She met each of his thrusts with a lift of her hips, craving ever more closeness. His face above hers became set in a grimace as he battled for control, not wanting to reach his release quite yet. "Sarah," he rasped. "Let yourself go, my darling. Let it happen."

He thrust again and again, and with each thrust she felt that pleasure building inside her again. "That's it, my love. Give yourself to me."

With a cry, she pulsed around his hard length, overcome with pleasure once more. And now, he pounded into her, chasing his own wondrous release and letting out a harsh groan as he flooded her with his seed. When finally, he lay still atop her, she held him to her tight, chanting words of love. If she could, she would hold him like this, his flesh inside her flesh, for an eternity.

As if he heard her silent prayer, he murmured, "I wish I could stay inside you for all time, my darling love." Then he added reluctantly, "But I cannot." Gently, he pulled out of her, then went to fetch a wet cloth. He came back a short while later and cleaned her carefully, lovingly. When it was done, he joined her under the covers, extinguished the lamp, and drew her into his embrace. "This is how it will be for us from now until we draw our last breath," he vowed. "Goodnight, my love."

"Goodnight, Benjamin."

And with the gentle swell of the waves rocking their ship, they both fell into a contented, restful sleep.

AFTERWORD

Dear reader,

I hope you enjoyed *The Bluestocking's Secret Obsession*, the third book in the series, *The Stanton Legacy*, which follows the lives and loves of the Stanton family. As you may perhaps have guessed, the next and final instalment in the series will be Daniel Stanton's story and his forbidden love for Ambrose Cranshaw. Read an excerpt in the following pages from *The Viscount's Forbidden Love*.

May I ask you for a small favour?

Reviews are the life blood of independent authors. Please could you help spread the word about this book by submitting a review on **Amazon, Goodreads** or any other book reader platform. Stay tuned for my latest book release news by subscribing to my newsletter on **mmwakeford.substack.com.** You'll also get access to exclusive freebies and discounts as well as some great book recommendations.

M.M. Wakeford

THE VISCOUNT'S FORBIDDEN LOVE

(AN EXCERPT)

A HISTORICAL MM ROMANCE

THE STANTON LEGACY
– BOOK 4 –

PROLOGUE

AMBROSE

January 1866

SHOULD HE GO to Ohio? There was one pressing reason to go, but he must not think of that. The question lay unresolved in his mind as he stared at a distant point on the horizon. Land had been sighted a short while ago and passengers had been informed that *The Scotia* would be reaching its destination—New York—within the next two hours.

Ambrose Cranshaw did not need to do much in preparation for this. His baggage was a meagre travel case with the few days' clothes that had been packed in a great hurry prior to leaving his home in Oxfordshire on this mad dash with his younger sister, Sarah, in pursuit of Benjamin Stanton. Ambrose had agreed to help Sarah on her quest to reunite with the man she loved before he sailed for America. They had travelled overnight on the mail train to Liverpool and reached *The Scotia* an hour before its departure, only to be told they could not get aboard without first purchasing a ticket.

So, at an expense that still made him shudder, they had bought a passage to America and boarded the ship. And now, Sarah was married to Benjamin, the ceremony having taken place a few days into their journey, presided over by Captain Fraser and blessed by Reverend Arnold, an elderly vicar who happened to have been a fellow traveller on the ship.

As the shoreline slowly grew from a minute point on the horizon to something more substantial, Ambrose assessed the situation he found himself in. Here he was, about to arrive in America, having never before set foot on this continent. He had only enough funds to cover the cost of his return journey to England plus a little more to spare. Once they disembarked, the newly married couple would be journeying onwards to their home in Ohio, where Benjamin's father and uncle had extensive landholdings.

And as for Ambrose… well, he should wish them a fond farewell and take the next ship bound back for England. His position as manager of the Stanton estate did not allow for him to absent himself for any great length of time. There were rents to collect, accounts to be done, works to be overseen. It was his duty to return as soon as possible and pick up the reins once more.

Yet there was another impulse tugging at his breast, and that was to accompany Sarah and Benjamin to Ohio. As her eldest brother and only sibling, he ought to ensure she was comfortably established in her new home before bidding her goodbye. He would not see her again for a very long time, and once back in England, they would be far apart from one another. His heart beat painfully in his chest at the thought. He would need to accustom himself to living alone at Ivy Cottage without his sister's cheerful companionship. It was not a heartening prospect.

The more he thought of it, the more he warmed to the idea of continuing on to Ohio. He had gone to the great expense of accompanying Sarah to America, therefore it would make sense to see the journey through to its end and to delay the final moment of farewell. He would ensure his sister was well settled and put his mind at rest as to her wellbeing before returning home. The Stanton estate would have to do without him for a few more weeks.

He refused to acknowledge the other reason why the idea of going to Ohio held appeal. It was nonsensical, not worthy of consideration. And yet, try as he might, he could not stop the thrill that coursed through him at the thought of seeing Daniel again. It had been over three months since he had last laid eyes on his friend, his employer and now also his brother-in-law. Three months since that forbidden kiss between them had spun his world on its axis. And much as he secretly longed for a repeat of that kiss, he understood very well that it must never, ever happen again.

THE VISCOUNT'S FORBIDDEN LOVE IS OUT NOW.
Available in e-book, paperback and audio.

ABOUT THE AUTHOR

M.M. Wakeford lives with her husband and son in a London terraced house that gathers dust while she loses herself in her writing. A lifelong reader of romantic novels, she writes in many genres including contemporary, sci-fi and historical romance. All her stories strive to capture that heady feeling of falling in love, with authentic characters whose journey to a happily ever after is lined with dilemmas to overcome. If you're looking for a page turning romance with high emotion and a good dose of spice, you've come to the right place.

ALSO BY THIS AUTHOR

MR TEMPLETON FINDS HIMSELF A WIFE
A Stanton Legacy Novella

Two jilted lovers find a second chance at love...

Life is not a bed of roses for Lexie Forbes. Abandoned both by her husband and her lover, she resigns herself to a quiet life with her two young children. Until one day, everything changes. Her husband dies suddenly, leaving both his fortune and children in the guardianship of his best friend, Philip Templeton.

Philip Templeton has lived a rakish life of hedonistic pleasure, but at nearly forty, he finds himself unaccountably dissatisfied. He resolves to marry, only to find himself jilted by his intended. And then to make matters worse, he is saddled with the guardianship of his friend's two young children. Not to mention the fact that the children's mother is not best pleased about it!

Mr Templeton Finds Himself a Wife is a spin-off novella from **The Stanton Legacy** *series. You do not have to have read the other books in the series to enjoy this novella. Set in Victorian England, this book is a steamy romance written for a mature audience. Although this is a male/female romance, there is one consensual polyamorous scene.*

Praise for Mr Templeton Finds Himself a Wife:

"The ebook and storytelling did not disappoint!" ★★★★★ Chirp review

"Nice and sexy." ★★★★★ Chirp review

MY CAPTIVE DUCHESS
Book 1 – The Reeves of Reeves Hall

"You cannot leave Reeves Hall again. Here you will remain."

Recently widowed, Jane, Duchess of Coleford, has moved to an isolated part of Cornwall with her young daughter. There she meets her nearest neighbour, Brook Reeves, a man with a seemingly permanent scowl on his handsome face who soon makes it clear that he wants her gone. Despite his many offers to purchase the crumbling house she inherited from her late husband, she stubbornly insists on staying.

It is not long before the two become adversaries, both determined to ignore the attraction that has flared between them. Until one day, Jane ventures uninvited into his domain and sees things she must never tell the world about. There is only one solution. At Reeves Hall she must remain, his captive duchess.

What you will get in this book:
- ♥ Forced proximity
- ♥ Enemies-to-lovers
- ♥ Grumpy/sunshine

♥ Mr Rochester/Jane Eyre vibes

♥ Slow-burn but steamy

♥ Regency romance with a sci-fi twist

My Captive Duchess is book one of the series, The Reeves of Reeves Hall, set around the mysterious Reeves family who are not what they seem. It can also be read and enjoyed as a standalone as each book in the series has its own featured hero/heroine and HEA. If you're looking for page-turning, heart-stopping romance with an original, fresh twist, then this story is for you.

Praise for My Captive Duchess:

"Absolutely outstanding writing... Original story with uncompromising storytelling that you will have difficulty putting down once you start reading." ★★★★★ Goodreads review

"I couldn't put this book down! It was a good story with steam and great characters... This is going to be an interesting series." ★★★★★ Goodreads review

"The most fascinating story I have read in a long while... a wonderful read!" ★★★★★ Goodreads review

"I found the story so engaging I couldn't put it down." ★★★★★ Goodreads review

"I applaud the clever plot in this story. I adore both Regency and Sci-Fi, but never expected to see a combination of my two favorites! Well done!" ★★★★★ Goodreads review

KRANTOR'S MATE

Book 1 – The Venorians and Krovatians

One day, on a planet far from Earth, I meet my fated mate.
The only problem is, he's in love with someone else.

Martha has enrolled on a six-month exchange program to the planet Ven, whose people have recently made first contact with Earth. Newly single and broke, Martha looks forward to this once-in-a-lifetime opportunity to find out more about the Venorians, an intriguing humanoid race of massive bronze-skinned people.

As the son and heir of the Kran, planet Ven's ruler, Krantor has four somars—men who are his lifelong bodyguards and companions. He loves them all dearly, but one of them, Prilor, he loves best of all. Krantor knows he's destined to meet his fated mate one day, but it's Prilor he wants to spend his days and nights with. And he certainly hadn't banked on his fated mate being a human!

Will Martha give up her life on Earth for a fated mate who already loves another? And what of the feelings she has developed for Shanbri, another of Krantor's somars?

260

Author's note: this is a standalone sci-fi romance with steam and spice aplenty, featuring FM, MM, and MFM relationships, and a guaranteed HEA for all.

Praise for Krantor's Mate:

"Trope busting. Loved it... M. M. Wakeford offers a completely new take on fated mates. With all the expectations that are set with a trope, the author blows it out of the water with her fabulous storytelling. I completely enjoyed this take on RH, fated mates, and deep-abiding love." ★★★★★ Goodreads review

"What a phenomenal read. The worlds, cultures, and species created were diverse and detailed. The characters were rich, vivid, and beautifully flawed. I went on such an emotional ride with this book." ★★★★★ Goodreads review

"An interesting and original approach to the reverse harem and fated mate tropes... Thought-provoking and provocative, with high heat throughout." ★★★★★ Goodreads review

"Ultra-hot and steamy... An interesting fated mate RH menage that explores individual pairings within the group, as well as a new partner trying to fit in and find their place within an existing strong and loving relationship." ★★★★★ Goodreads review

"This is a fantastic sci-fi romance... Fantastic story. I loved it and the characters and I highly recommend this book." ★★★★★ Goodreads review

"Loved it! This book takes a unique twist on polyamorous relationships AND fated mates... definitely give this a read!" ★★★★★ Amazon review

"An interesting and original approach to the reverse harem and fated mate tropes... Thought-provoking and provocative, with high heat throughout." ★★★★★ Amazon review

*"I really enjoyed this book. Great world building. I loved the different and connected relationships in this book between the males together and with Martha... Lots of yummy steamy scenes to keep me happy, too. *wink*"* ★★★★★ Amazon review

"What a phenomenal read. The worlds, cultures, and species created were diverse and detailed. The characters were rich, vivid, and beautifully flawed. I went on such an emotional ride with this book. It is so amazing to watch this talented author weave such a magical journey with such a balance of realism and fantasy. I can see myself turning back to this book time and time again." ★★★★★ Amazon review